Receive Me Falling

RECEIVE

ME

FALLING

A Novel

ERIKA ROBUCK

Elysian Fields Press
2009

Published by Elysian Fields Press
Elysian Fields Press (USA), Crownsville, Maryland, 21032, U.S.A

Robuck, Erika
Receive Me Falling/Erika Robuck
ISBN 978-0-9822298-0-4

PUBLISHER'S NOTE
This is a work of fiction. Names, characters, places, and incidents are
either the products of the author's imagination or are used fictitiously.

For Scott

"Thus was this place,
A happy rural seat of various view;
Groves whose rich Trees wept odorous Gums and
            Balm,
Others whose fruit burnisht with Golden Rind
Hung amiable, Hesperian Fables true,
If true, here only, and of delicious taste:
Betwixt them Lawns, or level Downs, and Flocks
Grazing the tender herb, were interpos'd,
Or palmy hillock, or the flow'ry lap
Of some irriguous Valley spread her store,
Flow'rs of all hue, and without Thorn the Rose;
Another side, umbrageous Grots and Caves
Of cool recess, o'er which the mantling Vine
Lays forth her purple Grape, and gently creeps
Luxuriant; meanwhile murmuring waters fall
Down the slope hills, disperst, or in a Lake,
That to the fringed Bank with Myrtle crown'd,
Her crystal mirror holds, unite their streams.

                    Paradise Lost, Milton

—And now, ye pow'rs! to whom the brave are dear,
Receive me falling, and your suppliant hear.
To you this unpolluted blood I pour,
To you that spirit which you gave restore!
I ask no lazy pleasures to possess,
No long eternity of happiness;—
But if unstain'd by voluntary guilt,
At your great call this being I have spilt,
For all the wrongs which innocent I share,
For all I've suffer'd, and for all I dare;
O lead me to that spot, that sacred shore,
Where souls are free, and men oppress no more!

                    The Dying Negro, A Poem,
                    Thomas Day & John Bicknell

RECEIVE ME FALLING

Nevis Island
February 1831

The slave woman fell over the cliff's edge toward the black swirl of water that churned over the boulders reaching up from the sea. Her mistress crawled to look over the ledge. The stones bit her shins and left smears of blood on their jagged surfaces. She was unable to locate the body amidst the swells and rocks, unable to see through her tears, and the night, and the rain.

Somewhere in the slave village, the woman's mother knew her only daughter was gone. In spite of the humidity, she shook in the hut with the rain dripping through holes in the thatched roof, patting her head and shoulders, and running down her legs into mud puddles.

She heard the scream—a sound she had heard before. Over the years, other slaves preceded her daughter over the cliff seeking escape, peace, deliverance, liberation. She heard the cry which now paralyzed her, because it came from her own, and it would haunt her forever.

1

Annapolis, Maryland
Present Day

Meghan stared down from the boat club railing at the river, revealed only in quick reflections from the low light over her head. There was no moon, and the wind filled her ears, muffling the sound the water made as it slapped against the pilings. The light over her head swung and flickered off briefly, before turning on again and casting an odd, yellow haze over the dock, like the light in an old basement.

Inside at the party, the governor had dropped his drink, sending shards of martini glass over the surface of the hard wood, and up Meghan's leg. When she had bent over to pull the glass from her calf, she had felt the effects of the wine on her empty stomach, and thought she'd be sick. It was good to get outside—in spite of the chill—away from her engagement party. She reached down and pressed a crumbled napkin to the cut on her calf, grimacing as she saw the smear of blood through her and Brian's names on it.

A high sound, like a woman's cry, pulled Meg's attention to the bridge that hung in the distance, higher than the pier where she stood. The cry was lost in the wind. It made her uneasy, and she rubbed her arms to smooth the chill that rose more from the noise than the wind. She looked up expecting to see the steady traffic moving from Annapolis to the eastern shore of Maryland, but saw that the bridge was empty and dark.

Meg scanned the water under the bridge, and thought she caught a movement in the grassy area at the shore. Then the sound again—a woman crying.

"It's almost over."

Meg jumped as her mother, Anne, touched her shoulder and turned her toward the boat club.

"You look tired," said Anne. "And Brian looks miserable."

Meg looked back under the bridge, but saw nothing. A low rumble of thunder started over the bay.

"I was hoping he'd end up having fun," said Meg, "but I'm afraid you're right."

"Then why are we doing this?"

"Because it's what you do after you get engaged," said Meg. "Isn't it what you and Dad would want?"

"What about you and Brian?"

At thirty-three, Meg had already seen most of her friends get married. Before they had gotten married, they had big engagement parties. It had not occurred to her to do it differently. Meg had taken her parents' silence on the matter of the party as acceptance, but now she could see that Brian was right. The big party was all wrong.

Lately, Meg was finding herself in situations that she'd orchestrated to fulfill some fantasy she had about who she was supposed to be. She loved the idea of pulling off a big event, but was finding out more and more that she hated attending the big events. She knew it was a result of her job working for the governor, and wondered how she had so carelessly disregarded Brian's disdain—and now her own— for large, impersonal gatherings. She wondered how she had let it get this far.

"I'll have the bartender make a last call announcement so we can all get out of here," said Anne. "Your father needs to be put to bed anyway."

Anne kissed Meg's cheek and led her back into the party. As Meg stepped through the door and into the boat club, she caught Brian's gaze through the crowd. His look fell somewhere between annoyance and misery. A lobbyist who worked with Meg's office had her arm through Brian's, and Meg could see that the drunken woman was falling all over him. She felt a pang of guilt.

"Are you okay?" asked Meg's father, as he put his arm around her and pulled her into a seat at the bar.

"I'm fine," she said.

"I think we cleaned out the bar."

"That's usually a sign the party's over," she said.

"Your mother will get them out of here. Look, she's putting a coat on the governor."

Meghan watched her mother guide the guests to the door. A sharp gust of wind blew in cold rain and the smell of early winter, and sent a pile of napkins fluttering to the ground. Her mother closed the doors quickly and smiled at Meg.

"One couple down. Sixty more to go."

❧

Meg dreamed of water. She was looking over the railing of her dad's sailboat at the black water in the Severn River, and saw fireworks reflected in its surface. Each time one dissolved, another appeared over the lightly rippled surface of the river.

Then she was looking at the Atlantic Ocean. She was standing in the sand, barefoot, staring out at the whitecaps under the stormy sky. She watched lightning hit the water far out at sea, and felt the wind knocking her off balance.

Then it was raining. Great, gray sheets of rain. The ocean dissolved, and Meg could only see the rain.

When the phone rang, it took her a few moments to lift her head off the pillow and look at the alarm clock.

4:13

Meg sat up and rubbed her eyes as the ringer stopped. Out of her waking confusion came fear. Her stomach became unsettled, and she climbed out of bed to her dresser to see who had called.

Only bad news came in the middle of the night.

Just as Meg was about to pick up the phone to check her caller ID, someone knocked at the door. She pulled on a sweatshirt and looked out the window to see who was at her door at four o'clock in the morning.

Two police officers.

Her fight with Brian came rushing back to her. They had left the engagement party not speaking. He was angry at the showiness and impersonality of it. He didn't know half the guest list. Was it her parents' wedding or their wedding? He dropped her off and sped away into the storm.

Oh God.

"Miss Owen?"

Meg nodded, unable to find her voice.

"Are you the daughter of Richard and Anne Owen?"

Meg nodded again.

"There's been an accident."

Brian was there within minutes. He wanted to drive, but Meg needed to feel as if she had control. She watched the streets slide by: Duke of Gloucester, West, Parole—their names steadied her nerves. Familiar names. Brian stared at her, saying nothing. There was nothing to say. The accident was over.

Her parents were dead.

When they reached the morgue Brian did the talking. They were led into the basement of the building. The hallway was sterile blue from the underground lighting.   An old man with stringy white hair cleaned the waiting room floor with a heavy gray mop that slid over the tile in a whisper. Meg watched him take a bite from a half-eaten candy bar and stuff it back into his pocket, getting sticky lines of caramel on his work pants. He looked at her without interest and then back at the wet lines he made on the floor.

Through the polished glass on the wall, Meg could see the two bodies on side-by-side tables. It was, indeed, her parents under the sheets. Their faces looked puffy and chalky, and like they had been on the losing side of a boxing match. Meg felt like she was outside of herself in a dream, watching the drama unfold.

Yes, those are my parents. My mom and dad.

In all the unreality of that moment, it was only when Meg had seen her mother's right toes sticking out of the bottom of the sheet—naked and tagged like some wax figure on display—that she lost her composure. It seemed wrong that her dignified and elegant mother should come to such an end. Meg saw that her mother's toenail polish was chipped, and she was fixated by that. She felt sure that it had to have happened during the accident, because Anne Owen did not walk around with chipped nail polish. Meg said as much to Brian, and he looked at her like she was crazy.

She didn't know what to do with these bodies that looked like her parents, but weren't her parents. She didn't want to leave them there, but she couldn't get away fast enough.

Meghan let Brian drive her home. She knew that she no longer had control. He came in with her and wrapped himself around her while she cried through Sunday.

Saint Mary's was a gothic-style cathedral with an ornate altar framed in saints, tall stained glass windows, massive columns, and a domed ceiling painted with the stars in the formation they were in the night the church was dedicated over two hundred years before.

Richard and Anne Owen lay in their caskets, covered in white baptismal linens, sprinkled with holy water, and bathed in incense. Brian sat with his arm tightly around Meg's shoulders as she watched the fragrant smoke drift over her parents' bodies and up to the ceiling.

Father Francis was a family friend. He and Richard had attended seminary together many years before—Richard dropping out after a year to marry Anne, and Frank staying on to marry the church. He spoke directly to Meg during the entire homily, assuring her of her parents' peaceful rest, offering her counsel, lightening the heaviness with humor as often as he could. But the truth of his words hit her hard. "This is only a temporary separation, but one you will have to bear the hardest."

It was a cold day, but a clear day. Brian led her through the funeral, holding her up as they traveled from church, to cemetery, to the wake at her parents' house. When all the guests had gone, Brian suggested that Meg get some rest.

"If it's okay with you, I want to be alone here tonight," said Meg.

"I don't think that's a good idea," said Brian. "Remember what Father Frank said."

"I haven't been alone since the accident. You've been wonderful, but I just need some time alone."

A flicker of hurt passed over Brian's face, but it was quickly replaced with understanding.

"Call me tomorrow," he said.

Meg reached for Brian and hugged him for a long time. Then he left, and she stood in the middle of the foyer, alone in the silence.

Meg walked to the kitchen and poured herself a glass of wine. She walked through the rooms in a trance, noting all the things that were just as her parents had left them. There was leftover roast beef in the refrigerator. Little hardened circles of mud sat around her dad's golf shoes in the garage. Her mother's dried lipstick marks smiled in little half-moons around the edge of a tea cup on her nightstand.

Meg carried a bottle of wine and her glass into her father's office and sank into the worn leather chair behind his desk. She looked at the picture of her and her dad on the boat and picked it up. They were Irish—dark-blonde hair with blue eyes—but her dad's hair was run through with white. Meghan had her mother's petite frame, but her father's lean face and blue eyes. There were fingerprints on the glass. Meg stuck her thumb in her sleeve and wiped the glass until it was clear. She put the picture back down next to a sculpture of a whale she had made in Kindergarten for her father. Its knotty surface was faded blue and held the imprints of her tiny fingers.

There was a stack of file folders on the desk. Meg opened the first and saw that it contained papers relating to a vacation home the family owned in North Carolina. There were settlement papers, a real estate contract, and photographs her mother had taken for the insurance company when the siding had blown off the eastern side of the house in a hurricane. In the background of one of the photos she could see the dune covered in sea oats that had been flattened in the wind, and she smiled.

Two years ago, Meg had read an article about how sea oat roots formed a network of support under a dune to protect the land from tidal surges. She ordered hundreds of seedlings, drew detailed maps of where they should be set, and enlisted her parents and Brian to plant them in early March.

The day had been unseasonably cold. Not expecting the chilly temperatures, they had not packed enough warm clothing for an all day, outdoor planting. Her father had on Brian's St. John's College sweatshirt and a painters' hat he had found in the owner's closet of the house. She and her mother had wrapped chenille blankets around their bodies and ears in an unstylish but toasty configuration. Brian had on two shirts and a yellow rain slicker.

At first, they all listened to Meg as she told them where to put the staggered, horizontal rows, but became impatient with her and began to plant them wherever they wanted.

"Don't complain to me when a tidal surge destroys the house because the sea oats weren't planted properly," she had said as she tried to keep her tidy rows going.

They ended up getting the sea oats in the ground much more quickly after that, and enjoyed teasing Meg throughout the rest of the process. The sea oats had done a fine job of keeping the dunes strong, and did end up holding out a tidal surge.

Meg closed the folder and turned to the next one that held the history of the house she lived in off of State Circle. Its original owner was a merchant and a minor political figure. There was a newspaper clipping of it as a featured home of the week, and a contract with the Annapolis Historical Society detailing its preservation.

Meg read through the folders for hours. She took comfort in touching her father's things and looking at photographs of places she knew well. She realized halfway through the pile that all this was hers now. It was overwhelming.

When the clocked reached midnight, Meg stood and stretched. She rubbed her aching neck and looked around at the empty bottles of wine standing erect in a monument to her grief. There was a small amount of wine left in the bottom of the bottle nearest to her, so she poured it into her glass and sat down to read through the last folder. In it was an old photograph of a dilapidated mansion.

EDEN, Nevis.

That was all that was written on the back of the picture. The house looked as if it had once been grand, but had fallen into disrepair. All signs of life around the place had vanished: vines grew wild over the portico, weeds had overtaken the fountain and driveway, broken, jagged, wooden shutters jutted out from old rotten frames.

According to the paperwork, her family owned a large amount of property on the Caribbean island of Nevis. She vaguely remembered her father mentioning the property some years ago, but never since. The photograph showed the remains of an old plantation home, Eden.

Paradise.

She finished her glass of wine and stumbled over to the couch. Her father's old, gray cardigan was draped over its edge. Meg wrapped it around her shoulders, inhaled its salty smell, and slept.

It was the vase of dead flowers that set off the panic attack. Twenty-four dried roses faded into various shades of brown, with heads drooping, looking at the black marble window sill and their own discarded bits of petal and pollen. The flowers had been from her father on her birthday.

Meg had only been back to work for two days after four days of leave, following the funeral. The Governor's

Office gave four days of mourning for family members, and a pamphlet dating back to 1972 outlining Kubler-Ross's five stages of grief: Denial, Anger, Bargaining, Depression, Acceptance. Meg figured that they allowed one day for each stage, banking on Acceptance falling on the first day of return from leave. She felt like she was still lost in the haze of Denial.

Meg looked from the flowers to her desk. There was a binder full of information on an upcoming fundraiser for the Governor, piles of unopened mail, a blinking light on her phone, a wedding planner--six inches thick with papers spilling out of it, and a file folder from her assistant jumping off the bookshelf with a note on the front of it that read: "When you get a chance." Her email had ninety-seven unopened messages—thirty-one with urgent marks.

Meg's assistant buzzed in.

"Your meeting with the Governor?"

"Oh, I forgot. I'll be right there."

The upcoming Nelson Night Fundraiser was Meg's biggest project, and had gone by the wayside during the past week. Governor Nelson was kind but made it clear that he needed her to refocus. She scribbled notes as he rattled off the guest list and the people he wanted to secure as speakers. Meg kept up but had little to offer in the way of suggestion.

The governor watched Meg chew the inside of her lip and draw a spiral on her notepad that got smaller and smaller. Her eyes were facing him, but she wasn't looking at him. She was looking through him at some memory that pulled her away, until he said, "You've had enough."

Meg blinked and shook off her thoughts.

"We can continue tomorrow," he said.

"I'm sorry." Meg stood and gathered her papers to leave while Nelson walked over to the door. He stopped her before he opened it.

"I'm very sorry for your pain, Meghan. If there is anything I can do for you, I am always available."

Before she could refuse, Nelson had her in a full embrace that didn't leave much of his form to the imagination. She extracted herself from his hold, mumbled something, walked back to her office, closed her door, and sat at her desk trying to process what had just happened. Meg felt uncomfortable, but knew that she wasn't thinking clearly.

He was just trying to console me.

But the way he loomed over her as he held the door knob—the way he gathered her into his chest. She could still feel his hands pressing into her back and his pelvis pushing into her body. She shuddered.

Meg looked at the vase of dead flowers from her father and felt her chest get tight. She was having difficulty catching her breath, and she began to feel lightheaded. She clutched the edge of her desk to steady herself, and tried to focus on something other than the flowers. Oddly enough, she was able to use the blinking light on the phone to regulate her breathing until her heart rate returned to normal. Once Meg regained control of herself, she walked to the window, picked up the vase of dead flowers, and dropped it into the trash bin by the door.

2

Insomnia had lately taken hold of Catherine. She blew out the candle and stared through the darkness at the various layers of black that now made her room. The bureau was coal-black, the walls were blackish-blue, the floor was brown-black, and the mirror looked gray-black. She went through her usual night routine of reading, praying, and lying with her eyes open to make the hours pass, hoping to fall asleep all the while, but eager for the morning light so she could stop trying. She thought of things she needed to do the next day. With each passing minute, she found herself feeling more and more awake. She finally got out of bed and opened the shutters to watch the plantation under the weight of night— the faraway fires burning on torches in cane fields where slaves worked to complete harvest, palms throwing around their leaves in the wind blasts.

Catherine crossed the room and slipped through the netting that hung from the ceiling to the floor around her bed. She flicked off several moths and beetles and again tried to rest.

The night was never silent in Nevis: shutters tapped the window casing in response to the wind, palm leaves hissed and rustled, the song of the bellfrogs reached frantic levels. Then there was the heat. The night was not hot, but the wood in the flooring of the house absorbed the sun all day and released its hot trappings as the wind blew the house at night. Catherine pulled her nightdress up to her waist under the light sheet, and wished she could remove it entirely. The sheet felt cool on her bare legs and she longed for the feeling to reach the rest of her body.

Just as she was about to let go and succumb to sleep, her door opened and Leah's dark form moved to her bed.

"The baby is coming," whispered the slave girl.

"Are you sure?"

"Yes—any moment now."

Catherine felt like she could manage to sleep if she were just left alone, but could not resist the birthing—her first. She dressed hastily, crept on bare feet down the staircase, and hurried to the back of the house holding Leah's hand. Catherine's heart pounded loudly enough, she feared, to wake her father, but she and Leah slipped out of the house unnoticed.

The darkness engulfed the young women as they tread away from the Great House to the slaves' path, and the moving clouds rolled thick over the moon. The girls moved along the dirt path in silence until a thumping of heavy boots could be heard nearby. They had only just ducked behind a group of oleander bushes when a large, shadowed figure passed them. They could smell the sharp salt of sweat and the stale odor of old alcohol, and knew that it was the overseer, Phinneas. Catherine felt Leah tremble as they waited for the sound of his boots to vanish. After a short time, the girls moved back onto the path and hurried to the slave village.

When they arrived at the thatched hut, a small fire crackled outside its entrance. Water was warming over the fire, and gasps and cries could be heard coming from inside the hut. Catherine took a deep breath and entered the hut to find Esther, her surrogate slave mother, wiping a young slave woman's sweating face. Esther's dark eyes grew wide upon seeing her young mistress in such living quarters, and she moved to Catherine and implored her to leave.

"You must go!"

"Mami, you know how I have longed to see this."

"You should not be here. This is not a scrape or insect bite. Childbirth is not something your eyes should see unless you are going through it yourself."

Leah stooped in the corner of the hut trying to sink into the shadows. Esther turned to Leah and began to hiss and curse at her in her thick African tongue.

"Please, Mami, do not abuse Leah," said Catherine. "I insisted she tell me when the baby was coming. I can be of assistance, and I assure you that Father will never find out what I have seen."

"It is not your father who will punish us," said Esther. "Mr. Sarponte knows all that goes on in Eden. He has eyes all over. Other slaves inform him of our goings on when he cannot be here himself."

"I'm already here. No one saw us arrive. I'll slip out once it is over, and no one will know."

An agonized scream pierced their conversation and forced the women to tend to Rebecca. Esther looked from Leah to Catherine, and finally said, "Catherine, continue ragging Rebecca's head. Leah, hold this knife over the fire. Hurry, this child is eager to enter the world."

"How long has she been like this?" asked Catherine.

"She has been laboring for many hours, but now the pains are coming close together. I feel that this child will be born before sunrise. She is moving quickly for her first time. That will be a blessing."

The women worked in silence, communicating only through gestures. An hour passed slowly as they rotated duties in the small room. The stifling heat inside the hut, combined with the odors of perspiration and childbirth nauseated Catherine and made her feel faint; but she was determined to be strong, and she fought through her own weakness. Leah, unable to stand the atmosphere, disappeared outside the hut, and returned looking ashen.

Another hour passed, when Esther announced that the child's head could be seen. Esther soothed Rebecca in her low, musical voice. She then gave Rebecca instructions, and Rebecca adjusted her position. Catherine strained to understand Esther's words.

"Leah, hold the stick in her mouth."

Esther turned back to Rebecca and gave her a command. Rebecca pushed and screeched, and the baby's head began to emerge from her body. The women encouraged her until she was overcome by fatigue. They continued in this manner for an interminable amount of time until the baby's tiny blue head emerged.

Catherine stared at the blue knob between Rebecca's legs. Panic seized her and she began to feel lightheaded. What if the child was born dead? How could she face Rebecca? What would they do with the infant? They would have to bury the tiny body swiftly since the slaves were superstitious about such occurrences. How could she take care of that without her father finding out that she was present at the birth?

Esther's voice became stern as she shouted at Rebecca. Rebecca pushed and screamed as the shoulders, stomach and legs of the baby slipped from her womb. Except for Rebecca's ragged breathing, the hut became silent. Esther's hands slid over the baby's slippery chest, around his neck, and into his mouth. She flipped him over and struck him on the back. Within seconds a thick, gurgling, guttural noise spewed from the child, followed by an angry wail. Catherine released her breath and smiled with relief as Esther placed the boy onto Rebecca's chest.

The child soon quieted and gazed at his surroundings. Catherine approached Rebecca and stroked the baby's cheek, while Leah pulled away the flap covering the hut's opening to let in the fresh, tropical air. After a few moments, the women cleaned the baby, and then Rebecca as she nursed her infant.

Esther suddenly exclaimed, "Catherine, you must go! Dawn is breaking! Go, while the shadows will still hide you!"

Catherine looked with alarm at the sky, and ran to the shelter of the trees. She moved toward her home under the protection of the shrubs, flowers, and vines. She passed through the banks of the lagoon and stayed hidden by the forest until she found the side door to the kitchen and entered the Great House.

Catherine tiptoed to the large staircase, but just as her hand reached the banister she heard her father gasp. Horrified, Catherine turned around to see her father passed out on the hall couch. He was grunting in a spirit-soaked dream. Her heart steadied itself as she crept up the staircase and into the safety of her room.

Catherine lit a candle and ran her eyes over her soiled clothing. Blood, dirt, and sweat matted the fabric and caused it to stick to her body. She peeled away the layers of stiff material and placed them in a pile behind her chest of drawers. Using a coarse towel and fresh water from her basin, Catherine began to rub the filth from her body, which was stiff and sore from crouching in the hut for hours amidst such tension.

Once the ruddy stain was bled from her body to the water in the basin, Catherine blew out the candle and collapsed into bed.

The candlelight flickered in the drafts blasting in from the shutters, which could barely hold out the wind. The men sat sweating in the small room at the heavy wood table.

"It will soon be over," said Albert Silwell.

"How can that be? Slavery is as old as the land. England is thousands of miles away—there's no way to enforce such laws," said Jonas Dearing. "The Nevis Council and Assembly are composed of the seven wealthiest planters on the island. Are they going to simply free hundreds of slaves and start toiling the land themselves?"

"English abolitionist politicians, like us, appointed by Thomas Clarkson and the Society for the Mitigation and Gradual Abolition of Slavery will continue to arrive on the island in droves over the next few months. Extensive research into the slaves' quality of life, the most effective means of phasing out the system, and planter compensation packages will be outlined and executed. Those unwilling to comply with the new laws will be dealt with justly."

"And how do you propose to find your way onto these thriving plantations for observation? Will you simply walk to the front door and ask the master of the house if you may stroll about the grounds?"

"Certainly not," said Albert. "Word has been sent to the three largest plantations on the island that we are businessmen here to observe their plantations at work so that we may start our own sugar plantation on the island of St. Christopher. We come as apprentices."

"Some may be suspicious of you. Cane on Nevis is a dying enterprise. Aside from a few lucky plantations, many have switched crops or abandoned the island completely."

The men looked at one another over the dull light of the dying candles. James Silwell stared between his father and the farmer. Their dialogue had been going on for hours, and James longed to plunge himself headfirst into the sea that he could hear crashing in the distance. His stiff, layered, aristocratic clothing was suffocating him. He thought with disgust of moving about in such clothing outdoors in the afternoon. James had been reluctant to accompany his father on the trip, but a motherless bachelor learning the business of English politics had no excuse to stay in Cornwall while his aging father made the journey across the Atlantic.

"May I ask," continued Albert, "if there are many farmers like yourself who we could trust as allies—men appalled by slavery, and angry over their inability to compete with the large plantations?"

"Most farmers and small planters, I fear, care not about the slaves or their unfortunate conditions. In order to gain their cooperation, you will have to exploit their outrage over the Council's attempts at destroying their homes and acquiring their land."

"What do you mean?"

"The Council passed a bill that those living in thatched houses have until April to shingle their homes or pull them down. They claim that it will prevent quickly spreading fires, but everyone is aware that the homes of which the Council is speaking are on valuable land adjacent to their properties. They offered an absurdly low price to buy the land as an alternative to shingling or rebuilding—an amount that would barely cover the cost of relocating a family. My home is one of the homes targeted."

"And you haven't the money or manpower to shingle your house."

"Precisely. If I have to destroy my home, I will be forced to return to England. My wife is with child and we have two other small children. There is no way we could make the journey at that time. And there is nothing for us to return to, even if we could."

James stared hard at Jonas. His face was deeply tanned and lined, and covered in grime. His hands were rough and calloused. James knew that in spite of his harsh, aged appearance, Jonas was probably no older than James' own thirty-three years. James wondered at the circumstances that would send a man like Jonas—who sounded reasonably educated—so far from his home, and into such miserable working conditions. Was it money? Trouble with the law? He said a silent prayer of thanks for his place and station in life, and suddenly felt that great familial altruism welling up inside him.

"I am very sorry to hear that," said James. "Your cooperation with us will afford you some compensation."

James pulled a leather pouch of money from his pocket. He then reached into his other pocket and added more to it. Albert watched as James passed the pouch to Jonas, who grabbed it and began to count the bills.

"We will ask for your advice often while we are here," said Albert. "Do not yet mention our conversations to anyone."

"I have no reason to betray your confidence."

The poor farmer stood and began to limp away from the table. Albert and James rose to escort him to the door.

"Before you go," said James, "tell us what you know of the Dall plantation—Eden. It is the most lucrative plantation on the island, but one that seems to invoke whispers and sniggers upon mention. It is the first we will visit."

"Cecil Dall and his daughter, Catherine, live there. Cecil acquired the land a number of years ago when he and his brother came from England with their wives. His brother died shortly after arriving on the island, Cecil's wife died birthing Catherine, and Cecil's sister-in-law died when Catherine was young. It may surprise you to learn that

Catherine has been managing the plantation almost on her own for the past few years—and quite successfully."

"Why, is Cecil ill?"

"He's ill with the illness that plagues many on these islands. One of the most profitable by-products of the sugar mills is rum. Cecil is consumed with the drink, and can barely manage to dress and dine on time, let alone run a plantation. He does, however, hold fast to the illusion that he is in control of Eden."

"You seem to know a great deal about the Dall family," said Albert. "How are you acquainted?"

"I'm the only person on the island able to tune and repair the pianoforte. I'm at the house often to service it."

"Now that I think of it, all correspondence we have had with the Dalls has been signed C. Dall," said Albert. "I wonder if it is Catherine who has been writing to us."

"You may be sure it is Catherine. The only other person of authority at Eden is their chief overseer, Phinneas Sarponte. Cecil appointed him after Catherine's aunt died. Miss Dall—though she would not admit it—would be quite unable to get on without him."

Albert and James looked at one another, and then at Jonas.

"Thank you, Jonas. Your assistance has been invaluable."

A strong wind thrust open the shuttered windows of Catherine's bed chamber, awakening her with a start. She made her way over to the window and looked out at the sun dawning over the horizon. Catherine inhaled and could almost taste the mangoes hanging ripe from a nearby tree. Her eyes followed the slope of the land away from the Great House passing over tropical foliage layered in deep greens, splashes of color, insects, birds, and creatures out to the cliff overlooking the sea—shadowed and strange in the still half-light of dawn.

Catherine turned away from the window and approached her dressing table as the humidity began to press itself upon her. How long had she slept? It could not have been more than an hour. She noticed that her soiled clothing had already been removed from her room, and fresh water filled the basin. Only the soreness in her limbs and the dark rings below her eyes suggested what she had participated in under the cover of night.

Catherine bent down and splashed the cool water on her face, allowing it to run down her neck and into her nightclothes. Fanning herself, Catherine dressed and swept up her hair.

The aroma of fried eggs and fresh bread drifted up the staircase as Catherine descended to the dining room. Her father had not yet arrived at the table, and for that Catherine was grateful. She was not yet awake enough to put on the façade of the obedient daughter, and was afraid her guilty countenance would betray her.

Leah appeared from the kitchen carrying a pitcher of freshly squeezed juice. Her eyes were half-closed and her caramel colored skin appeared pale. She started upon seeing Catherine at the table so early, and quickly crossed behind her to pour her drink.

"You're awake early," said Leah.

"The wind woke me. I'm still running on last night's energy."

"Mami is tending to Rebecca this morning. She and the child are doing well."

Catherine reached for Leah's arm. "Thank you for getting me last night. I hope Mami has not been too hard on you."

"She hasn't yet had the opportunity, but I am sure it will only be a matter of time."

The girls laughed and Leah turned back toward the kitchen.

"Shall we meet in the grove after sewing tomorrow?" whispered Catherine.

Leah nodded and disappeared around the corner.

Catherine was alone only a moment before Cecil stumbled into the dining room, trailed by his butler, Thomas. She put on a smile as he crossed the room and kissed her on the head.

"How are you this morning, my dear?"

"Fine," said Catherine. "How did you sleep last night?"

"I spent some of the time on the hall couch, I must confess. It was a late night at the Ewings. But I awoke before dawn and was able to continue my slumber in the comforts of my bed, until Thomas insisted I come down to eat."

Catherine exchanged a smile with Thomas as he pushed her father's chair to the table.

"I, for one, can't wait to get home from Services today," said Catherine. "I've found a particularly mossy and unexplored region by the lagoon where I hope to find some medicinal plants for Mary."

"Aren't the Englishmen joining us today?" asked Cecil.

"They're not due here until four o'clock. I've invited them to dine with us this evening to secure them introductions with the Ewings and the Halls. Our three plantations will be the focus of their observations."

"Do these men have the upfront capital necessary to start their own sugar plantations on St. Christopher?"

"It would appear that they are very wealthy and very motivated," said Catherine. "I do, however, find their timing a bit odd."

"Why?"

"You know as well as I do that Britain is close to banning slavery in its colonies," said Catherine.

"It will never happen. The British economy relies too much upon our exports and debts to them. Abolishing slavery would be the equivalent of pulling the supports from underneath the entire capital system. You take too much stock in those bumbling Quakers and Evangelicals."

"Perhaps, but it would be foolish to ignore such rumblings. After all, we must plan for what might be inevitable. And what the Quakers and Evangelicals say about our slaves does strike a chord—in my mind, at least."

"That's because you are the embodiment of compassion without sense."

Catherine looked at her father and then out to the back lawn.

Cecil stood up from the table. "A slave gave birth to a healthy boy last night, and I would like to inspect him before Phinneas adds him to the register. I will have the carriage brought around in an hour's time."

Catherine's eyes dropped to her plate, and she studied it until Cecil exited the dining room. After he left, she finished her breakfast and gazed out of the window.

Palms fanned in the ever-blowing breeze, partially obstructing her view of the back lawn. Sunday stretched itself wide and lazily before her, and as she chewed the sweet fruit from her plate Catherine tried to send her mind to wander into the cool, moist landscape which she hoped to explore in solitude after church. Instead she could only think of her father's words, and the chores that needed done, and Rebecca's baby, and Leah's fatigue.

Childish shrieks and laughter snatched Catherine from her thoughts. Three small slave children were chasing one another down by the path that led to their huts. Catherine grinned as she collected various treats from her breakfast table and wrapped them in a napkin. After glancing around the dining room to make sure she was not seen, Catherine ran from the house and charged after the children into the dark path. Leah's eyes smiled after her in the shadows.

~~~

James stared out at the sea as the carriage brought him closer to the drive off the main road. An insistent breeze blew away the harsh edges of the heat that had begun to settle on the island. His eyes could not take in enough of the surrounding landscape: golden apples, coconut palms, fern, bamboo, all color and array of blossoms, and countless other varieties of vegetation all teeming with warblers, finches, doves, swifts, lizards, beetles, butterflies and monkeys. And standing above it all, a grand mountain steeped in clouds and drizzled in miles of rainforest.

The great roar of noise from the crashing waves, the trade winds, and the morning symphony of island creatures, combined with the magnificence of the visual landscape assaulted and intoxicated James' senses. He looked at his father sitting next to him for a reaction, but saw only the steady and placid look that always characterized Albert Silwell.

The Silwells were in Nevis under the direction of Thomas Clarkson. Clarkson and William Wilberforce were two leading British abolitionists working to persuade their country to end slavery and all its associated practices. Clarkson was honored by Wordsworth in a poem written after Clarkson had helped to get the Slave Trade Bill of 1807 passed—which had effectively banned British ships from involving themselves in the slave trade. His drawing depicting how the slaves were arranged below deck in transatlantic crossings influenced many people of the time to reconsider their views on the practice of slavery. James and Albert Silwell were on the island gathering evidence to assist Clarkson and Wilberforce in their anti-slavery crusade.

James' eyes moved to the large dark-skinned man driving the horses. His neck shone with perspiration. He was thin, but the muscles on his forearms and the spread of his back showed his strength. He looked stiff and uncomfortable in the white blouse and black breeches that he was wearing. As the sun warmed and illuminated their backs James drew in his breath. He noticed knotted scar tissue creeping up the back of the slave's neck that he had originally mistaken for a shirt's ruffle. The vine-like scars fascinated and repulsed James enough to capture his attention for the remainder of the ride to the Great House.

The sharp crunch of crushed shells aroused James from his trance. The slave directed the men to the veranda wrapped around the lower level of the house, and then disappeared around the corner. Moments later, a round, glassy-eyed man with wind-swept gray hair pushed his way passed a haughty, well-dressed slave at the front door and invited the Silwells into the hall.

"Greetings, gentlemen. I was just on my way to have the carriage brought around when I learned of your early arrival. I trust your journey afforded you a breathtaking view of our beautiful island paradise."

"It did indeed," remarked Albert. "We apologize for taking the liberty of venturing to your home before we were scheduled to arrive, but several gentlemen at the hotel assured us of your hospitality."

"We are never bothered by visitors—especially those coming to learn the sugar system. We take great pride in our production and look forward to any opportunity to boast about it," said Cecil as he led them to the front parlor.

"We understand that your plantation houses the most abundant and productive slave population on the Leeward Islands," said Albert. "This is the first time we've gazed upon these exotic Africans. It is a much less dramatic prospect than the stories have foretold."

"I know that many grizzly tales have surfaced about slavery, but I assure you that our slaves are treated kindly and accommodated fairly. There are a small number of plantation owners who have abused these poor beasts beyond what is reasonable, but I believe that you will find it to be a much more humane prospect than you had imagined. The slave is, after all, physically and mentally designed for such servitude. He is happiest when productive and well cared for."

James glanced at the man who had driven them to the Great House who had materialized in a dark corner of the front hall, and the man quickly shifted his eyes to the well-polished wood floor.

"I would like to look around while the two of you talk," said James.

"Certainly," said Cecil as he filled three glasses with rum. "Unfortunately, my daughter and I will be leaving soon for Services. You were a bit earlier than I had anticipated."

"I won't venture far. I plan to do a more thorough investigation later in the week. I'm eager to explore some of this landscape on foot."

Cecil hesitated a moment and glanced out toward the back of the house. "The doors off the dining room will allow you passage to the back lawn."

"Thank you, Mr. Dall."

James approached the doors and stepped out into the morning sunlight. The lawn was quieter than the road. Birds and insects could still be heard, but their music was much more reverent, tame, and muted. He passed over the trim green grasses and onto a well-trodden dirt path. Vines, leaves, and flowers entombed the passageway, and the cool, dank smell of moss and earth was pungent in the air.

James heard laughter flutter through the vegetation. He crept into a clearing bathed in sunlight where he saw three slave children running in circles around a blindfolded woman. The children shrieked with delight as she tried to chase and grab them.

Large fruit trees formed a circular grove veiled in the evaporating dew of the morning. Hummingbirds and insects flew from their shelters as James stepped out into the sunlight. Upon seeing the white man, the children started and scattered like birds, leaving the blindfolded and breathless Catherine asking after them as she felt the air around her.

"Children, I am going to find you," she teased.

James stared at Catherine with fascination. She was tall for a woman, slender in form, and flushed from the heat. Her fair hair was swept up, but many curls escaped their confinement.

Catherine heard James' movements over the lawn and began creeping toward him, feeling the air around her with her outstretched arms. James did not want to startle her, but she was soon within inches of his face. He reached for the blindfold and removed the covering from her eyes. She blinked as her eyes adjusted to the sunlight.

"Now, yours is a face I do not know."

"I'm sorry if I've frightened you. My name is James Silwell. You must be Mr. Dall's daughter."

"And you must be the entrepreneurial businessman."

James laughed. "My father Albert is probably the entrepreneurial businessman. I am just a businessman."

"Well, Mr. Silwell, I am sure my father would be horrified to find that I had been carousing before church with the children, so shall we keep this between the two of us?"

"Your secret is safe with me."

Catherine smiled and led James out of the clearing.

"You're here early," said Catherine.

"Our ship arrived at Nevis from England several days ago, and we have been staying at the Bath Hotel. After some inquiries we were ensured that our early arrival would not trouble a man like your father, so we set out this morning."

"Father troubles himself about very little, so you should find yourselves quite welcome."

Catherine and James arrived at the house and entered the parlor as Albert and Cecil were preparing to depart it.

"Ah! You have found my darling imp, Catherine. Was she up a tree, or elbow-deep in mud?" said Cecil.

"I assure you, she was acting every bit the lady," remarked James.

Catherine smiled.

"A distinct pleasure, Miss Dall," said Albert, as he bowed.

Catherine nodded.

"If it would not be too much trouble, we will accompany you to church," said Albert.

Preparations were made, and the small party took leave of Eden.

St. John's Anglican Church was set on Main Street in the port city of Charlestown. It was newly built, beautifully landscaped, and surrounded by a stone wall that appeared to frame the church rather than separate it from the road. The

Dalls and the Silwells pulled up in front of the entrance, and Cecil helped his daughter down from the carriage. She led the group toward the entrance of the church, but stopped and turned when a loud voice could be heard crying over the crowds.

A Quaker, whose face and hair were as sun-bleached and lined as his clothing, stood on a large rock with his thick hand on the shoulder of a large African man.

"Brothers and sisters, I have seen the error of my ways," called the Quaker.

Cecil tightened his grip on Catherine's arm and pushed her toward the door of the church.

"I have freed my slaves, and William, here, has agreed to work with my family, for wages, as any man should be entitled to do."

Catherine resisted her father's pressure and strained to listen to the speaker.

"William is a full man—not a beast as we have been led to believe for so many years. He has a wife whom he cares for, and children he loves, and is a hard worker and a good, God-fearing Christian."

"For Christ's sake," mumbled Cecil.

Much of the crowd that had stopped along Main Street resumed their travels and called out insulting remarks to the Quaker as they passed.

"I pray for you all, that God enlightens you, as he has enlightened me."

Catherine looked from the Quaker to the freed slave. William's face was shining with perspiration and he shifted his weight from foot to foot. His posture was erect, but his quivering mouth betrayed his confident appearance. She met his eyes, and suddenly felt a lump rising in her throat. She could not account for the heaviness in her chest, nor could she understand why she suddenly felt so ill. Cecil urged his daughter forward and mumbled about getting her out of the heat, but Catherine continued to watch the African as Cecil pushed her toward the church. Just before passing through the arched entrance, she looked over her shoulder and saw James and Albert exchanging smiles with the orator.

~ ❦

"Then the Lord God said to the serpent: 'Because you have done this, you shall be banned from all the animals and from all the wild creatures. On your belly shall you crawl, and dirt shall you eat all the days of your life.'" The reverend wiped his brow, closed the Bible, and began speaking of the first sin. As his voice rose and fell over the assembled congregation, Catherine stole glances at James and Albert, increasingly curious about the newcomers.

It was difficult for Catherine to concentrate on the sermon, and she was grateful when the closing hymn began. At the end of the service, her father led her by the arm out of the church and into the blazing midday sun, followed by Albert and James. The Dalls exchanged a farewell with the Silwells, and remarked on their pleasure at having them to dinner later that evening. Cecil helped Catherine into the carriage, and as it moved away from the church, she peered from behind the canopy at the Silwells until they were out of sight.

~ ❦

The golden glow of evening settled over the island, and a curious quiet fell over its inhabitants from the mountainside down to the shoreline. The night song of the bellfrogs started with one tiny call that grew to a hushed conversation between thousands of creatures.

As Albert and James approached Eden, Beethoven's somber Sonata reached out and drew the men into the house. A slave led them to a large, high-ceiling room where Catherine sat playing the pianoforte, watched by a small audience.

James took note of the lavishly dressed men and women sitting in the room. The women fanned themselves through sweaty layers of costume and shifted in their chairs. The men smoked in the corner while one stared through the smog at Catherine. Cecil sat in the back row swirling the liquid in his glass and smiling at the others as if to say, "Isn't she talented?" Catherine sat at the instrument, deep in concentration. A fine layer of perspiration wet her face and chest, and her hair stuck in curls to her neck. The conclusion of the song brought applause and much commendation. Catherine bowed and proceeded to James and Albert.

"Welcome," said Catherine. "We are delighted to have you here."

Cecil stood up and motioned for the Silwells to join the men in the corner.

As they walked into the group Catherine said, "I must apologize on behalf of my father. Several of the men have been over since we returned from Services."

"You need not make any apologies," said James.

Cecil introduced the Silwells to the owners of the neighboring plantations, the Ewings and the Halls. Then dinner was announced.

James waited for the guests to make their way into the dining room, and followed behind. As he turned through the doorway he was stopped at the sight of the massive floor to ceiling mural of the fall of Adam and Eve. It took his breath away to see the life-sized figures of Genesis in living color before him. Eve had already bitten the apple and was passing it to Adam. She was dark with windswept hair. Adam was light, except for his arm reaching for the apple. The devil with its snake's tail and cherub head leered behind them. James strained to see the signature on the wall.

"West," said Catherine. "Benjamin West of America. He painted it before I was born. It's a pity I was never able to question him about it. There is much about it that warrants discussion."

"Perhaps you would ask about Eve's startling likeness to you?" asked Edward Ewing, the man who had been staring at Catherine earlier.

"No, only your startling resemblance to the snake."

The company giggled and Edward nodded.

James saw that the seat next to Catherine was empty and that it was intended for him. Edward sat on the other side of Catherine.

"You mustn't be shocked by our banter, Mr. Silwell," said Catherine. "We've known one another since childhood."

"I would not presume to be shocked by anything."

"Miss Dall often tries to shock with her tongue," said Edward, "but it's only the attention she wants. She's quite harmless."

"There is certainly nothing I would do to encourage more of your attention, Mr. Ewing; I have more than I care to of that."

Edward turned away from Catherine for the remainder of the meal, but kept an ear on her conversation with James and his father.

James was overwhelmed by the opulent displays of fine plates, silver, goblets, urns, and candlesticks that glittered over the abundant feast of game, fruits and vegetables. Four finely dressed slaves—two men and two women—served the meal. The men carried, the women cleared, and James scarcely would have noticed their presence if he had not been looking for them. One of the slave women was young and beautiful under the shadows that hung over her face. She and Catherine exchanged many looks throughout the meal. He once caught them smiling conspiringly at one another, but as soon as a smile touched the woman's face it was gone, leaving James wondering if she had smiled at all.

Throughout the meal, James learned that Edward and his father, Bartholomew, lived at the neighboring plantation, Goldenrise.

"So named because of the curious golden hue pervasive in the area at sunset," said Edward.

"I noticed that coming in," said James. "It would seem that all of Nevis is a Garden of Eden—rivers flowing to the sea, the gold of Havilla, the trees and fruits."

"The snakes," said Catherine.

"And delinquent women," said Edward. The group laughed and the meal continued.

Course after course of steaming and sumptuous fare sedated the company into a drowsy silence. For dessert, James tasted his first Bananas Flambe. The shredded coconut was crispy with brown sugar, and complemented the soft, warm fruit.

After dinner, in the billiard room, James was uncomfortable from the large meal, the heat, and the smoke. He opened the buttons on his jacket and watched the curtains move in the breeze, which disappeared as soon as he reached the open window. While he stared out the window and watched the world alive and crawling with the wind that refused to enter the house with any regularity, he listened to the men's conversation. Every now and then he turned to look at Catherine, who was also straining to catch bits of the conversation over the drone of the women.

"England has no jurisdiction over any of the big planters in the Caribbean," said Bartholomew. "We will continue practicing slavery, if banned, after their removal."

"Wilberforce is a fool," said William Hall. "It has been twenty-five years since he persuaded Parliament to ban slavery on the mainland. He will never succeed in persuading them to abolish slavery throughout the empire."

"Parliament only agreed to ban slavery on the continent because they knew slaves served little use in such a climate," said Bartholomew.

"I fear our timing is off," said Albert. "It is little wonder we were able to purchase the land at such a bargain. Planters on St. Christopher are fearful of their futures and are selling out."

"Our neighbors on the island of St. Christopher have always been skittish," said Edward. "I, for one, am glad to form a relationship that could lead to a formal alliance between the two island Council's. Be sure to involve yourself politically on St. Christopher as soon as possible. Our opinions will hold more stock in Britain if we have larger numbers."

The gentlemen continued their discussion until Cecil suggested an evening walk to the cliffs. Catherine was eager to remove herself from the stale air of the house and mind-numbing conversation of her counterparts, but the other ladies in the party elected to stay indoors on account of her neighbor, Mrs. Hall, remarking that the tropical night air was dangerous for the lungs.

"Catherine, you really should heed my warning," instructed Mrs. Hall. "It is already scandalous that your skin is so burnt by the sun, but you will truly do yourself an injustice by exposing yourself to the nighttime elements."

"Your advice is falling on deaf ears, I'm afraid," replied Cecil. "It is certainly my fault for not enforcing more feminine restrictions upon my motherless daughter, but I fear it is too late to impose such rules."

"You are correct in that assumption, Father," said Catherine. "I do appreciate your concern, Mrs. Hall, but I am sure my father will send me indoors the moment he fears for my health. Besides, it is he who needs looking after."

James stifled a smile as he watched Mrs. Hall ruffle herself in agitation on the settee. She remained indignant as Catherine and the gentleman proceeded out of the house.

The night air was, in fact, invigorating. James inhaled the sea air and watched the sapphire sheen on the folds of Catherine's dress ahead of him in the glow of the moonlight. He became transfixed in its motion and thought back to his travels across the Atlantic, looking over the deck of the ship into the water below.

He thought back to his third week onboard The Clarkson with Albert. The surface of the ocean had swirled and churned blackish-blue in the night. Shimmers of moonlight had flashed at him on the curling waves below. The fluid liquidity of the waters was both mesmerizing and frightening, and he was filled with dread as he thought of falling overboard and being stranded in the middle of the ocean.

The wind had cried around his ears, and pale, dead faces seemed to rise and fall in the waves beneath him. He sickened at the thought of the child who had been buried at sea just days before. Little George Painley—the one-year-old son of a shoe maker—died of dehydration after several weeks of violent seasickness. James shook his head to rid his mind of Mrs. Painley's agonized cries as the body of her small son slipped beneath the waves of the Atlantic.

James' time onboard the ship had been awful. Slight food and water rations, cramped quarters, poor hygiene, and the mind-numbing monotony of the voyage took their toll. He was thankful that he at least had his father with him to pass the days. James had always admired Albert Silwell, and was able to enjoy their philosophical and political discussions to pass the time.

But time still crept on slowly.

"Do you know that these cliffs are said to be haunted by the ghosts of dead slaves?" asked Catherine.

James blinked and shook off his memory.

"If you are trying to scare me away, it won't work," he said.

"I was trying to bring you back."

"I'm sorry. Readjusting to society after the long sea voyage has been difficult. Who told you of these slave ghosts? Or have you experienced the specters yourself?"

"It has been told that slaves used to throw themselves from this cliff when their lives became unbearable. Many slaves believed that they would journey home to the mountains of Africa to live out eternity after death. On stormy nights some say the cries of the dead pierce the wind."

Catherine and James continued on in silence until they reached the edge of the cliff. Sweet perfume drifted up from the large tropical flowers growing on it, and the waves crashed over boulders one hundred feet below. Catherine and James stared into the dark abyss. The wind was a low, mournful wail around them.

3

Every slave story is a ghost story.

That's what the man at the Nevis Historical Society had said over the phone. His words played over in Meg's thoughts as she sat stuffed in the stifling backseat of the van—wedged between a rusty door and a pile of her own luggage. She noticed that a large, wet stain growing on one of her bags had attracted several flies, and wondered which cosmetic had exploded.

Maybe this was not a good idea.

Meg tried to imagine the surprise of the three hundred guests upon opening the announcement calling off the wedding. Brian was initially sensitive to Meghan's distress, but when he came to understand that Meg wished to cancel rather than postpone the wedding, his injury was acute.

My God, Meghan, of course we should call off the wedding—I never wanted all that to begin with; but you can't mean to call off our marriage.

Meg no longer knew what she wanted. Her parents' deaths had sent her into shock, her job and her wedding had become too much to bear, and after the episode with the governor, Meg thought a trip would help clear her head. The house in North Carolina was too close and too full of memories. Meg needed to go somewhere new and far away— a place that her life and her obligations couldn't reach. She thought that removing herself from the physical setting of her life would allow her to become an objective observer. She could make decisions without feeling the need to please anyone. Brian had accused her of running away.

"Where you going, again?" called the driver.

Meg looked at her map. "Just past Gingerland. The plantation's called Eden."

The driver turned around and looked Meg as if she were mad.

"You going alone? Ghosts in that place."

Drew Edmead, the historian to whom she had spoken on the phone, reacted similarly when she told him of her destination. She had called him before making the trip to see if the Historical Society had any information on or claim to the property. He had assured her that it was hers to do with as she pleased, but expressed his keen desire to accompany her to visit the property if she would allow him access. Meg said that she would think about it.

"How long you here?" asked the driver.

"Two weeks."

"I don't think that place is fit for visitors."

"I'm actually staying at a small villa just off the property called Havilla," said Meg. "Drop me off there, and I'll find the plantation house on foot after I get settled."

"You not scared?"

"I don't believe in ghosts."

The driver made a clucking sound and shook his head.

In a short time the tires crunched over a driveway of crushed shells leading to a modest, single-storied villa of pure white; white shutters, white columns, white porch, white flowers. It had a small plunge pool and sweeping views of the island. Meg thought it was perfect. She helped the driver remove her luggage from the van, gave him a tip, and stepped into the villa.

The inside of Havilla was quaint and smelled of coconuts and sea water. The purity of color and design extended throughout the dwelling. It was simple, but comfortable. The wood was dark, the curtains were filmy and white, and the views extended from the side of Mount Nevis down to the Caribbean Sea.

And the bar was fully stocked.

Directly across from the full wall glass sliders leading to the covered back porch she discovered a wet bar complete with refrigerator, wine cooler, and blender. Meg ran her hands over a white binder resting in front of an assortment of bottles of rum.

Rum Recipes.

19 pages of rum recipes spread out before her. Beachcomber, Fog Cutter, Pink Paradise, Rum Toddy, Van Vleet—delightful names to say. Meg felt her mood lighten just thinking of the playful drink titles. She settled on *Casa Blanca* in honor of the villa, and raised her glass to the white walls.

"Cheers."

***

Meg reclined in a padded lounger by the pool and watched the sun set. She had flown from Washington D.C. to St. Kitts next to a woman heading to the islands with her husband for their thirtieth wedding anniversary. The woman was not sophisticated enough to read Meg's reluctance to engage; she misinterpreted Meg's silence as an invitation to divulge her life story.

After the flight, Meg had some time on St. Kitts while waiting for the ferry to Nevis. Under any other circumstances this would not have been a bad thing, but her nerves were frayed, and her need for solitude was making her frantic. Meg's relief was considerable when she realized that she was the only passenger on the ferry, and the captain was a reserved, polite old man who sensed and respected Meg's need for silence.

The short boat ride aboard the Halcyon was like a massage for her soul. Blue-green water lapped against the vessel, balmy breezes carried marine smells and birds over the water, and Mount Nevis' jungle-covered slopes filled her view as she approached Charlestown. The jerky van ride, however, planted her back into reality.

Maybe I should have taken a cruise.

Meg drained her glass and fell asleep.

~⊙

Something awakened Meg.

Piano music?

She glanced at her watch.

At 3:00 in the morning?

She sat up as quickly as her stiff muscles would allow, ground at her eyes with her fists, and strained her ears to hear over the breeze and the night song of the bellfrogs. Palms whipped in the wind, and the ocean whispered in the distance. Her eyes scanned the property, surveying the foliage along the fence for signs of life. A vague feeling of uneasiness crept over Meg. She shivered and crossed her arms.

Meg heard a thump in the grass nearby, and stood up from the lounger. Her heart began to race.

The piano music stopped, as if a distant music box had quickly been shut.

Meg began to back up toward the house, when a large piece of fruit thumped out of a nearby tree and landed on the grass in front of her. Meg laughed at herself and released her breath. As she turned and opened the slider, the sound of piano music once again froze her. It sounded canned, slow, melancholy. Meg looked over the yard once more, went into the villa, and locked the door behind her.

Unable to sleep, Meg decided to explore Havilla's eclectic library. The Bible, Byatt, Austen, Poe, Woolf, *Swords, Ships and Sugar, Nevis: Queen of the Caribees, Sugar & Slaves*—the owners not only had good taste in literature, but were thoughtful in the reading selections provided. Meg poured over the historical books and guides into the early hours of the morning, finding herself fascinated with the slave past of the island.

Black Devil, Fogcutter, Nightcap—after Meg's third rum drink she finally passed out on the ottoman covered in books. Not long after, the morning light made its way into the villa through the sheers. Diaphanous silk—though beautifully decorative—was a useless barrier to tropical sun. Under a heavy hangover, Meg found her admiration of the window treatments wane.

After a shower, glass of water, and a double dose of pain medication, Meg felt ready to start her vacation. Her headache prevented her from wanting to sit in the sun, but she was eager to explore the plantation home. Meg filled a bag with a camera, notebook, pen, bottled water, pain relievers, and the old photograph of Eden, and began walking out to the road from the villa. Though it was early, the sun was already bearing down on the island. Meg wiped the sweat from her neck and twisted her hair into a knot which she secured with her pen. She admired the vegetation and began a mental catalogue of the plants she had read about last night in the guide to Nevis. Allamanda, African tulips, bougainvillea, calabash, coconut trees, lilies, and white cedars—always a list running through her mind.

Meg's talents at research, organization, and persuasion, along with her heavy familial connections, had helped her secure a sought after position at the governor's office in Annapolis. She was in charge of fundraising, event planning, and general public relations on behalf of Governor Harold Nelson.

Unfortunately, after young staffer Mindy Newcomb went public with pictures and video clips from a year-long affair with Nelson (father of 4, husband of 18 years), Meg's job had become nearly impossible. But Meg—fiercely loyal and always determined—assisted the governor and his staff in uncovering enough skeletons in Mindy's closet to destroy her character, humiliate her, and undermine her allegations. A child born out of wedlock, an arrest in high school for marijuana possession, and a father in jail for tax fraud contributed to the case Nelson's office presented: Mindy Newcomb was a street-smart, loose, drug addict who used her pitiful situation to gain the sympathy of and seduce the governor—a compassionate but weak man.

His ratings had dipped in the thick of the controversy, but had recently surpassed earlier highs after Mrs. Nelson and the governor were interviewed on a local television station discussing the renewal of their marriage vows, and commitment to the future of their family and the state of Maryland.

It wasn't until her uncomfortable embrace in the governor's office that she had felt remorse for her role in pardoning him. She thought of the day she'd seen Mindy Newcomb at Quiet Waters Park playing with her daughter, Lucy—a sturdy five-year-old, buoyant with energy. Lucy was chattering away as Mindy pushed her on the swings. Mindy looked frail and tired, but attempted a feeble smile for her daughter. This struck Meg as pitiful, and caused a knot to form in her stomach that still hadn't worked itself out.

"Shit!"

Meg's ankle twisted into a mud-baked groove in the ground, and it took her several yards of limping to walk off the pain.

And suddenly, there it was.

Set at the end of a long, overgrown drive, laden with vines and plants, half-shadowed in the mid-morning sun stood Eden. Meg felt the weight of that great, skeletal, abandoned, plantation home settle over her as she stepped into its shadow.

Meg recalled a passage she had read the night before from Poe's *Fall of the House of Usher*. Looking upon the house gave the narrator "a sense of insufferable gloom...the vacant eye-like windows."

Meg searched through her bag until she came across her photograph of Eden. Though the photograph was old, not much had changed since it was taken. Slightly more plant growth pervaded the ancient place, but it was mostly preserved. This, in itself, was astounding considering the history of hurricanes and earthquakes on the island.

After snapping several photographs of the front of the house, Meg approached the stairs leading to the front door. She checked each of the stairs before putting her full weight on them, but found them to be sturdy. Naturally, the front door was stuck, but a hard push opened it, releasing the stink of mildew, rotting wood, animal droppings, and that familiar musty smell that emanates from anything old. Meg waited for the creatures and birds who had taken residence in the abandoned house to scurry away before crossing into the foyer.

Even through years of neglect and filth, it was easy to see that Eden had once been a spectacular house. The two-story foyer opened to a massive staircase straight ahead, which led up to the second floor. High-ceilinged rooms—a parlor, library, dining room, billiard room, and sitting room encircled the foyer. A dark passage off the dining room led to a kitchen which, though attached to the house, was set far enough to the rear of the plantation to keep the cooking smells and heat from the stone ovens contained.

Meg was surprised at the amount of furniture, wall hangings, and décor still inside of the home. Someone must have either left the house in a great hurry many years ago, or intended on returning and never did. Of course, it was all damp, half-eaten, and completely unusable to anyone but small rodents, but still a marvel to see in such a condition. The Historical Society would salivate if they knew the level of preservation.

Meg shot picture after picture, thankful she brought a new memory card for her digital camera. As Meg made her way into the parlor to begin a room by room catalogue of the house, she began to think of the monetary possibilities of selling the house and land. Would the Nevis Historical Society be able to give her fair market value for the property, or would an outside investor be the best option? If she sold the property to a developer a grand hotel could be built, with the house as an historical site that could be restored and used for tours.

As she thought and walked slowly through the parlor, Meg found herself in front of a piano whose legs looked as if they were moments away from collapsing under the burden of the instrument. The bench had already given out, and rested heavily on the floor. The spine of a music book peeking from under the bench caught Meg's eye.

Beethoven's "Moonlight Sonata."

Her years of piano training as a child came rushing back to her as she thought of the somber sounds of the piece in her head. A sudden chill seized Meg.

That was the piece played last night.

Suddenly aware of how dark the house had become, Meg felt a sudden urge to leave. She carefully lifted the bench to remove the music book, and stood in a hurry to exit the house. As she rose, a small pamphlet fell from the pages inside the book. It was yellowed and very brittle. A note was scribbled in old-fashioned script and almost illegibly on the inside cover:

Miss Dall,

You should find this writing most interesting, as Mr. Alexander Hamilton was one of yours, that is, a Nevisan.

Yours,
James Silwell.

Meg turned the pages, scanning its contents as she went. The pamphlet provided a biography of Alexander Hamilton and catalogued his efforts as an officer of the New York Manumission Society. Meg was interested to learn that Hamilton was born on Nevis, and his early observations and experiences that exposed him to the slave system (though he never personally owned slaves) helped form his abhorrence of it.

The second half of the pamphlet provided a brief biography of Benjamin Franklin and his involvement in the abolitionist movement. In 1789, Franklin became president of the Pennsylvania Abolition Society and worked to make meaningful transitions to freedom for slaves. He advocated education, training and support for free men and women, noting that simply freeing droves of people and sending them on their way did little to help their situations.

Meg was interested to read an excerpt from a letter to George Washington from General Lafayette:

> *Now, my dear General, that you are going to enjoy some ease and quiet, permit me to propose a plan to which might become greatly beneficial to the Black Part of Mankind. Let us unite in purchasing a small estate where we may try the experiment to free the Negroes, and use them only as tenants—such an example as yours might render it a general practice, and if we succeed in America, I will cheerfully devote a part of my time to render the method fashionable in the West Indies. If it be a wild scheme, I had rather be mad that way, than to be thought wise on the other tack.*

Suddenly, a shell fragment flew through the window, missing Meg's face by inches. She ran to the window to locate the perpetrator, and nearly scared a boy of about twelve to death.

"Are you a ghost?" he asked.

"No, are you?"

The boy laughed. His white teeth flashed in the sun against his black skin.

"I'm Hamilton"

"Like Alexander?"

"Yes. Who are you?"

"Meg."

"You know that place is haunted."

Meg smiled and rolled her eyes. "I've heard."

Hamilton ran his toes over the shells. His feet were bare. He wore tan shorts and no shirt. He was slender in frame, but appeared robust, active, and strong. His confident demeanor was one that adults warmed to and children would follow. He had a kind and familiar way of speaking—one that instantly made others feel at ease.

A distant rumble of thunder caused Meg to place the music book and pamphlet in her bag and leave the house. She pulled the door closed behind her and walked down the stairs to join Hamilton.

"Do you often come here to vandalize the house?" teased Meg as they started wondering along the drive.

"Not usually, but I thought I saw a ghost in the window."

"So you threw a shell at it?"

"A silly choice of weapon, I know. But it was all I could come up with."

They turned off the drive onto an overgrown path that led around the west side of the house.

"So where do you live?" asked Meg.

"Just up the road. My dad says I shouldn't play here—it's trespassing. But I like to spend time in the lagoon. I don't think the owners have ever been here before, anyway."

"I'm here now."

Hamilton looked worried and stopped walking.

"Don't worry, I don't mind you playing here—as long as you stay away from the ghosts, that is."

Hamilton smiled.

"Why did you wait so long to come here?" he asked.

Meg couldn't explain why she felt so comfortable talking to this young stranger, but for some reason it felt natural.

"I didn't even know I owned it until a few days ago," she said. "My parents recently died, and I was their only child. I found an old picture of the plantation home in my father's office, along with some documents relating to things I've inherited. I guess I've come here to decide what to do with the land, and my life."

"I'm sorry about your parents. I hope you find what you're looking for."

Meg looked at Hamilton. He seemed so grown up. In some ways she felt like she was speaking to another adult, yet his candor and openness were typical of a child.

"Me too."

The wind which had been building, called attention to the approaching storm.

"I'd better get going," said Hamilton. "You should too, if you don't want to get caught in the storm. They are quick and fierce in the Islands."

"Thanks. It was good to meet you. Feel free to play in the lagoon anytime."

Hamilton smiled and disappeared down the path. Meg watched after him, and then made her way back along the drive.

⁓

Half-way to the villa the downpour began. It came from out of nowhere and caught Meg off-guard. She tucked her bag up her shirt to protect her findings and ran the rest of the way back to the villa.

Out of breath, soaked, and limping on the ankle she had twisted, Meg placed the old book on the table, removed her wet clothes, and changed into a dry pair of shorts and a shirt. The wind had ceased to blow so violently, but the rain continued to fall in a great gray sheet. Meg opened the slider and let the sweet smell of the wet earth fill the villa in little gasps. Quick flashes of lightning followed by soft rumbles punctuated the hushing of the rain. It was as if someone had flipped the "Thunderstorm" switch on a stage for atmosphere.

Meg walked over to the bar and briefly debated whether or not to make herself a drink. She considered the

Hurricane recipe on page 8 of Rum Recipes a sign to proceed. Not that the little storm could be considered a tropical storm, but it amused Meg, nonetheless.

Meg sat with her cocktail on the couch facing the slider and opened the music book. She poured over each page hoping to find something else to go with the abolitionist handbook, but found only piano sonatas. Perhaps Miss Dall shoved the pamphlet into the music book one day in a hurry to hide it from someone entering the room, and then forgot about it.

Next to the music book was a Nevis history book she had been reading the night before. Meg remembered reading something in *Swords, Ships, & Sugar* that now reminded her of Eden. It was an excerpt from a journal of some kind that an American had written in 1895.

> "…we came upon the ruins of a great stone mansion, bare and desolate, with its eyeless windows boarded up. On the hill behind it rises the tower of the windmill, still intact, with its huge arms motionless in the air."

Had the author seen Eden all those years ago, or was he referring to some other place?

Meg rummaged through her purse until she found the number of the Historical Society. Before deciding on the future of the house, Meg needed to find out more about its past.

4

Monday dawned overcast and stormy, reflecting Edward's mood. From where he stood on his balcony he had an excellent view of his land and the surrounding neighbors. Edward was displeased at the size and quality of his plantation compared to Eden.

It was the topography of Nevis that afforded Edward such a view. At the center of the island swelled the peak of Mount Nevis. Its cloud-covered summit reminded Spanish explorers of snow—"nieves"—resulting in its name. The densely vegetated land of Nevis sloped downward in steps, upon which the largest plantation homes rested near the top, and the lesser homes on the low-lying areas. The base of the island plunged into the sea at various cliffs and beaches.

Owning an entire expanse of land from Mt. Nevis down to the sea was quite an accomplishment. Only the Dalls, Ewings, and Halls belonged to that class of planter. Most of the major plantations had failed due to the poor, stone-infested earth. The three great plantations remaining on the island, however, thrived due to a rich deposit of volcanic soil.

The sugar plantations in the Caribbean were advanced manufacturing machines. An army of slaves planted, harvested, clarified, cured, and distilled cane through a network of mills, boiling houses, curing houses, distilleries, and storehouses. Sugar cane was a particularly difficult crop since it required well over a year to ripen and would rot if production did not occur within several hours.

Edward contemplated these things as he walked down the dirt path to the mill. He was beginning to resent his mental output over such details as keeping enough cows to provide sufficient dung for the fields, equipping the slaves with enough tools to be efficient at harvest time yet busy during the off-season, and constantly having to replace the boiling house slaves when they would get burned or killed by the scalding sugar. Edward's chief overseer had died several months ago after falling from his horse, and Edward had yet to find a suitable replacement.

~❧~

"I don't understand the drop in production," said Catherine to her father as she brought him the columns of numbers. "The sugar output of Eden has fallen by thirteen percent since last season. I know our strongest harvest season is just beginning, but I can't see how this could be."

"My dear, I wish you wouldn't trouble yourself about such things. It is not becoming in a lady of your stature," said Cecil as he reclined in a hammock on the back porch. A half filled jug of rum and empty glass lay on the table next to him, and his beard and shirt ruffles glistened with spilled alcohol.

"It must be the rats," said Catherine. "Phinneas said that the good weather and plentiful crops are allowing them to multiply beyond reason. I have organized several slave rat-catchings, but none have been effective."

"Well, what do you suggest?"

"I have been reluctant to employ this method, but I feel we have no choice. We must lure the rats to the center of one of our fields, and burn the field from the outside inward. It's the only way to thoroughly wipe out a pesky rat population."

"Catherine, you must be mad. Burn an entire field? That would cost us more than a slight slip in production due to a few troublesome rodents."

"I disagree. Field D is about to re-sprout for the third time. The sugar it would yield would be less than half that of newly planted cane, and it would be of an inferior quality. Field D is also more isolated than the others, and would pose less chance of catching other fields on fire. If we lure the rats to the center of D, and burn the field from the borders inward, we will not only eliminate our rat population, but we will create soil rich in nutrients for a brand new planting."

Cecil looked at his daughter in perplexed amazement.

"Well, by all means, let's proceed. I'll inform Phinneas of the plan. You be sure to get word to our neighbors so they know what's going on."

The conversation was interrupted by the announcement that the Silwells had arrived.

"Ah, gentlemen—you've arrived just in time for a great rat bonfire," called Cecil as he poured himself another drink.

James and Albert looked at one another with confusion. Catherine rolled her eyes and explained what they were about to do.

"The bonfire will not be held until a future date, I'm afraid. We must prepare the field, lure the rats, wait for the weather to clear, and wait for the sun to go down. The fire will be better managed if we can see all its embers, and the moist night air will aid us in preventing the fire from spreading. Also, our neighbors must be notified of what we are going to do. I wouldn't want them rushing over with buckets of sand and water in their nightclothes."

"I hope you brought your journals, gentleman," said Cecil as Catherine helped him out of the hammock. "You will learn much about life on the sugar plantation from my daughter."

Catherine thanked her father and excused herself to the parlor so that she could begin composing notes to her neighbors. The Silwells turned to accompany Cecil to the cane fields.

As Catherine sat at her writing desk, a noise caused her to turn.

"Miss Dall," said James.

"Yes?"

"Word of your advanced knowledge of plantation life has reached us from many different sources. You are known for you business savvy."

"I know more than I care to," said Catherine as she turned back to her desk.

"I beg your pardon."

"I would not have chosen this role. It has been set upon me."

James shifted uncomfortably and again attempted to lure Catherine into conversation. "I hope to speak with you at length about how you manage. There is much I wish to learn about the sugar system."

"Certainly."

Seeing that Catherine was intent on beginning her letters, James turned to leave until her voice stopped him.

"Interesting, really, Mr. Silwell."

"What's that?"

"St. Christopher has put a hold on land purchases for plantation development in light of Britain's recent coolness toward slavery. I hope to speak to you at length about how your father managed to secure such an estate."

Catherine looked hard at James as he wiped a sweaty line of perspiration from over his eyes. A wooden clock over the fireplace mantle began an eerie tinkling to announce the half-hour, and a gust of wind blew into the room, sending Catherine's writing papers blowing about all over the parlor. James rushed to gather the papers as Catherine watched him with amusement, and she was grinning at him as he rose from his knees. James relaxed into a smile.

"It is an interesting story," he said. "However, I must catch up with our fathers. They will fear the wind has thrown me over the cliff if I do not join them shortly."

Catherine smiled and turned back to her desk as James left the parlor.

~~⁓⌒~~

Dust thick with mud and blood was clumped in hunks of coarse, sweaty, black hair and puffed skin. Dust was curdled in black eyes under lids swollen and stiff above a broken, crusted nose. Dust filled her mouth with its arid, earthen taste and lined her teeth like moss on filthy gravestones.

Esther breathed in staggered gasps on the dirt as she awoke from her black-out to the sound of male voices on the nearby path. The thick foliage blocked the faint light of the cloudy morning while concealing Esther in the shadows like a forgotten animal crawled away to die.

But I will not die, she thought. For her injuries—though throbbing and fresh—were shallow. It had been so long since her last beating that she had forgotten how tender skin could be. Her last beating came before Leah's birth, before Catherine, before Eden, on a slave ship carrying her to Nevis, more than twenty years ago. Of course, she had been abused and violated for the last twenty years—but not beaten.

Esther felt every muscle in her body groan as she began to push herself to a sitting position. She closed her eyes once she was upright to block out the spinning trees before her. Once the world seemed to steady itself, she again opened her eyes as much as possible and looked over her battered body to survey the damage.

Sharp pains upon inhalation alerted her to a broken or bruised rib, and bloody welts ran up the back of her legs and back. Mercifully the switch had been applied with some degree of restraint. The wounds would heal quickly. *Just a warning,* he had said.

But the pain of the beating was not what frightened Esther most—it was the anticipation of Leah and Catherine's reactions to the beating that most sickened her. Leah was thin-skinned and tender from her own demons. She would be further damaged once she knew the source of her mother's suffering. Leah had grown up too close to Catherine, too comfortable for a slave, too educated for her lot—her recent violations had nearly pushed her over the edge.

And Catherine's illusion of control was about to be shattered. Esther feared Catherine's reaction when she learned of the beating—she feared the head-strong girl would place herself in a dangerous situation. Perhaps she could hide herself from Catherine, but not from Leah. Esther just hoped Leah had already gone to the Great House to begin her work for the day.

Shuffling behind the vines and bushes, Esther made her way to the slaves' lane. The stiffness in her body was sliding off her bones as the strength of circulation returned with each passing step. The smells of cornmeal browning over fires, the curious babble of the slaves, and the shrill scraping of knives on stones foretold her arrival at the slave village.

Esther crept behind Mary's hut and waited for an opportunity to sneak unnoticed into its shelter. She was forced to wait before the slaves moved off to their stations and the morning bustle subsided. Before Esther could sneak into the hut an ancient, African voice whispered behind her.

"I smell you, Esther, under all that hurt."

Startled, Esther turned too quickly and gasped from the pain in her rib.

"Don't speak."

Mary handed Esther a patched, threadbare quilt and instructed her to cover herself as she snuck with her wounded patient into the small, thatched dwelling.

Esther felt stronger as Mary eased her onto her stomach in the soft bed of straw. She could smell the pungent aromas of the herbs that hung from Mary's ceiling in tight bundles—bundles scavenged and dried by expert hands.

"Is Leah gone?" asked Esther.

"She is."

Mary crouched and shuffled her way across the hut to a small bowl. She hummed with a voice deep and thick like molasses as she crushed the long grass, bee bush, and water into a thick paste. Her aged fingers pressed into the paste to feel its consistency. Once it felt like lagoon-bank mud and smelled sickly sweet she turned and moved back to her patient.

Mary helped Esther remove her worn, filthy, bloody, cotton dress and ran her hands over Esther's skin. Esther peered out of half-shut eyes into Mary's eyes—glazed-over and frosty-white like the clouds on Mount Nevis. Mary's sightless eyes, coarse white hair, and deeply lined black skin gave her the appearance of a witch. Her healing powers convinced the village children that she was a witch, and caused some to fear her. Most, though, revered and loved Mary—especially Catherine, who spent hours at Mary's side filling countless journals with her healing remedies, plant sketches, and general wisdom.

Esther knew that Mary could heal her body. She lay patiently as Mary's fingers moved like zephyr over her abrasions without disturbing them. Esther tasted the sharp acid of the soursop on her tongue, and allowed Mary to feed her the sedative before beginning treatment.

As her body relaxed, Esther could feel the warm water dribbling into her wounds. Mary's fingers peeled away the crusty film from her cuts, exposing virgin skin that tingled in the light breeze that crept into the hut through the door-flap. Once she was clean, Esther felt the sting of the paste as Mary pushed it deep into her cuts, followed by a numbing sensation that grew like roots down to her bones. The numbness traveled through her body, up to her eyes and head, and brought on a dreamless, peaceful sleep.

$\sim\!\!\infty\!\!\circ$

The needle bit Catherine's finger, startling her out of her sewing trance. A tiny red bead oozed out of her fingertip, and Catherine put her finger to her lips, tasting the sharp metallic flavor of the blood.

"That's the third time you've done that in an hour. Do you need a break?" asked Leah.

"No, I'm fine. We have to finish these shifts for the field women. I will not have female field slaves working bare-breasted next to their male counterparts, and under the eye of Mr. Sarponte. Besides, now that I've convinced Father to allow the use of this extra material for slave clothing, I want to get it finished before he has time to change his mind."

"It is good of you to do this."

"It is nothing. Decent clothing is the right of any human being. It is scandalous the way the Ewings and Halls allow their women to walk around half-naked. It is dangerous for those poor things. Men cannot be trusted around such a display of flesh. Why tempt them?"

Leah continued to sit in silence as the young women finished the dresses.

"I wish I could throw one of these lightweight garments on during the day," said Catherine. "Layers of corsets and petticoats are ridiculous in such a climate. Could you imagine the look on Father's face if I appeared one morning wearing this?"

Leah smiled as Catherine held the plain, short garment up to her figure. She folded it and added it to the enormous pile that she and Leah had already sewn. The women had worked side by side sewing the shifts for weeks. Catherine had promised Cecil that she would only take one slave from her chores to complete the garments made from leftover bolts of fabric. A tremendous amount of clothing had been completed in such a short time.

"I'll have Joseph take these to the slave village," said Catherine as Leah folded the final dress. Then she dropped her voice to a whisper. "Meet me in the grove shortly."

Leah nodded and packed up the sewing materials as her young mistress exited the room. She worked slowly and paused frequently to wipe the cold sweat from her brow. A sudden wave of nausea stopped Leah and sent her into a panic. Stumbling over to the window, she was just able to heave her breakfast out of the window and wipe the spittle from her mouth before she heard male voices entering the room. She hurried back to the sewing chest to finish as Cecil, Albert and James strode into the room.

"Ah, Leah, fetch us some tea before you're off," instructed Cecil.

Leah nodded and moved from the room. She nearly collided with James, and looked into his face to mutter an apology. What was it that she saw in his eyes? Was it pity? Had he seen her sickness? He smiled at her and moved aside to let her pass.

Catherine stepped out of the Great House and moved over the back lawn. Until she felt the cool darkness of the lagoon trees, she did not slow her step. After making her way through thick plants and vines, Catherine emerged into a small clearing. Doves cooed near her head in the branches of the surrounding trees and a small vervet monkey ran across her path to the other side of the clearing. Catherine moved over to a small stone bench framed in fern and bougainvillea.

As she waited for Leah, Catherine's thoughts turned to Esther. It was unusual that Esther would still be tending to Rachel and kept from her household duties. Catherine planned to visit Esther at the slave village once she and Leah finished. She also wanted to speak to Mary about the birthing. After having written copious notes in her journal detailing each stage of the labor, Catherine wanted to speak to Mary about several questions she had regarding the care needed for mother and child following delivery.

The hiss of rustling bamboo announced Leah's arrival. The slave girl emerged—secretive and panting—from the great, straight stalks to join her mistress. She carried a basket of fruit and kept it on her lap as she sat next to Catherine.

"I hope no one saw me run across the back lawn."

"I am sure no one did. Everyone is attending to their duties, and I believe Father is showing the Englishmen the sugar buildings."

Leah produced a small, worn Bible from under the bananas. Catherine opened the book and the girls moved close together. Leah began to read aloud from Genesis, and Catherine coached her pupil through the first chapter. The girls leaned into one another as the silent mutiny was executed.

"You've been practicing," said Catherine.

"It has been difficult keeping it from Mami but I have managed a bit each day."

Leah read slowly but clearly through the first three chapters of Genesis. The thick vegetation of the grove trembled around them under the weight of birds, small animals, and swift breezes, and concealed the figure who was watching them.

The lagoon began under a gushing cataract that surged into shallow pools and bubbled up to the surface of the water where it moved noiselessly to a large boulder. At the boulder the waters divided into four streams that drained down to meet the sea. Large flowers colored like lapis lazuli covered the shadowy banks. The murmuring plash of the waterfall, the drone of the insects, and the brief communications of the birds were the only sounds that pierced the stillness.

After finishing with Leah, Catherine escaped from the scorching afternoon by entering the lagoon for a bit of exploring. She descended over fallen branches and through dense floor covering to the banks of the water and began to scour the earth for various medicinal plants. On the ink-spotted pages of her journal, she sketched the plants and their locations before moving on for more explorations. As Catherine moved closer to the waterfall, she slipped and nearly fell into the water. Upon regaining her balance she smiled and thought of the day in her early adolescence when she and Leah had romped through the lagoon. She had recited Tennyson—

> "Day and night to the billow the fountain calls;
> Down shower the gamboling waterfalls
> From wandering over the lea;
> Out of the live-green heart of the dells
> They freshen the silvery-crimson shells,
> And thick with white bells the clover-hill swells
> High over the full-toned sea."

She had climbed onto the large boulder and had begun to recite to her companion a poem of her own composition. "Oh, Waterfall, what beauty you possess! But your sopping sprays make the mud soil up my dress. If you would but spray the other way, you would not make a mess."

Catherine had jumped down from the boulder amidst much laughter and applause as Leah climbed up and began: "Rushing waterfall; dangerous dashing font, how I wish you would drown that monstrous man Sarponte. Unless of course, that means, he would be back to haunt!"

The girls' laughter had evaporated in the rush and splash of the water, and Leah jumped down from the boulder. They had knelt by the water to see if any manner of creature could be observed. As Leah had peered into the water, Catherine pushed her from behind. She came up sputtering mad.

"You wicked girl! Mami will be furious!"

Leah climbed out and began to chase Catherine. She caught Catherine and forced her into the lagoon under the spray of the waterfall. Upon doing so, Leah lost her balance and fell into the shallow pool. Both girls splashed and plunged one another under the water until they were out of breath.

They grew silent and began floating on their backs as they stared into the canopy of tropical trees. Only the sound of the waterfall could be heard as they floated like water lilies. They spun in the gentle current until their hands touched.

"Why can't every day be Sunday?" Leah had whispered.

Catherine shook her head as Leah's words came from her memory and whispered ghost-like around her. They hung in the air, jumped from behind bushes, and splashed off the water. Catherine's eyes swept the trees with foreboding. She began trembling and a lump rose in her throat.

The rumbling of distant thunder urged Catherine to gather her journal and bundles of plants and hurry to the slaves' village. She walked quickly, watching the sky for signs of the incoming storm, but soon relaxed her step when she saw the storm was far off on the horizon.

The smell of oranges and boiled sweet potatoes greeted Catherine as she stepped into the slave village. The very young, the very old, and the infirm were the only beings populating the village at this hour, and many waved at Catherine as she made her way to Rebecca's hut.

Piercing high over the wind, cooking sounds, and humming was the shrill cry of the infant. The flap was pulled back, exposing a tearful and agitated Rebecca rocking her newborn son.

"I don't know what's wrong. I've tried feeding him, but he won't drink. He cries like he suffers some illness."

Catherine took the child from Rebecca and looked into his furious face. She whispered to the baby as she laid him on the bed of leaves and began to undress him. Upon careful inspection, Catherine found the source of his irritation—a large, red welt on his left thigh.

"An insect bite."

Catherine broke open an aloe leaf and squeezed its milky salve into her palm. She then rubbed a yellow dad leaf into the milk, and applied it to the child's insect bite. His crying ceased, and he watched Catherine.

"Apply this whenever he seems uncomfortable. It should be gone in a few days."

"Thank you, Miss Catherine."

Catherine smiled and turned to leave, until she remembered her purpose.

"Have you seen Esther today?"

"I've not seen her since yesterday evening."

Catherine's brow furrowed. She thanked Rebecca and moved down the lane to Mary's hut.

The ancient blind woman was sitting on a log in front of the thatched dwelling, weaving kush-kush grass into a mat. Her gnarled fingers—worn from decades of ceaseless industry—moved nimbly through the stalks. Catherine watched her deeply lined fingers on rough, skillful hands. Strong hands on a powerful body used up almost completely. Mary turned toward Catherine with her empty eyes and greeted her young mistress.

"How do you know when I approach?" asked Catherine.

"Your step sounds like one on its way to something else. It's different from all the others."

Catherine smiled, dropped her bundle of plants, and embraced the old woman who smelled of coconut, herbs, and smoke.

"Wild cilliment, joint wood, seagrape, hog plum— you've brought me a good selection today," said Mary.

Catherine gazed into the old woman's face. The milky blobs in her eye sockets seemed to stare back. Over the years, little by little, a film had slid down the gold-brown of her eyes like mountain mist, eventually rendering her sightless. Her visual palette had deteriorated from the light glory of day, to the sneak-shadow of dusk, to the tar-stain of night. Yet here in her pitch-black afternoon, Catherine felt that it was not Mary who lacked for anything.

The women spoke for some time about Rebecca's birthing. Mary mumbled her wisdom in her husky voice as Catherine's ink-pen blackened her journal and fingertips. When Catherine noticed that the storm clouds had inched a bit closer, she bade Mary farewell and moved down the lane to Esther's hut. Finding it empty, Catherine traveled to the path leading to the beach, hoping to secure a bit of coconut palm to bring to Mary before the rainstorm began. As she was running down the path, she collided with James Silwell.

"I'm sorry. I'm in a hurry to explore a cave down by the water before high tide. It's inaccessible once the tide comes in, and some useful plants are to be found around it."

"It looks as though it's going to storm," said James.

"I'm sure it will just be a light soaking. Would you like to join me? You can take notes on the excursions of a planter's daughter."

"You enjoy mocking me," remarked James as he followed her down the dirt path.

She smiled, turned away from him, and continued her descent to the shore. James saw the turbulent, blue waters frame Catherine's form as she moved ahead of him. When they reached the sand, Catherine pointed to a dark cave overgrown with vines. The two of them made their way toward it and fell into step beside one another.

"Forgive me if I've offended you," said Catherine.

"I'm not easily offended. I was teasing you."

Catherine stopped and picked up a starfish that had washed up onto the sand. She pulled off her boots, hitched up her skirts and waded out into the shallow pools toward some rocks offshore where she placed the small creature.

Once she was back on shore she rung out the bottom of her skirt and picked up her boots. James tried to suppress a grin.

A bolt of lightening followed by a sudden downpour of rain sent Catherine and James running toward the cave.

"I'm sure this will pass as quickly as it has come," said Catherine. "Is your weather at home as unpredictable and sudden as it is here?"

"We do see quite a bit of rain, but rarely does it announce itself in such a way. My family comes from Cornwall in the Southwest of England. It's very mild during all seasons, but our winds blow strong and steady, as do yours."

"If I'm not mistaken, my father's family comes from those parts of England. Do you have a large family at home?"

"I do," smiled James. "My younger brother is a clergyman at a neighboring parish, and I have three younger sisters. All of my siblings are married and have children, except for me. I am the victim of much good-natured teasing in my family."

Catherine looked at James. His brown hair was worn shorter than most, but it suited him. His eyes were light in color, but set deep in his face and rimmed in dark circles. His features were sharp and serious, but very attractive. Catherine wondered why he wasn't married.

"And may I ask of your mother?"

"Mother died when I was sixteen. She was a kind and loving woman, and I'm afraid we've all never quite recovered from her passing. She was full of life, and very spirited."

"You were blessed to have had her in your life."

"Tell me about your mother. Did you ever know her?"

"No, she died during my childbirth," said Catherine. "My Aunt Elizabeth helped to raise and educate me, but she died when I was twelve. Esther is really the only constant mother-figure I've had."

The pair sat watching the storm in the damp cave that smelled of soaked moss and salt. It was close and humid and sheltered from the sharp blasts of wind tossing the outside landscape into a wet frenzy. A small hermit crab crept around the corner from the beach and inched its way into the cave for shelter, leaving a little lined path in its tracks. Coconut palms rippled along the opening of the cave like underwater seaweed.

"Are these the plants you need?" asked James. "I'll get them for you."

Catherine watched James pull a blade from his jacket and slice down the great, wet leaves. He shook them out and passed them into the cave.

"I told Mary in the slave village that I would take them to her," said Catherine. "Now that the rain is slowing down, I think it's safe for us to venture out. A search party will be organized if I don't report to my father as soon as possible."

They moved out of the cave and proceeded up to the Great House. As they emerged from the path, Phinneas intercepted them. Catherine recoiled as Phinneas looked over her soaked figure.

"Where have you been?" he demanded. "Mr. Dall has been frantic. We were about to assemble a search party."

"A storm overtook us as we walked on the beach," said Catherine.

"It is not dignified or ladylike for a woman like yourself to be alone in the company of strange men," said Phinneas.

"I assure you it was a totally innocent mistake. If you will excuse us, we must go and tell Father that we are unharmed."

Catherine and James stopped by Mary's hut and delivered the palms before returning to the house. Leah greeted them at the back door and led Catherine upstairs to assist her in changing her wet clothing. James found Albert and Cecil in the parlor and recounted their adventures.

"I'm sorry you were forced to worry," said James. "The cave was really an excellent shelter."

"I'm only glad Catherine had you to keep her safe. She probably would have danced in the rain if you hadn't pulled her to safety," said Cecil. Phinneas scowled and retreated into the shadows of the room. Catherine returned and Leah followed with tea.

"Won't you stay for dinner?" asked Cecil.

"We don't want to cause you any trouble," answered Albert.

"It's no trouble at all. Guests are a wonderful diversion. One gets to feeling very isolated in the islands without frequent visitors."

"Then we would be glad to accept."

Thomas led James away to change his clothing and dry him off while the rest of the company sat down to enjoy afternoon tea. Phinneas slipped out of the room and returned to the fields.

The day's storms left behind the sweetly pungent aroma of rain-soaked flowers and earth. A breeze blew into the dining room, carrying with it the pleasant fragrance of the gardens. Thousands of winking stars appeared between the moving clouds, and a luminous full moon glowed white and round above the island.

"Catherine is adored by our slaves," said Cecil. "You may have noticed that she has acquired quite an extensive knowledge of the medicinal uses of plants on the island. She helps sick slaves, neighbors, and her father to stay healthy."

Catherine colored.

"And do not think I have not noticed you smuggling food to our slaves in spite of the fact that they are well-fed," teased Cecil.

Catherine looked down at her plate. She did not understand why she felt embarrassed. Her father's tone was light, but there was something behind it—something that made her feel like a child who had been caught doing something wrong.

"Yes, Catherine is about the only untamed creature on this island."

Albert addressed Cecil in a serious tone: "I beg your pardon, sir, but are you not concerned with Miss Dall interacting with the slaves, unsupervised?"

"Mr. Silwell, of our two hundred slaves about half are women. Of the remaining men, sixty percent of them are children or elderly. Of the forty or so able-bodied men, I assure you that not one would dare harm a fly. They are all quite docile—not to mention the fact that they are fearful of Mr. Sarponte."

James and Albert exchanged knowing glances.

"How long has Mr. Sarponte worked as an overseer here?" inquired James.

"Phinneas was hired around the time that my deceased brother's wife died, and it became too much for me to look after the slaves, my daughter, and the plantation. He was referred to me by a neighboring planter who was leaving the island. I've recently expanded his duties to include buying and selling slaves. I'm getting too old to participate in the trade, and Catherine has no place in such business. Phinneas is efficient, stern, and knows all that goes on in Eden."

At the conclusion of the meal, as another soaking downpour began, the party retired to the parlor where Cecil solicited Catherine to play the pianoforte. She sat down at the keyboard and began Chopin's *Nocturne in E Minor*. Cecil's glass soon dropped to the floor as he passed out to the slow, monotonous tones of the piece. James looked at Albert as the song continued, thinking back to the day that his mother had died.

A fire had crackled in the room where Jane Silwell lay dying in her bed. Heavy rain and winds assaulted the windows in the room, and Chopin's *Nocturne* drifted up the stairs as James' sister played.

"Open the windows, James. Do you see how the air begs to come in?"

"You will catch a chill, Mother."

"James, the chill of the rain will not reach me before I've already gone. Please let in some fresh air. I haven't been out of this room in weeks, and I long to feel the air in my lungs again."

Albert nodded from his chair by the fire, and James pushed open the streaked glass. A blast of mist covered his face and the air filled the room. James returned to his mother's bedside and held her hand. Jane turned her head and looked out the window. She inhaled deeply and regularly. James reached for her hand again, and watched her chest rise and fall.

When Catherine's song concluded all were silent. The rain had ceased, and only Cecil's snore could be heard. Catherine escorted the Silwells to the front door, wished them a safe trip back to the hotel, and returned to the parlor where her father was sleeping. She crossed the room to pick up the empty glass on its side by the fire—its light flickering along the walls and over Cecil as Catherine placed the glass on the table beside him.

Catherine took her father's hand and told him to wake, but he could not be roused. Catherine stared into his lined face. His once ruddy complexion was pallid and old. His breaths came in irregular wheezes. Her father's failing health could not be denied under such scrutiny, and fear crept into Catherine's heart.

What would become of her if Cecil died? With no other living relatives, she would inherit all of Eden. Catherine knew how to run a plantation, but without her father's protection, predators would abound. The men of marrying age on the island—none of whom interested Catherine in the slightest—would have to be beaten away constantly; but it was Phinneas who most frightened her. His lurking, leering figure was everywhere, and was only kept in check because of Cecil's presence.

Catherine looked into the fire and thought of her future until the last ember was extinguished. Only then did she leave her father's side to retire for the evening.

5

Meg and Hamilton stood side by side looking down into the water crashing below the cliff. Though it was a beautiful day, the storm left behind a trail of gusty wind that made Meg's heart race as she stood close to the cliff's edge.

It wasn't a straight drop down to the water—the cliff formed a series of long, steep, vine-covered steps that ended where waves crashed over massive boulders and rock fragments about one-hundred feet below.

"So they say that the slave girl took her life here and now haunts the plantation house?"

"That's what I've heard," said Hamilton. "I don't know if it's true."

"And that keeps people away from the property?"

"People are superstitious."

"Well, for whatever reason, I'm glad the house remained largely undisturbed. It will be worth more in its present condition than if it had been vandalized or looted."

"Or hit with broken shells," said Hamilton. They laughed and turned back toward the Great House.

"And what about the owners of the house?" asked Meg.

"It is said that a woman and her father, along with many slaves, died of some sickness a long time ago."

"So maybe if the house is haunted, it's the ghost of one of them."

"Maybe."

"When it's said to be haunted, what kind of stuff are we talking here?"

"Oh, the usual," said Hamilton, "lights flickering at night, moaning or crying sounds, a scary feeling around the house..."

"Nothing a couple of kids with a candle couldn't manage."

"Yes, but there's also the piano music you can hear in the middle of the night."

Meg stopped walking and looked at Hamilton.

"You've heard it?" he asked.

She nodded.

The two continued walking along the palm-lined path. Meg had returned to the property early in the morning to survey the grounds, and had met Hamilton on the back lawn. He had been acting as her tour guide through the property. He pointed out the remains of the old mill, storehouse, and well. He showed her the coast, the lagoon, and the acres of overgrown land that had once been cane fields.

"In one of the Nevis historical books it said that the Caribbean is made up almost entirely of slave descendents," said Meg. "The Carib Indians and Arawaks were the only native people, and they were mostly killed by early settlers."

"My teacher said that the word 'hurricane' comes from the name of the Carib god "Hurican," who sent floods and storms when he was angry."

"I'll have to put you in charge of tours when I open the place to the public."

Hamilton smiled and looked at the ground.

"I suppose I'll lose you tomorrow to school," said Meg.

"Yes. I won't be able to come until the afternoon."

"That's all right. I'm going into town tomorrow to check through records at the Historical Society Building and Government House. I want to learn more about the people who lived here."

"Do you plan on relaxing while you're here?"

"I'm going to the beach this afternoon, and to Jones Bay this evening for dinner. The owners of the villa where I'm staying posted a list of recommended dining spots on the fridge, so I'm going to start checking them out."

"Well, have a good afternoon. I'll see you tomorrow." Hamilton turned back toward the lagoon path, when Meg called out to him.

"You know, you don't have to help me if you have something better to do."

"Something better to do? Do you know how long people have been wanting to get inside that house? I'll be the envy of the island."

He smiled and was swallowed up by the trees.

Meg spent the afternoon relaxing on the beach. She was sure that she had never seen a more beautiful island than Nevis, and briefly entertained the idea of relocating.

Now that would be running away.

Brian had called seven times since Meg had arrived. Every time she got back to her cell phone she had a missed call from him. He hadn't left any messages.

That night Meg prepared for dinner. She straightened the villa, showered and got ready, and made herself *A Day at the Beach*.

As she sipped her drink, her cell phone rang.

Brian.

On the fourth ring she answered. He sounded startled to hear her voice.

"I was expecting your voicemail," he said.

"I'm sorry. I haven't been in the villa much."

"You know, you could carry the phone with you. It is a mobile phone."

Brian's tone was light—not at all what Meg had expected. Just hearing the kindness in his voice sent a wave of warmth over her.

"I'm sorry to have left so suddenly without you," said Meg. "I just needed to be alone. How are you able to be so kind after what I've done?"

"If I had gotten you on my first try, the conversation would have sounded a lot different. It's good you didn't pick up the phone."

"I must have sensed that."

"Look Meghan, I know this is hard. I don't judge you for wanting a retreat. I just wish you would let me know what you plan to do before you actually do it. I mean, you sent out the cards calling off the wedding before we'd finished discussing it. You called me from the runway to tell me that you were going to the Caribbean for two weeks. I think I deserve a little more input than that."

"You're right, I'm sorry. I was reeling—I'm getting better now."

"I understand. I mean, I can't imagine what you must be feeling, but I understand how you could be out of sorts."

Meg suddenly felt very guilty and very alone.

"I wish you were here," she said.

"Good," he teased. "Maybe you'll stop taking me for granted."

"I know. I'll make it up to you when I get home."

Maybe it was her friendship with Hamilton, her phone conversation with Brian, the kind men who delivered the rental jeep to her door at the villa earlier that day, or the engaging and warm exchange with Miss June Mestier at her exceptional restaurant—whatever it was, Meg felt very peaceful for the first time in a long time.

Miss June's was a restaurant run from a private home. Cocktails and hors d'oeurves were served at 7:30, followed by a five course meal including soup, an abundant buffet sampling a massive cultural array of dishes, and dessert. Miss June presided over the whole evening leading conversation with her culinary expertise, colorful anecdotes, and fascinating stories. It did not take long for Meg to feel at home in the intimate setting which ran more like a personal dinner party than a restaurant.

There were eighteen guests dining at Miss June's. Most were tourists, but several people were Nevisians. It was with the locals that Meg fell into conversation, and was the eager pupil of a group of people who clearly loved their island home. Throughout the evening, Meg was given information on the history of the island, the best places to dine and shop, historical sites, botanical gardens, beaches to visit, and which hotels to avoid. She was very interested to hear the perspective of the Nevisians at the table on the increase in tourism.

"Tourism is what currently sustains the economy here," remarked a local school teacher named Betsy. "That will only increase with the new hotel and resort being built. Sugarcane used to comprise a good segment of it, but the industry was recently closed."

"Why?" asked Meg.

"Nevis was losing more money on its production and export than she was making, not to mention the fact that cane working was a brutal reminder of the slave past of the island."

"Yes, but the sugar workers have all just lost their jobs without any alternatives," remarked Davis, a retired fisherman. "A good plan for re-employing these people was never put in place before the industry was closed. For many of them, sugar is all they know. Their fathers worked before them, their grandfathers, great-grandfathers, and so on— what will they do now? Serve drinks at the Grand Hotel?"

"That's a good point," said a local artist named Miles. "These big hoteliers come in here thinking they are noble with all the jobs they provide Nevisians. While the jobs are good, I can't help but feel that it's like the past."

"How so?" asked Meg.

"The Nevisians are the life-blood of the hotel industry—they are the cooks, maids, waiters, security, concierges, landscapers, spa workers—but they only make a minimum wage. The majority of the revenue goes to the rich hotel owners—many who don't even spend any time on the island."

"So you think it's like a modified form of the slavery of the past."

"Precisely. There is good, sure. The hotels are safe, respectable, clean, comfortable places to work. But is it in good taste to have black Nevisians dressed in historical costume catering to rich, predominately white tourists at places with the names 'Plantation Inn' in their titles? It's rather degrading, if you ask me."

"Many of the hotels are mindful of the sensitive nature of the slave past of the island," said Miles' companion Louise. "Tours are done respectfully. The plantations are part of the history of the island. There's no denying that. If the hotels didn't conduct tours some tourists wouldn't even realize that slavery took place here.   I used to work at a Plantation Inn."

"I know. That made me uncomfortable."

"What are tourists to do? There are few options when it comes to staying on the island. Nearly every place has "Plantation Inn" in its name," said Louise.

There was a brief lull in the conversation. Meg felt the color rising in her face, and didn't know if that could be attributed to the wine or her shame over these thoughts never having occurred to her.

"If the government of Nevis or some wealthy Nevisian could only sponsor its own hotel—one not owned by people from a thousand miles away, but by the citizens of the island—then Nevisians could truly benefit from tourism," said Meg.

"That would be something," replied Davis, "but there wouldn't be any way the government, or even a private citizen, could outbid a foreign source of capital for land to complete such a project."

"—unless the seller recognized the significance of such an endeavor," said Meg.

"I love your optimism," said Davis. "Waiter, another drink for the lady."

The table toasted each other and continued their feast. The party dispersed at 11:30, and Meg was home and sleeping soundly by midnight.

The cell phone woke her up. She ignored the first call when she saw that it was only 6:30, but by the third round of rings, Meg knew something must have been important.

Brian.

"I'm sorry to wake you, but there's a problem."

"What's wrong?"

"I just got a call from Howard."

"Dad's lawyer?"

"Yeah, he said he needed you to call him right away—something about the estate."

"Did he mean 6:30 right away, or as soon as possible?"

"Right now. He sounded awful."

"My God, I wonder what it could be."

"I don't know, but he left his number at home—said you could call him there."

It was worse than Meg could have imagined. Simply put, Richard Owen was a thief. Meg's father had been a stockbroker and financial planner for forty years. He had a loyal, distinguished, and enormously wealthy client base, and had been stealing their money for eighteen years. With so many clients worth so much money, they had never even noticed. It was a young lawyer Richard recently hired who discovered what Richard had done, and who had no choice but to report it. He had tried to be discreet about it, but it didn't take long for the local papers to stumble upon the information. The young lawyer called Howard to explain that the Owen estate would probably be sued by numerous sources for at least as much as Richard had stolen from them. The sum of the stolen money that he was able to track down already totaled in the tens of millions of dollars. Meg was shaking so violently by the time Howard was able to relay the information that she had to sit on the floor.

"Meghan, I can't tell you how sorry I am to have to tell you this. Your father was a good man. There must be some explanation for this."

But there wasn't any explanation—none that would explain it away, anyway. Meg began running over her father's—no, her—estate. One waterfront home in Annapolis, a restored, historic row-house in downtown Annapolis (where Meg currently lived,) a beachfront house in North Carolina, two boats, three luxury cars, a Monet, and the land in Nevis. Howard had said he would look into the matter and fight it if he could, but he did not sound confident. He sounded defeated.

Meghan had thought her father the kindest, most generous man she had ever met. The charity work, the entertaining, the family vacations—Richard was always doing something for the assistance or enjoyment of others. That is why he had encouraged Meg to pursue her interest in politics. He had told her she could be a public servant, and change the world.

But he was a liar. He had used his best friends' money to host dinner parties in their honor, to fund his charitable campaigns, and to take his family on several vacations a year.

And did Anne know? Had Meg's mother known what was going on? Did she know why she never had to work outside of the home—that her husband was a crook?

Meg didn't think it possible that her mother could have known. She was a devout Catholic—a model of moral behavior. Anne had always thought herself a failure because she was unable to have more children. She had devoted all her energy to helping the underprivileged youth of the community succeed in and outside of school—had set up Big Brother/Big Sister programs, completed a fundraiser to renovate a community center in one of the worst neighborhoods in Annapolis, sponsored parenting classes, tutoring, rec. league basketball, and music programs through the center, and gave generously of her time and resources to a women's shelter on West Street—no, Anne couldn't have known.

Meg took a deep breath and tried to think. She paced around the villa trying to decide if she should leave the island early. Howard told her to stay put until he learned more, but now she really felt like she was running away from her problems. She looked over at the picture of Eden and the abolitionist pamphlet on the table. If she did stay, she could work on selling the property.

Without thinking, Meg pulled out her cell phone and stared at it through her tears. She opened it, scrolled down the list of saved numbers to her father's name, and hit *call*.

After four rings, his cheerful voice answered and told her to leave a message.

Meg dropped the phone and ran to the bathroom to get sick.

~~~

The phone in the villa rang.

"Meghan Owen?"

"Yes."

"My name is Desmond Foxwell. I am with Grand Star Resorts. How are you this morning?"

"I've been better."

"I'm sorry to hear that. We actually met last night—at Miss June's?"

Meg thought over last night's introductions. This was not a Nevisian—he had a British accent. There were a group of British people at the next table. Meg had assumed they were tourists. Two of them were men. One was about sixty, the other about forty. Yes, he was introduced as Desi. Thick black hair, blue eyes, good-looking. Meg had thought he was pretentious and hadn't spent much time speaking to him—

though now, in retrospect, she remembered him spending a lot of time looking at her last night.

"Yes, I remember."

"I have a business proposition for you. Would you be willing to meet with me this evening for dinner?"

Grand Star Resorts—had he overheard her talking about the land she owned last night? Did he want to buy it? In her thoughts, she suppressed the conversation she had at Miss June's about outside investors and echoes of slavery. She didn't feel good about it, but everything had changed.

"Where would you like to meet?" asked Meg.

"The Overlook at The Plantation Inn, say 7:30?"

"I'll be there."

Meg had made an appointment at the Museum of Nevis History to search the archives before hearing of the recent drama concerning her family. Since she had a lot of time before dinner, she intended to keep her appointment. Meg got into her jeep and drove to the small building in Charlestown. A plaque on the building announced that it was the birthplace of Alexander Hamilton. Meg climbed the gray stone steps to the green shuttered door and pushed it open.

The museum could be found on the bottom floor of the Government House of Assembly. The building smelled stale and ancient, and Meg again wondered at the ability of air to remain in a place for centuries in spite of its natural flow.

The Museum was empty when Meg entered. Archive cabinets and artifacts lined the walls, and classical piano music played from an old radio behind an empty desk. Meg cleared her throat, and a tired looking man of about sixty emerged from a side door.

"Miss Owen?"

"Meg, yes. We spoke on the phone."

"Yes, you are wanting to look through the archive collection."

"I am. Are you Mr. Edmead."

"Yes, please call me Drew. If you'll sign our visitors' book and take a look around, I'll be right with you."

Drew went to his desk and made some notes in a binder while Meg scribbled her name in the book and walked around. There were many items and documents on display to do with Alexander Hamilton, but there were also ceramics from indigenous people, and a display dealing with environmental conservation on the island.

"I hope we are able to help you find what it is you are looking for."

"I hardly know what it is I'm looking for. As I told you on the phone, I have come to own the property that was once the Eden plantation. I'm curious about the early inhabitants of the plantation, the lore surrounding the place…"

"Unfortunately, it is very difficult in our geographical location to preserve history. Hurricanes, earthquakes, volcanic eruptions, strong tropical weather in general wipe away all traces of those who came before us. Nature is still in command, here. But what we do have we take good care of, document carefully, and limit its handling. You'll have to wear these gloves when searching through the archives."

As Meg reached to take the linen gloves from Drew, she noticed his left hand looked as if it had been badly burned. He was missing three of his fingers, and the others looked as if they had been fused by some terrible heat. Chalky patches of virgin flesh moved up his arm and disappeared beneath the tan sleeves of his shirt. Meg averted her eyes, but Drew had seen her studying his wounds. Meg grasped for something to say to hide her embarrassment.

"Eden is a miracle, it would seem," she said. "It's amazing how much inside is still in tact."

"Really? Perhaps, if you find anything historically significant you could show it to me or donate it to the collection."

"I'll let you know."

Drew led Meg to a large cabinet and opened its locked doors.

"In here you'll find old documents: tax records, slave lists, parish records, even the occasional letter or journal. Take as long as you'd like. We're open until four."

"Thank you."

Meg watched Drew walk back to his desk. His black hair was graying at the temples, his skin was dark and lined, and he favored his right foot when he walked, creating a slight limp.

Meg checked her watch—*10:15*. She took out her notebook and set it on the table by the cabinet.

~~~

The first hour passed slowly. She sifted through ancient tax records she could barely decipher and found nothing on Eden. Several references to debt caused Meg's stomach to churn, and she thought of her father. Tears burned behind her eyes. Meg blinked back her tears and looked up at Drew. He sat hunched over his desk with a magnifying glass, pouring over some document. He didn't notice her at all. Meg looked at the tax record and then back at Drew. She smiled suddenly at her memory.

St. John's College—one of the oldest Liberal Arts colleges in the country—was a short walk from Meg's house in Annapolis. Housed in the basement of one of its dorms, Humphrey's Hall, its tiny bookstore was an abundance of literary treasures—well-known and unknown. Meg enjoyed picking up coffee from The City Dock Café, strolling up Prince George Street to College Avenue, and wondering through the shelves of the old bookstore to find new reading material.

One autumn day, Meg had walked to the bookstore. It was the kind of day when every leaf of every tree seemed to hold on in all its warm-hued glory before shedding itself. Meg had wandered into the bookstore and saw someone new working behind the counter. He looked young—mid-thirties, maybe—and erudite. He was wearing glasses and was hunched over some musical text with a magnifying glass. He looked up when Meg entered, smiled, and said some words of welcome.

Meg could feel him watching her as she scanned the shelves, and found that she could scarcely remember why she was in the bookstore. The weight of his eyes on her back was paralyzing her. She concentrated on the books again, and as her ability to read returned she noticed, with some annoyance, that the book she wanted was out of her reach. She did not wish to make the awkward jump necessary to secure it in front of the new clerk.

"May I help you with something?"

Meg felt her face color as she turned to him.

"I can't reach. Do you have a step ladder?"

"I'll help you."

The man stood and crossed behind the counter to help Meg. He was very tall—much taller than Meg initially observed—and thin. His hair was light brown and disheveled—as though he had been running his fingers through it all morning. He was not handsome in a conventional way, but something about him was attractive—perhaps it was the accent. It sounded British, but slightly different.

"Austen—*Sandition*."

He made a face.

"You don't recommend it?"

"I personally detest Jane Austen. I suppose that would be due to extreme overexposure. But don't allow me to dissuade you."

"Well, I can't possibly buy it now," said Meg. "Do you have any other recommendations?"

"I'm partial to Homer, Dante, Dostoevsky...but it all depends on your mood."

"It's more about the period, for me. I'm most interested in the nineteenth century."

"Have you read Flaubert—*Madame Bovary*? Wilde's *Picture of Dorian Gray*?"

"No, I haven't."

"Excellent selections. Those are my recommendations."

"I can reach those, thank you."

The man smiled, returned to his desk, and resumed his magnifying glass inspections.

After Meg browsed around a bit longer, she carried her selections to the cash register.

"Ready?" He put down the magnifying glass and rang up the books.

"You might need a stronger prescription."

He laughed. "I desperately need a stronger prescription. I've not been able to find an ophthalmologist since I arrived."

"Where are you from? You don't sound exactly British."

"You've single-handedly dismantled my prejudice against Americans with that observation."

"What do you mean?" asked Meg.

"Well, to Americans, foreigners tend to fall in broad categories. I'm extremely impressed that you detected something else in my accent."

"Thanks, I think."

"Thank you. I'm Welsh."

"How long have you been in Annapolis?"

"Since August. I head a preceptorial on Milton's *Paradise Lost & Paradise Regained*. Are you a student?"

"I'm not, actually."

"Good, then it won't be considered sordid if I ask to you join me for coffee sometime. You can let me know about the books."

"When I finish them, I'll let you know."

The man smiled and handed Meg her bag.

"Thank you." She left the store and started up the stairs to the campus lawn, but turned around and peeked back into the store.

"Meghan Owen."

"Brian Hyer."

Cecil Dall.

Meg snapped out of her reverie. Dall, Cecil Dall. And under his name was Catherine Dall followed by Eden, 1830. Pounds of sugar cane and currency were listed, acreage, location, number of slaves: 202.

My God.

Meg's heart raced. The Dalls owned 202 slaves—an entire village. How was she related to these people? Were the Dalls father and daughter, or were they married? No, James Silwell's note was addressed to a "Miss Dall," and Hamilton had mentioned that a father and daughter lived at the plantation.

"Drew, I found something. Cecil and Catherine Dall lived on the plantation in 1830. Do you know how I could find out more about them?"

"I could check my computer. All of our archived material has been entered. I may have a cross reference for you. Give me a minute."

Meg watched Drew go to the computer and use his good hand to navigate through the search engine.

"You'll have to forgive me," he said. "My hand slows me down quite a bit."

"What happened to it?"

"Common sugar boiling injury."

"Were you a cane worker?"

"I was."

"How long ago were you injured?" asked Meg.

"It was two years ago. It was a blessing in disguise. I had only worked part time at the Museum before the accident. Now I'm able to be here all the time with a full time job. My friends are not so lucky right now."

"The sugar workers who are now out of jobs?"

"Yes. Are you familiar with island politics?"

"Not as much as I'd like to be. I learned a bit from conversations at a dinner at Miss June's last night. How do you feel about the close of the industry?"

Drew paused and looked out the window. "That is an interesting question. From my position, I'm inclined to say it is a good thing. As a cane worker, there was always something nagging me about my job—something that did not feel right."

"Because its origins were in slavery?"

"Yes. But it was what my father had done. He supported my whole family well. He worked very hard. I wouldn't want to shame his name by saying that it was not honorable work. But it was brutal."

"And your burns?"

"From boiling cane juice. Once you get it on your body it sticks like tar—it is nearly impossible to remove before it removes your own skin to the bone."

Drew held up his stump of a hand.

"But I was lucky. Many have died as a result of cane juice burns. My wife was glad it happened. She said it was good I was injured just enough to get me out of the industry without killing me."

Drew turned back to the computer screen. His search revealed that Cecil was on the Nevis Council and Assembly from 1826-1831.

"I will check the church records we have to see if I can find out when Cecil and Catherine died," said Drew.

"What would have happened to the slaves and land if the owners of the property died?"

"If there wasn't a will, the plantation could have been taken over by the Crown. Many of the planters of the day were in heavy debt. If not, a neighboring planter may have purchased it. Since planters in the West Indies were very far from home, it would have been difficult for anyone in England to lay claim to the land. But a plantation Eden's size would not have been overlooked. I could keep checking on the property if you'd like."

"I would appreciate that—if it wouldn't be too much trouble."

"Not at all."

The telephone rang. Drew answered it, and his eyes darkened.

"Meg, I'm afraid I have to go. My wife—she's been sick. I nearly forgot that I have to go with her to the doctor this afternoon. Can you come back to the museum another day?"

"Sure. I would actually like to get back to the house to look around some more before I go to dinner tonight."

"Good. I will call you if I find anything. May I have your number where you are staying."

Meg gave Drew her number and helped him close up the Museum. They walked out to the parking lot together, and then Drew turned and began walking down the road.

"Do you need a lift?" called Meg.

"I usually take a bus."

"It would be no trouble for me to take you home. I don't have to be anywhere until tonight."

Drew looked down the road and considered her offer.

"Thank you. That would be nice. Actually, Havilla is not far from my home at all."

As they drove to Drew's house, he pointed out various landmarks and points of interest. The road was winding and rustic. Cows and goats wandered along the dry patches of brown dirt, looking with mild interest at the Jeep. It was the custom while driving in Nevis to stop often and greet friends, so by the time Meg returned Drew to his home, she had been introduced to four very friendly people who teased Drew that they were going to call his wife, Dorothy, to tell her he was riding around with a pretty, young woman.

Drew's house was very close to Havilla—so close, in fact, that Meg could have seen the house if there had not been a thicket separating her from it.

"Thanks for the ride, Meg. I'm sorry it took so long. You can never be in too big a hurry when you are driving around here. "

"I didn't mind at all. I just hope Dorothy doesn't give you any trouble."

"Oh, she knows how it is. If I had taken the bus it would have taken twice as long."

"Do you need me to take you to the doctor's office?"

"No, thank you. We do have one car, but I like to leave it with Dorothy in case she needs to go somewhere.

For some reason, though, she does not like to go to the doctor alone."

"Ah, a gentleman."

Drew nodded and closed the door to the jeep.

It was a bright, cloudless day. Light winds played over the island causing a shiver in the vegetation. It was ideal for exploring Eden.

As Meg moved through the house, shafts of sunlight followed her through the rooms. She looked around the foyer and walked through the parlor. A worn writing desk was positioned on the wall opposite the great windows at the front of the house, but it had nothing in it. Several mildewed pieces of furniture were set in the room in no particular arrangement. Meg stepped over the rough, wooden floor and passed into what must have been a library. Large, built-in shelves lined three of the walls, but Meg's disappointment was acute when not a single book could be found. She traveled further into the room to check the shelves more closely when the sharp clang of the keys of the pianoforte sliced through the silence. One note continued to ring until overpowered by the ruffled flutter of wings. Meg's initial terror was overcome by her need to determine the source of the sound. She approached the room and passed through the archway.

A pigeon fluttered from the pianoforte to a high backed chair when Meg entered the room, again leaving the strange, out-of-tune clang hanging in the air. Meg walked around the room running her eyes from the floor to the ceiling. The pigeon heaved itself from the chair back to the piano as Meg passed. It was disturbed by her presence but unwilling to vacate.

Something caught Meg's eye from behind the chair. She moved it and found a large, framed canvas leaning against the wall. The hole in the wall above the chair indicated that the picture had ripped down some of the wall when it fell. Meg lifted it and placed it on the floor where she could get a better look.

A young woman with white-blonde hair, dark brown eyes, and tan skin stared out of the painting. She looked bored. The toes of the shoe on her right foot could be seen peeking out of the bottom of her dress slightly elevated, as if the artist captured her impatiently tapping her foot. She was attractive, and her posture was confident. Her hand rested on the shoulder of an older man with gold-gray hair, sitting in a chair. His face was soft, lined, and relaxed. His eyes were glassy and blue. He too had tan skin.

Was this a painting of the Dalls? The clothing they wore certainly had a nineteenth century look about it, but it was curious that their skin would be so tanned—especially the lady's. Weren't women of that time expected to keep their skin white? Were these people fond of the outdoors, or did their plantation lifestyle force them out of doors?

A sudden knot formed in Meg's stomach. She thought of the picture on her father's desk at home. It was very similar to this painting. Taken after a long day sailing along the Severn River and the Chesapeake Bay with her family, Meg stood leaning against her dad, who sat on a chair on the boat. Her mother had taken the picture, but she did not know how to work the camera. Meg had been instructing her on which button to push, so when it was developed, Meg was not smiling. It looked as if she was talking to someone out of the picture—she was talking to someone out of the picture. But Richard loved the photograph. He and his daughter, tanned, windswept, and tired after a long day on the water.

The knot in Meg's stomach traveled to her throat. She covered her mouth to stifle a sob, but realized that she was alone—completely alone. Meg moved down to the floor in front of the painting and cried out something that had been stuck inside her for days.

Meg wiped her eyes and was left with a strange, heavy, peaceful feeling. She picked herself up from the floor and looked at her surroundings. She glanced back at the painting for a moment, and then gathered her things to leave for the day.

2:00.

Meg thought she might go back to the beach—there was still plenty of time before dinner. She decided to exit though the back of the house and walk to the beach through the back of the property along the path that Hamilton had shown to her. Meg had to pass through the dining room on her way out of the back of the house. It was the most decomposed room in the Great House thus far—it was completely overgrown with a dense covering of vines that had crept in through the window. It was a massive room with a heavy table running the entire length of it. The table was dark cherry and was supported by opulently carved legs. The vines that had climbed into the back window reached down the back walls and to the table, where they had begun coiling up the legs of it. The entire room was darkened from the foliage that blocked the windows, creating the appearance of a subterranean cavern lined with the roots of some great tree. It smelled earthen and musty, and the vines looked like snakes.

Meg stepped through the shadowed room, careful not to entangle herself in the growth. As she was about to pass into the stone hall leading to the kitchen and out of the back of the house, something caught her eye.

It was a painting of an apple in a hand, cracked and peeling on the wall beneath the vines. Meg scanned the perimeter of the wall and thought that she could make out other sections of what must have been a mural: an unclothed leg, a tree, a cloud. She was reluctant to tug at the vines fearing to disturb the creatures that may have lived within the coils, but her curiosity to see the painting overcame her squeamishness.

The vines proved much stronger than they looked, and it was with some effort that Meg cleared a section of the mural.

A serpent, a woman, a cherub.

Meg continued pulling at the growth until the entire painting was exposed.

The Garden of Eden before the fall.

Eve stood lustily gazing at the apple with the serpent coiled up the Tree of Knowledge and around her arm. Adam wore a look of innocence because he had not yet bitten the apple. The serpent's head was that of a cherub—a sinister and disturbing representation meant to depict the beguiling and charming attributes of the beast. The likenesses of Adam and Eve were somewhat familiar. Meg searched for a signature on the mural, but the limited light made it very difficult to find. Eventually she located it—*West, 1811*. Meg knew of an American painter, Benjamin West, but she could not recall the time period in which he painted.

If this mural was the work of a famous painter, the selling price of the property would climb significantly. She took pictures and jotted down the name in her journal. She planned on researching West when she got back to the villa. Meg had not yet unpacked her laptop—she had been reluctant to bring it. Now, she was glad that she did.

Instead of going to the beach, Meg spent the remainder of the afternoon on the computer. Benjamin West was an American painter and a Quaker. He had traveled to England in 1763, and spent the rest of his life there. She found a great deal about his upbringing, his life in London, and the provenance of many of his works. Many of his paintings were listed, but nothing caught her eye. The colors and figures he had used were similar to those in the mural at Eden, but that could have simply been a result of the elements and the passage of time.

5:00.

Meg stood and stretched.

Cocktail Hour.

She mixed herself a *Planter's Cocktail.*

Meg's alcohol consumption had lately been on the rise. Graduation from college saved Meg from what was about to become an alcohol problem. She had taken her job very seriously and limited herself to a single glass of wine on weeknights. But the recent events involving the governor, the wedding, and the death of her parents brought about Meg's return to familiar bad habits.

Richard Owen had been a heavy drinker. Meg could scarcely remember a time when her father was without a tumbler of Scotch or a glass of wine. He was a jovial drunk, and quick to pass out. It had been Anne's routine every evening to scoot Richard off to bed before he could pass out on the couch. She had been able to figure out the precise right moment of intervention after too many nights of missing the moment and having to leave him snoring in the family room.

Meg's mother was driving the night of the accident. She usually drove Richard. The paper said that the rain and the wind were what caused them to slip over the cliff along the Severn River. The pictures were terrible.

Meg thought she must be crazy to be sitting in her villa on the Internet on a tropical island. She finished her cocktail and went over to the table to disconnect her laptop, but as she leaned over the screen, something caught her eye. She scrolled down the screen to reveal a picture of the entire painting.

An angel, a woman, a man, a serpent.

The woman's face was nearly identical to the face on the mural in the house.

The Expulsion of Adam and Eve from Paradise.

The restaurant at The Plantation Inn was located in the dining room of the hotel. The entire hotel was designed and decorated to resemble an early plantation home, with each of its rooms arranged as large-scale replicas of what an historic plantation home in the Caribbean would have been. Named The Overlook because of its fabulous views of the Atlantic Ocean side of the island, the entire outside wall of the restaurant was hung with magnificent floor-to-ceiling windows.

"Grand Star Resorts designed and built this hotel six years ago. It is one of the most lucrative on the island. Tourists love that authentic plantation experience."

Meg stifled a laugh as she silently wondered if brutal beatings and near starvation were included in the vacation packages. Yesterday, Meg would have said such a thing out loud, but everything was different now. She needed to sell the land, and if Desmond was going to make an offer, she didn't know how she could refuse.

"It is a beautiful hotel."

"Beautiful, yes, but not very large. The Plantation Inn has only fifty rooms, and doesn't even have enough acreage for a full-sized golf course. The spa is only half the size of spas at competing resorts, and our Ballroom can only seat eighty people comfortably. We are unable to book large weddings and conventions, but have been approached by countless groups looking to do just that."

A young Nevisian woman approached the table to fill the water glasses.

"Return this soup to the kitchen and bring us some that is warmer than room temperature."

Meg looked up startled at Desmond, and then back at her half-empty bowl of soup.

"I'm terribly sorry, sir," apologized the waitress as she cleared the dishes. Meg was left with her spoon in mid-air and quickly placed it on the table top. Bisque from the spoon seeped its pink stain onto the white tablecloth.

"As I was saying, there is a growing need for hotels and resorts to accommodate larger functions—particularly on Nevis—which brings me to why I asked you to dine with me this evening."

"You overheard my conversation last night about the land I own."

"I did. And I wanted to approach you and see if you would be willing to sell it."

Meg was silent for a moment. She surveyed the room and listened to the pleasant din of the diners, the clinking of silver on china, the hum of the symphony music playing from speakers in some unknown location. The waitress returned and placed two steaming, hot bowls of bisque before Desmond and Meg.

"I would have to speak with my lawyer first, and get an independent appraisal of the land." *And an art historian to look at that mural.* "I could let you know after that."

"So selling isn't out of the question?"

"No."

"That pleases me tremendously," said Desmond. "Now, I hear there is also an abandoned house on the property—Eden?"

"Yes."

"What a name for a resort: The Plantation Inn and Resort at Eden. The Paradise Plantation Inn at Eden. Maybe Eden: Paradise Resort and Spa. What a marketing dream. The old house could be restored for historic tours, lavish gardens would abound—the possibilities are endless. Is there a beach?"

"Yes."

"Splendid. We could put up high gates or do mass plantings on either side of the property to keep the locals from using the beach, and truly make it a getaway. There's nothing worse than enjoying a daiquiri on a resort beach and having to deal with islanders."

Meg smiled half-heartedly as Desmond rambled on. The only pauses in his palaver came while he ate—which wasn't nearly enough. Meg had lost her appetite after the bisque and could only choke down enough to keep from being embarrassed.

"You know, the land wasn't the only reason I asked you to join me for dinner," he said.

Oh God, here it comes.

"You are very attractive, and I can't help but notice that you are unattached." His eyes shifted to her left hand and traveled back to her face.

Meg glanced down and saw that she had forgotten her engagement ring. She had taken it off before her shower, and now regretted that it was still lying on the dresser.

"Thank you, Mr. Foxwell—"

"—Desi."

"Desi.   Thank you, but I am actually engaged to be married. I forgot to put my ring back on after getting ready earlier today."

The smile left Desmond's face.

"Pardon me."

The check seemed to take an interminable amount of time to arrive, but once it did, Desmond made a big production about paying for the meal. Meg practically ran to the jeep, but Desmond stopped her before she could leave, and passed her his business card.

"Call me after you speak to your lawyer," said Desmond, "or whenever you get lonely while on the island."

Meg shut the door and drove back to the villa as quickly as possible.

6

Under the cover of night, the group that was once three had grown to six. The Silwells and Jonas Dearing were the original members, joined by another small farmer, the orating Quaker from outside of the church, and his cousin—a nervous, twitching man who looked strongly as if he would rather not be there. They met at three o'clock in the morning in the Silwells' hotel room. The outsiders had snuck into a side entrance to the Bath Hotel so suspicions were not aroused.

After introductions were made, Albert Silwell questioned each of the men regarding slavery practices, law-breaking plantation owners, and insurgents. The newest small farmer, Caleb Whitting, was passionate in his hatred of the Hall family. Mr. Whitting was convinced the Hall's overseers were sabotaging his small tobacco crop and gardens at night, and had taken to sleeping with his militia musket in hand, ready to shoot and kill any trespassers.

"All the big planters' slaves live in thatched huts within walking distance of the cane fields—yet they don't have to replace them," said Caleb. "There's some exception in the law regarding the size of the dwelling. My house isn't much bigger than a slave hut, but I still have to tear it down or re-shingle. It will ruin me. I know many as angry as I who have come up with a plan to ruin the big planters."

"Taking the law into your own hands would be dangerous and foolish," said Albert. "My son and I did not come here to raise rebellions. We are working within the confines of the law."

"That could take years! We don't have time."

"The Council reconvenes at the end of the week," said James. "We have spoken to several of the lesser plantation owners on the Council. There is a chance that the law will be overruled."

"The three largest planters have the most leverage," said Caleb. "The law will not be overturned because they want our land. You are a fool if you think they can be persuaded otherwise."

"Caleb," said Jonas.

"I am not wasting any more of my time here. Your kind of help won't do any of us any good."

Caleb's chair scraped against the hard wood floor of the hotel room as he stood. Grabbing his hat, he crossed the room and slammed the door behind him.

"I'm sorry about that," said Jonas. "I had no idea he would be so unreasonable."

"No apologies necessary," said Albert. "I just hope he doesn't do anything foolish. Have you any idea what his plan is for the Hall's?"

Jonas looked at the floor and shook his head. He turned his hat around in his hands like a wheel and slouched in his chair.

The Quaker said that he agreed that they should work within the confines of the law. He had heard many rumblings amongst the small planters and other Quakers about revenge, and had persuaded many to reconsider.

"It seems that these angry farmers want to strike at the hearts of the large plantations."

"And what exactly would that entail."

The Quaker looked at Jonas and back to the Silwells.

"They want to burn the mills and boiling houses."

"Don't they realize that many of these large planters have slaves and overseers working around the clock during the major harvest seasons?" said James. "They'll surely be killed."

"They know that, but they are desperate. Besides, no slaves work in the mills on Sunday nights. If they strike, they will do so on a Sunday night."

~⌒⊙

Catherine was relieved to see the light of the sun blazing in through her shutters the next morning. She thought that she would tell her father that the field burning should be done later that night if the weather cooperated.

Catherine washed and dressed for the day, and made her way downstairs to see if Esther had yet arrived. As she was coming down, she met Leah carrying a large basket for collecting soiled linens.

"Good morning, Leah."

Leah looked at Catherine out of shadowed eyes rimmed in red. She mumbled a reply without stopping, leaving Catherine staring after her. Catherine continued down the staircase and into the dining room, where her father sat at the table.

"I trust you will have me tell Phinneas to prepare for the rat-burning this evening?"

"Yes, thank you," said Catherine as she sat at the table. "Today I'll be in the food storehouse taking inventory to plan for next week's menu and prepare a list for the market."

A soft shuffling sound drew Catherine's eyes to the door of the dining room. Esther stiffly entered the room bearing the breakfast tray. She kept her eyes down as she set the food on the table and filled the glasses with fruit juice. She refused to meet Catherine's gaze, and exited the room as swiftly as possible.

Cecil stood and announced that he was not hungry.

"I'm meeting with several Council members in town this afternoon, so I'll eat then."

Catherine knew that Cecil's meeting would likely take place in a Charlestown pub, and that the only nourishment he would get would be rum, but he was out the door before she could protest.

She ate her breakfast as her thoughts returned to Esther. The soft clink of Esther's preparations in the kitchen summoned Catherine out of her chair and out of the dining room.

Eden's kitchen was attached to the house, but separated from the dining room by a long, cool, stone hall. This was an unusual arrangement as most kitchens of the day were located in outbuildings to keep away the danger of fire. The hall had been designed, however, to isolate the kitchen enough to lessen the danger of fire, while increasing the convenience of having it just off the dining room. The smells of baking bread, citrus, and herbs hung perpetually in the hallway and stirred in Catherine the warm familiarity of her childhood play. She and Leah had spent hours running through the hall and kitchen, stealing bits of food and bothering Esther. Somehow they had both managed to learn a great deal about cooking in spite of their endless mischief.

As Catherine stepped down into the heat of the kitchen, she spied Esther moving around in the shadows. The oven cast a strange, orange glow about the room, but largely it remained dark as a cave. Even the light of day just through the door leading outside was kept from entering the grotto.

"Good morning, Mami."

The whites of Esther's eyes were all Catherine could see.

"Good morning," she replied.

"Are you well? You were not here yesterday, and I could not find you at the village."

"We must have just missed one another."

Catherine continued to stare at Esther, trying to make out what it was that troubled her about Esther's appearance. Her dark brown face and black hair blended with the shadows. Her white, cotton dress appeared to hang in midair and float from place to place, like that of an apparition.

"I'll be back after I inventory the food storehouse to go over next week's menu with you."

Esther nodded and seemed relieved to be left alone.

Catherine crossed the room and stepped out into the daylight. She began to walk away from the house and thought of how strange everyone had behaved that morning. Leah had been quiet and sullen, her father seemed in a hurry to get away from her, and Esther seemed stiff and peculiar. Catherine's heart began to pound, and she pivoted back toward the kitchen. She crept to the doorway and stepped back into the dark room.

Esther had not heard her enter. She was standing by the oven—its flames illuminating her back, revealing long welts scraped down her legs like the claw marks of some ferocious animal. Catherine could not stifle a gasp. Esther turned quickly, failing to look down and hide her swollen eyes and nose.

"When did this happen?" asked Catherine.

"That is not of your concern."

"Why did this happen?"

Esther was silent and began chopping vegetables.

"It was because of me, wasn't it? Someone found out that I was present at the birthing."

Only the sharp, wet crunch of the blade slicing through raw potatoes could be heard.

Catherine stepped closer to Esther and saw tears running down her face. Catherine's misery transformed to anger, and she charged out of the house and toward the sugar fields. She plunged into the darkness of the path through the rain forest and out again into the scorching island sun. Acres of fields lay below her as she sprinted down through the slave's quarters, passed the sugar mill and boiling house, and toward the coast. Slaves watched her with curiosity as she dashed toward the dark figure on the horse. Her pace slowed as she neared Phinneas.

Phinneas was in his late thirties, but looked much older. His face was scarred from a bout with smallpox he suffered as a child, and his skin had the hue of burnt ochre from so much time spent in the sun. He had fair hair that looked dark due to a lack of washing, and squinty green slits for eyes that gave him a menacing look. It had been widely thought about him that he had no conscience.

After being born in a brothel in Paris, Phinneas was taken care of by his mother in her dirty little room for several months, but Madame made her give up the child. His crying could be heard throughout the house, and it made the patrons uneasy. Reluctantly, Phinneas' mother wrapped him in blankets, asked Madame (the only literate person in the house) to write his name on a piece of paper, carried him in secret to a nearby convent, laid him on the stoop, rapped at the door, and disappeared into the night.

Sister Marie L'Cour, a sweet, young woman who had only recently joined the convent, found the infant and added him to the growing nursery of illegitimate children. The nuns quickly learned that young Phinneas was trouble, and as he grew to boyhood, he became loathed and feared throughout the orphanage. Sister Marie tried to bring him up learning and living God's law, but he did not appear to respond to love or nurturing. He was motivated by greed and by fear, and he only feared Mother Superior because it was her job to administer corporal punishment when necessary.

He was beat often and hard with a cane for various misdeeds including theft, brutality, and a disturbing incident that left the convent cat dead. Mother Superior and several of the other nuns were convinced that he was possessed by a demon and kept him secluded from the other children. Sister Marie was inclined to believe that all human persons possessed some good and valiantly attempted to reform her young charge, but by the time Phinneas had reached his twelfth birthday, even she had given up hope.

One foggy morning in April when Sister Marie went to fetch Phinneas for breakfast, he was not to be found. His room was empty, his few belongings were gone, and the cross on his wall was found floating in the waste of his chamber pot. Sister Marie had fainted when she found her Jesus covered in the child's excrement, and even Mother Superior was shaken. The room was cleaned thoroughly, blessed by Father Jaques, and turned into a storage closet. Phinneas was never spoken of again by the nuns, but Sister Marie prayed daily for forgiveness at her inability to reform the child, and for her relief at his absence.

As Catherine approached Phinneas, she saw that he was nothing but a black form on a horse against the sunlight behind him. Catherine moved into Phinneas' shadow and stared up at him through defiant, bloodshot eyes. As she panted, he smiled down at her.

"You seem quite out of breath, Miss Dall," said Phinneas. "Allow me to give you a ride home. You are well aware of the fact that you should not be near the slaves' quarters. It is no place for a lady."

"You will not get away with this."

"Whatever are you talking about?"

"I will tell Father as soon as he returns."

"Miss Dall, when is your father sober enough to hold a coherent conversation? And furthermore, what makes you think that your father does not know of and even endorse my methods of issuing consequences?"

Catherine began to tremble.

"Are you sure I cannot escort you home?" he asked.

She backed away from Phinneas, and turned toward the Great House.

* * *

Bartholomew Ewing, William Hall, and Cecil Dall sat around a small, wooden table overfed, overdrunk, and overdressed. The surface of the table glistened with gems of spilled rum, catching the light like little, irregular jewels. The pub was largely empty at this hour—all the small planters were laboring and all the middleclass planters were overseeing their small properties.

"When we meet formally at the end of the week, we'll finalize the law and get those wretched little planters off this island," said William Hall.

"I think they'll find the small sum of money we offer to buy their land a much better option than having to linger on Nevis and sabotage their own homes," said Bartholomew. "I know Edward is convinced that absorbing Caleb Whitting's small acreage between our plantation and yours, William, will be key in pushing us into a much greater profit next year."

"I, for one, feel left out," said Cecil. "The small falls and lagoon just east of Eden will prevent me the pleasure of growing my estate by acquiring others' land."

"Cecil, you already own the most prolific plantation on the island. Be content with what you've got."

"Our production is down a bit, though, gentlemen. Catherine thinks it's the rats, so don't be alarmed when you see one of our lower fields on fire tonight. We're going to try to burn them out."

Bartholomew and William looked at one another.

"Cecil," said William, "I know Miss Dall has demonstrated a keen business sense in the past, but do you think that this is a wise idea?"

"Phinneas supports the decision, therefore, I feel entirely comfortable with it myself. Besides, it will be quite amusing."

The other gentlemen nodded in agreement and drained their glasses.

~~∽⌒

Edward Ewing stood at the pianoforte in Eden's luxurious parlor. He ran his hands over the keys as he crossed behind it to the mantled fireplace. A great portrait of Catherine and her father hung over the room. He grasped the marble mantle and gazed up at Catherine's likeness, allowing his eyes to travel up her legs, over her body, to her face—whose eyes were alert and direct.

Catherine's portrait held none of the awkward or demure looks typical of the ladies of the day. She was all confidence, self-assurance, certainty. Only a slight look of boredom—which the artist had captured perfectly—made her look anything but in complete control. Edward knew Catherine's boredom, however, must have been at waiting for hours while a painter fretted and flattered over her. He grinned as he imagined her being reprimanded for tapping her foot or looking out the window as she thought of all the work she had before her.

Edward's eyes traveled down Catherine's arm to where it rested on Cecil's shoulder. Cecil stared out from his glassy eyes with a look of dumb satisfaction on his slightly amused face. It was Cecil's perpetual look of amusement that made him look like a fool—or a child, aged in body alone.

Edward knew that his father was supposed to be asking Cecil to dinner at Goldenrise that evening, but had no confidence in his ability to carry out the simple task. Edward, however, had no intention of standing around the Dalls' parlor all day waiting for Catherine. Overcome by boredom, Edward scribbled a brief dinner invitation to the Dalls on his card, placed it on the parlor tray, and left Eden.

Esther was still working in the kitchen when Catherine returned. She looked up briefly as the girl entered the room, but continued with her duties. Catherine watched Esther's dark hands coated with white flour-gloves kneading the thick puff of dough in the bowl. The rhythm of Esther's hands working was soothingly monotonous. The scrape of the bowl as Esther turned it around and around on the wooden table had the pleasingly muffled quality that had often coaxed Catherine to take over the chore as a child. She crossed the room to do so now.

The women fell into synch—weaving in and out of one another in a noiseless dance as they prepared the bread. Esther hummed some sad, low song as she fed the oven, while Catherine wiped the sweat from her forehead with the back of her arm.

Once she finished preparing the dough, Catherine looked at Esther's back as she slid the loaves over the fire. Tiny, red dots began to reach through the white fabric of Esther's shift in several places along her back—wounds opening in the heat as she worked, bleeding blood-tears on her garment.

Catherine crossed the kitchen and took the great peel from Esther's hands. She led Esther down the hall, through the dining room, up the staircase, and into her mother's bedroom, where she told her to wait. After a few moments, Catherine returned with a healing paste, water, and a towel.

Esther sat on the large bed, framed in white curtains, looking unsure of herself. Catherine eased Esther down onto her stomach and peeled down the white cloth, revealing her slashed and bloody back. Catherine had to look away and gather herself so that Esther would not hear her weep. As she dabbed Esther's back, Catherine thought of a bad fall she had as a child that she had secured while hunting for sea stars along the slippery rocks that edged the coastline. Catherine had sulked over her cuts as Esther had reminded her of her previous warnings to avoid the rocks. But Esther's instructions on the healing plants she used, laced through her reprimands, took the sting from her chastisements.

"Next time, you must hold my hand, Mami."

"That is not the lesson I had hoped you learned."

By the time Catherine had finished, Esther was asleep, breathing deep and regular breaths. Catherine lay down next to Esther on her mother's bed and gazed into her face—peaceful with repose. Her own face was lined with worry. There were now consequences to her actions. Phinneas was taking more liberties. Cecil was fading into the background. She knew that she could never speak of this to her father, whether or not what Phinneas had said was true.

As much as Catherine longed to remain at Esther's side, she felt the overwhelming need to go on with her day as planned. Perhaps it would not be so bad. Perhaps her father's health would improve. Perhaps this was just a hard lesson. Resolved to push forward, Catherine kissed Esther's hand, closed the door as she exited the room, and again set out to inventory the food storehouse.

The Ewing plantation came into view as Catherine and her father rounded a bend on the road in their gig. Catherine was ill at ease, uncomfortable in her finery, and glum at the prospect of enduring such an evening as her father rambled on about the magnificence of their neighbors and the charms of young Edward. His recent escalation of effusions of the subject of Edward Ewing was beginning to concern Catherine. She found Edward conceited in his manners, full of self-importance, haughty to those around him, and cruel to his slaves. His charming façade did not fool Catherine, and she found evenings spent dodging his flattery to be tiresome.

A finely dressed slave led the Dalls into the massive Ewing foyer and went to fetch his masters. Catherine gazed upon the lavish surroundings with distaste. Everything was in overabundance at Goldenrise. Massive, expensive furniture cluttered every room, vast feasts spilled off the table at every meal, a profusion of alcohol was consumed, and the most decadent and impractical clothing were worn.

As Catherine looked around the room she was confronted with her reflection in the massive, gold-gilded mirror that hung in the foyer. Her skin was tanned, her hair was bleached white from time spent in the sun, and her dark eyes were hung with shadows—a slave with white hair. She smiled with irony at her likeness and realized how scandalous it would be to mingle about society in England with such a face.

"You are a dazzling sight to behold, Miss Dall," said Edward. "I see you've even charmed yourself."

Catherine colored with embarrassment as Edward took her arm and led her to the dining room. She cursed herself for allowing Edward to witness and misinterpret such a moment.

"It was amusement at my appearance that you witnessed," she said. "My skin is shockingly dark for an Englishwoman. Mrs. Hall would be mortified if I were her daughter."

"What you say is true; however, tanned skin is strangely becoming on you."

Catherine ignored his remark and pulled her arm from his grasp as the small party sat at the table to dine.

As the dinner progressed, Catherine moved the food about her enormous gold-rimmed plate as the men laughed and conversed around her. Edward, noticing her displeasure, urged his Father to quiet himself.

"We are in the presence of a lady, Father," said Edward. "I apologize. We are not accustomed to the fairer sex."

Catherine exchanged glances with a timid female slave who hurried out of the room.

Cecil and Bartholomew continued to try and outtalk one another while Edward leaned closer to Catherine.

"I'm delighted you could join us this evening. We need a proper feminine influence to smooth some of our rough edges."

Edward could see that he was not charming his guest, and searched for another avenue to conversation with Catherine. "I am touched by your sweetness in attending to the slaves. Do the beasts even acknowledge your sacrifices on their behalf?"

"The men, women, and children I assist are always very grateful if that is what you are asking."

"Have you been speaking to the Methodists? You are beginning to sound like an abolitionist."

"I am merely acknowledging that to deny a slave is as human as you or me is foolish," said Catherine.

"Your childish optimism is very refreshing—overly simplistic and idealistic—but refreshing."

"You need not patronize me."

Before Catherine was able to continue her argument with Edward, a strange, unpleasant odor crept into the dining room—one of scorched hair and burning vegetation. Cecil urged the group to move to the back of the house to watch the rat-burning, which he announced must be commencing as they spoke. They all moved to the back veranda and beheld the breathtaking and frightening sight of the burning field.

Ten feet of land had been cleared and filled with wet beach sand around the entire perimeter of the field. The flames rose high into the air, smoke blotted out the stars and a potent stench arose from the hellish inferno. They watched the fire for a long time in silence as it blazed inward to the center of the field and smoldered out along its edges. Dark figures like little demons could be seen raking over and stamping out tiny fires left burning in the cane.

The revolting smell indicated that many rats were indeed burning. Seizing the opportunity to hasten their departure, Catherine complained of a headache. The party moved back indoors and approached the front entranceway. Catherine and Cecil boarded the gig, and Bartholomew stumbled back into the house as Edward watched the carriage until it disappeared from view.

7

Meg's head was throbbing. She took her pain medication, showered, and waited for the headache to subside while turning over last night's conversations. She had phoned Brian on her way back to the villa to tell him about the dinner and her plans to sell the estate. He had been mostly quiet, but seemed to be in agreement with her on the need to sell. Meg had convinced herself that selling to Grand Star was the best way to secure money to start paying back her father's debts. They could offer the best possible price—maybe even enough to take care of all of her father's debts. Then she could keep her other assets, and put it all behind her.

Brian had seemed distracted on the phone. He had not said much about the sale of the land, but did seem interested in hearing about Drew. Brian had told her about some places of interest in Nevis he found on the Internet that she might want to visit during her stay, and peppered her with questions about the villa, but then got off the phone in a hurry.

After her conversation with Brian, Meg called Howard at home to discuss her meeting. He had said that a class-action suit had been filed against the Owen estate for sixty-eight million dollars.

"Meg, are you there?" asked Howard.
"Yes."

"Worse than you expected?"

"Much."

"You know, I've had several hours to digest this and have spoken extensively on the phone with their attorney—who, I might add, I have done business with in the past and have a very good rapport. Their attorney said that all of the parties listed in the suit are pained over this and are simply seeking their losses—nothing more. It's amazing, really. Your father may have stolen from these people, but they still consider him a friend."

Meg flinched.

"If we are able to quickly turn over these assets, we may be able to settle rather soon," he said. "Of course, that won't leave you with much of anything."

Meg had thought about that, and it wasn't sitting well. She had just learned that she was a multimillionaire heiress, only to learn that she might end up broke. Meg was accustomed to a certain style of living and did not look forward to making any adjustments to it.

Howard said that he would set her up with an agent to survey the property as soon as possible. Meg was grateful he was taking care of that. In the meantime, Meg told Howard that she would do some more research on Benjamin West and how she might get the painting assessed.

"I'm sure you'll want to keep the press out of this as much as possible, Meg. We will get through this as quickly as possible."

Meg hung up the phone, and feeling rather helpless, and with nothing else to do, she fixed herself a *Night Cap*.

Meg slipped into the warmth of the plunge pool to watch the night move over the sky. She heard the far-off waves crashing and the singing of the bellfrogs. A faint breeze played on the leaves. If the air had not cooled so much, she could have stayed out there all night. As it was, she was chilled and could not keep her eyes open.

Her sleep was fitful. Since the accident, Meg had been dreaming vivid dreams that her parents were still alive. Always out sailing on the bay with her mom, dad, and Brian. Usually on the Fourth of July—the day Brian proposed—while they watched fireworks from the Annapolis Harbor. They were all sunburned from a long day on the water, and a bit tipsy. Brian disappeared below deck for a minute. Richard gave Anne a knowing look and dropped the whaler into the black water. Brian came back up and asked Meg to take a ride out away from the other boats with him. Zigzagging between the throngs of holiday boaters until they were at least a hundred yards from anyone. Watching fireworks over the harbor from the distance. Masts rocking back and forth, water lapping, thunderous explosions muffled from the humid air. Meg almost didn't hear Brian over the fireworks. She saw the ring first. When they got back on the boat she hugged her parents. They hugged Brian. Richard turned back toward the display and mumbled to himself, "And just like that, she's gone." But Meg had heard. And that was how she woke up each day. And each day she had to remember that it was not she who was gone, but them.

The worst part of grieving, Meg often thought, was waking up each morning and having to remember over and over again that her parents were dead. There were those few precious, innocent seconds, followed by that stab of pain. She wished she could just know that they were dead.

❧

The knock at the door was tentative, as if the person on the other side of it was not confident that he had the right place, or wasn't sure it was his place to be there. Meg opened the door to Drew. She had called him earlier that morning to invite him to accompany her to the plantation. She felt that she could trust Drew and knew that he would take a keen interest in exploring Eden. He may even have some advice for her on what to do about the artwork. She told him that she would drop him off at the museum when they finished.

"How's Mrs. Edmead doing?"

"Oh, fine," said Drew. "Thank you for asking. She is diabetic and was feeling a bit under the weather yesterday. She needed some adjustment to her medication."

"I hope she doesn't mind that I'm taking you away from her for some adventure this morning."

"I did tell her that the beautiful young lady who gave me a ride had asked me on a date, but she didn't seem too worried. She thinks I'll be back soon. She thinks I won't be able to keep up with you."

Meg laughed as she packed two bottles of water and her camera in her bag.

"I've found a way to take the jeep up the drive, so you won't fall in any holes and twist your ankle like I did the other day," said Meg. "The house itself seems surprisingly sturdy. You'll be just fine."

Meg drove Drew out to the main road and down about a hundred yards. A rusted gate sat buried in the foliage on the side of the road. She hopped out of the jeep, pushed the gate open, and proceeded down the long, overgrown path to the plantation house.

As Eden came into view, Drew's face grew shadowed and serious.

"Are you okay?"

He paused a moment, but then answered. "I'm fine, yes."

Meg turned off the jeep and stepped out onto the crushed shells by the remains of an aged, cracked fountain.

Drew walked to her side and they stared up at the Great House.

Meg said, "Can you imagine what this place must have been like in the 1800s?"

"Can you imagine what its inhabitants would have thought to see us here together today?"

They were quiet as they entered the house. Meg showed Drew around each of the downstairs rooms. Just as Meg had suspected, Drew was thrilled by the condition of the house. He was most interested in the pianoforte. Meg thought of the piano music she heard in the night.

"Would a slave have been able to play the piano?" she asked.

"That would be unlikely, unless she learned from watching her mistress get lessons. Sometimes, slaves were educated right under their masters' noses. Many slave owners thought slaves to be subhuman beasts of little intelligence. They would tell secrets, get educated, and learn instruments in front of their slaves not suspecting that the men, women, and children serving them could learn too. Why do you ask?"

"It's silly."

"Are you thinking of the piano music that can be heard in the middle of the night?"

"I am."

Drew walked over to the pianoforte and played a few sour notes on the tuneless keyboard.

"The music I've been hearing sounds much more melodic," said Meg.

"You have trouble sleeping?"

"Lately."

Drew began to play *Moonlight Sonata*. It sounded strange played on such an old instrument, but it was still recognizable.

"Me too."

Meg smiled at Drew.

"But your hands—"

"My right hand is fine. My left still has two working fingers. Since the right hand plays the melody, I'm able to improvise with the left. It's not so difficult, really."

"Amazing."

"It is amazing how people adapt. It could have been much worse."

Drew stopped playing and gestured to the painting.

"This must be the Dalls?" he said.

"I would imagine."

"Beautiful girl. She looks very much in control of her surroundings. Do you see how she holds her father's shoulder? She's in charge."

"He looks amused, glassy-eyed."

Drew knelt down and lifted up a piece of the painting that had been torn. He fit it back into place.

"Do you see this?"

Meg looked carefully at Cecil Dall's left hand. He held a glass of amber colored liquid.

"Rum?"

"It would appear that way."

"He couldn't part with it for a portrait?"

"Not surprising. The plantation owners in the Caribbean were notorious for their alcoholism. These men were likely unwelcome in their homeland, adventurous enough to embark upon a treacherous ocean journey to exotic islands where they came into money quickly and lorded over massive populations of slaves. They had no one to keep them in check."

"Except, perhaps, their daughters."

"It looks that way."

"Look at her face," said Meg. "She's bored. And her skin is so dark. She must have been an active plantation owner. I don't see her spending much time lounging about indoors."

Meg looked around the room.

"So how could this place have remained so undisturbed over the years?"

"Nevisians are respectful of others' property. You know, there's another Eden that's haunted on the island—the Eden Brown house. A woman's fiancé shot her lover the night before they married. No one ever disturbs that place. Plus, the history of this house and the land is enough to keep most people away."

"Do you mean the alleged haunting?"

"In part."

Drew's face again grew dark.

"Is there more?" asked Meg.

Drew looked around the room and ran his hands over the pianoforte.

"About fifteen years ago, some children were playing around the house. They were horsing around on the cliff down on the back lawn. There was a terrible accident."

"What happened?"

"A child went over the cliff. He was standing too close to the edge, and the ground gave way under his weight."

"And that's why others have stayed away?"

"Yes."

"And that bears the unfortunate coincidence involving the slave who went over the cliff."

Drew turned from Meg and walked out into the hall and toward the back of the house. Meg followed him and directed him to the dining room. Drew stood in the doorway for several minutes taking in the mural. It was quite impressive from a distance to view the entire scene.

"The fall of Adam and Eve," said Drew.

"Look down here—West, 1811."

"Are there any famous artists named West? I don't know much about art."

"Benjamin West was an American painter and Quaker alive during the late 18th and early 19th century," said Meg. "He moved to England in 1763 and is said to have lived the rest of his life there. But the date on the painting, 1811, suggests that he may have spent time on the island."

"What makes you think Benjamin West is your painter?"

"He completed a painting in 1791 entitled *The Expulsion of Adam and Eve from Paradise*. The face of Eve in *The Expulsion* looks exactly like her face in this painting. The colors, the style—it all matches. Unfortunately, I was unable find any information on Benjamin West in 1811. By all the accounts I could find, he was in England."

"You said West was a Quaker. There was a large Quaker population on the island in the 18th Century. Is it possible he was visiting a relative? The Bath Hotel was quite a popular resort for the wealthy during that time period as well. Perhaps he stayed there."

"I'll look into it further. In the meantime, I'm going to contact the National Gallery of Art in Washington DC. *The Expulsion* has been there since 1989, and I'm going to see if they have any recommendations on West experts who could help me."

As they moved throughout the rest of the house, Drew seemed to be tiring. Meg suggested they stop for the day, and drove him back to the museum.

"I'll contact you if I find anything significant while I'm at work," said Drew. "Thank you for taking me into the house."

Meg smiled and watched Drew limp into the building. Then she drove back to the villa.

Meg was falling in love with Nevis. The temperature was perfect, the humidity was low, and a light breeze kept the edge off the heat. She walked close to the tree line in the cool, soft sand to get a good look at the flowers, shrubs, and trees on the beach. Much of the vegetation comprised some form of coconut palm, but a small grove of trees that looked like apple trees caught Meg's attention.

Meg walked closer to observe the leaves and fruits hanging from the tree. It looked like the tree of knowledge from the painting in the house. It had thick, waxy, green leaves, and shiny, plump, green fruits. It looked very inviting, and Meg reached up to pluck one of the fruits.

"Stop!"

Meg jumped and turned around to see Hamilton approaching her. He was running and wore a look of concern.

"What's the matter?" Meg asked. "Does it bite?"

"Yes—well, sort of."

"I don't understand."

"That's a manchineel tree—poisonous."

'The fruit?"

"The whole thing," said Hamilton. "The sap will blind you. The leaves will give you blisters. The fruit is deadly."

Meg walked out from under the tree.

"Thanks for the warning," she said.

"Most of the manchineel trees are marked with signs, but since this is on your land, it's considered wild."

"I'm lucky you found me here. Aren't you supposed to be in school?"

"It's a holiday."

"Thank God for that."

Meg and Hamilton fell into step along the beach.

"I've spent so much time inside the plantation house that I haven't been able to explore the land," said Meg. "This is the real treasure."

"Do you see that cave? It is a great hiding spot—except when the tide comes in. You'd have to swim to get out. And the boulders below the cliff—those are great for finding sea creatures, but you must be careful. The water is rough and the boulders are slippery."

"So much danger with so much beauty."

"That's the trouble with Paradise."

Hamilton led Meg over some of the low, flat boulders to look at the sea life. They found a sea star, several varieties of tropical fish, and anemones. The water was warm and calm—even around the boulders. Hamilton remarked that it was unusual for the water to be so still. After exploring the rocks, Hamilton raced over to a banana tree and scaled it to pick a bunch for Meg. They were pure yellow, without a hint of spoiling, and deliciously sweet.

Meg looked at her watch and was frustrated to see that her appointment with the real estate agent was fast approaching. She thanked Hamilton for saving her from the manchineel and hurried back to the path that led to Eden to meet with the agent. Hamilton stayed on the beach, tossing shells into the water and humming to himself. Meg smiled and started up the path. She thought she would like a picture of Hamilton on the beach and turned back to capture him against the water.

She fished her camera out of her bag as she came to the clearing on the shore. She was prepared to take his picture with his back to her, facing the sea, but when she got to the beach, he was gone. She looked around, but did not see him anywhere. A movement over by the cave drew her attention away from the water, and she thought he must have gone in the cave to explore.

I'll get his picture later.
Meg turned back up the path and hurried to Eden.

Henry Kingston, the real estate agent, was effusive about the quality of the land. He took pictures, measured, sketched, and completed forms for almost two hours. Meg saved the plantation home for the end of the tour, and Henry never once closed his mouth as he walked through the house. Meg had to show him the mural, and notified him that she was consulting an expert.

"The value of the land and plantation home will be in the tens of millions of dollars," said Henry. "My only concern is that there may not be a single buyer out there who could afford it all."

"I've actually spoken to a man from Grand Star Resorts. He thinks the company would be able to purchase it no matter what the cost."

"Have you considered subdividing the land into smaller parcels to sell to local developers?" he asked. "Much of the land on Nevis is being converted for tourism so Nevisians are finding it increasingly hard to find housing of their own."

"I hadn't considered that."

"I will go back to my office and work up some numbers and possible ways to market the property. I would love to list it."

"My attorney said you come highly recommended, so that would be fine with me."

During Meg's tour of the Great House, she realized that she had not yet been upstairs. Her explorations on the lower level were keeping her so busy that she hadn't yet been able to explore the second floor. Meg led Henry up the massive staircase. The rooms were almost empty except for a great deal of plant and animal life that had settled there. One of the rooms in which they glanced still had a large, four poster bed with a mildewed mattress, a vanity, and a bureau.

"This is unbelievable," said Meg. "Once this place is restored it will be magnificent."

"If the buyers don't tear it down."

"That would be a sin."

At the end of the meeting, Meg stood on the front porch of the house until Henry was out of sight. The wind was picking up and the sky was beginning to cloud over, but Meg was anxious to investigate upstairs alone. She walked back up the staircase running her hand along the balustrade. Meg's heart raced as the floorboards creaked under her weight, and thought that she would not venture upstairs again. She turned down the eastern hall, came to the room with the bed, and entered.

Clouds outside covered the sun and the room grew dark and shadowed. Meg opened the drawers of the bureau. They were empty, and the wood smelled damp and rotten. She walked across the room to the vanity and gazed at her reflection in the spotted, tarnished mirror.

Suddenly, Meg noticed a woman's face in the mirror behind her. Meg jumped and turned to face what she thought might be a ghost. Instead, she laughed at herself as she gazed at a portrait of a woman dressed in wedding clothes. She looked somewhat like the woman in the picture downstairs, but not exactly the same.

Is this Catherine's mother?

No reference had been in the tax records to indicate that Cecil had a wife. Perhaps she had died during childbirth or when Catherine was young.

Meg walked over to the bed. Its yellowish-gray mattress gave off an unpleasant odor. She looked at the intricately carved bedposts. They were cut with flowers and wildlife from top to bottom. The headboard was also carved with large flowers and trees. While looking at the bed, something caught Meg's eye. It was wedged between the mattress and the headboard. Meg reached over and pulled an old book from the bed. Meg carefully flipped through its pages. Blue ink on crispy yellowed pages. Some pages were ripped out, others smeared, but most were in tact.

April 1809...December 1811...

It was a diary.

8

The morning brought torrential rain and winds. Catherine opened her shutters to see palms bent in the wind, petals ripped off of flowers, and blinding sheets of rain. Thunder rumbled and vibrated Eden and lightning crackled with electricity over the island. The pungent smell of saturated earth and vegetation hung in the humidity of the Great House.

The roof hung enough over Catherine's window to allow her to sit and watch the rain fall. She reclined in silent meditation, watching the storm. Truthfully, it comforted Catherine to sit indoors and be still with nothing but the constant downpour to distract her thoughts. She dressed slowly, and moved like a phantom through the upstairs rooms of the house, obtaining different views of the sodden island from each window.

Upon entering her mother's chambers, Catherine moved to the chest of drawers and began looking through her mother's old clothing, trying to find items of clothing proper for the slaves to wear. It had never occurred to her until this moment how bizarre it was for her father to have insisted this room be kept as a shrine all these years. Moth eaten, old-fashioned garments were folded and stacked in the musty drawers. Dusty, corroded toiletries still sat at the old vanity in the same order in which they were placed so many years ago.

Catherine sat at the vanity and picked up her mother's hairbrush. Fine dusty strands of golden hair still coiled around its bristles. Catherine gazed into the mirror before her, and over her shoulder was able to see the painting of her mother. The elder Catherine gazed at her daughter through faded brown eyes. Catherine had seen the portrait hundreds of times, but had never studied it before this moment.

She moved to the wall and placed her hand upon the canvas in her mother's lap. Her mother sat straight, beautiful, and serious in her wedding clothes. Catherine knew that her mother was reluctant to come to the islands, and was only married a year before Cecil transported her to this strange place. Cecil spoke little of her, but through what Catherine could ascertain, her mother spent many hours indoors to keep away from the intense heat of the sun and the strange dark-skinned slaves.

Catherine moved to her mother's bed and lay down upon it, thinking with a shiver of the day she cleansed Esther's wounds. She ran her hands over the bedspread and under the feather pillows that had collapsed with years of neglect. Deep under one of the pillows, leaning between the edge of the bed and the headboard, Catherine felt the leather surface of a book. She pulled it out and turned it over in her hands. Upon opening the book, Catherine saw pages of small, fine handwriting.

Catherine sat up with excitement. After reading several passages, she realized that it was her mother's diary. Catherine could scarcely contain herself. Cecil surely did not know such an item was in this room or he would have removed it. Judging by some of the diary entries, Cecil may not have even known it existed. After hurrying across the room to close the door, Catherine returned to her mother's bed and began reading the diary.

April 1809

We have finally arrived at this Godforsaken Island after two and a half months of sheer torture. Plagued by illness, filth, and a serious want of supplies we managed to survive our long voyage away from my beloved England to this strange tropical place. My poor sister-in-law, Elizabeth, nearly died from her seasickness. I nearly died of fright from the profusion of squalls through which we had to suffer.

My first glimpse of Nevis came early during the morning of our 10th week onboard the ship. A soaring mountain obscured by dense mist loomed over the entire island. Though the waters were pristine and the vegetation resembled that of Paradise itself, the ship was docked in a vulgar and dirty town called Charlestown. I almost kissed the dust of that grimy town, however, because of my joy at making land.

I was thrilled to find such fine accommodations at the Bath Hotel, and wish with all my heart that we were only spending a holiday here. I would gladly endure such a sea voyage again to see the shores of England, but Cecil and his brother, William, are quite intent on settling here.

July 1809

It is astounding how much has occurred since we arrived at Nevis. We are now living in a hastily constructed dwelling that I fear will not last a fortnight. Cecil and William work all day and night with fifteen African slaves re-cultivating the land of an overgrown sugar plantation. Cecil and William are trying to convince Elizabeth and me that a good sugar crop will provide us with more wealth than we could ever imagine—enough to return to England after a stay of 10 years.

The promised riches and the ten year time table are the only reasons Elizabeth and I agreed to allow Cecil and William to drag us to this place. I shall make marks on a wall counting down the 3,650 days I am forced to live here.

August 1809

The heat is unbearable, the winds don't allow me a moment's peace, the slaves are frightening, and it is a scandal how much work I am forced to do each day to make this hut a home. Cecil assures me that after the first crop we will be able to buy an entire legion of slaves to perform all of the house and field work, but I must suffer until then. And I am not overly pleased that we are using slaves at all. It does seem a bit cruel to work such beings so hard with no compensation, but Cecil assures me that they were designed by God to serve. I have begged Cecil to hire at least one white servant to help with the household duties. I would like for my household to be run proper and English, but he insists that all plantation labor will be done by slaves. I do not know if I will ever become accustomed to living around such savages.

And to make matters worse, William has become ill with some dreadful tropical illness. I only hope it passes soon so he is able to again assist Cecil.

September 1809

William has died! Elizabeth is beside herself, and Cecil now has yet another burden to bear. I have tried to persuade him to allow us to return to England, but he is insistent that we stay here.

I do secretly know that the political climate in England is not friendly to him, so he stays here more out of fear than desire. He and several of his cohorts angered some important people, and I suspect we are in some sort of temporary exile.

I can only pray that God will have mercy on us and help us survive these difficult times.

March 1810

Much has happened in these few months since our arrival and William's death. A large and beautiful plantation home has been built up all around us with the help of the sixty slaves we now own. Elizabeth and I now have much relief with our own troupe of house slaves. I am particularly fond of Esther—a quiet, respectful, and mature young woman. She and Mary, an older but hard-working slave, attend to the household duties of cooking, cleaning, and laundering. Mary is quite an experienced cook, and our meals have become nothing short of spectacular!

I was taken to the auction when we purchased Esther and Mary, and I must say that it was an unpleasant scene. The slaves looked quite humiliated and devastated to be separated from one another, but Cecil assures me that any slave would be lucky to live under our care.

I still have not adjusted to the intolerable heat— Elizabeth and I spend most of our time indoors. I try to stay far away from any sort of tropical moisture, but that is nearly impossible with the humidity.

My life, I must say, is slowly returning to the level of comfort and luxury to which I am accustomed. I try to be positive for Cecil, but I still look eagerly forward to the day when I can return home.

Catherine paused in her reading and rubbed her eyes. She was hungry to continue working through the diary, but was becoming upset by her mother's spoiled and haughty manner, and her attitude toward the slaves. Catherine's previous ideal of her mother was dissolving with each passing word from the diary. It was becoming apparent to Catherine that her mother was a shallow creature concerned primarily with her own physical and emotional comfort.

Catherine read through the entries of 1810 as her mother catalogued the expansion of the plantation, the acquisition of more slaves, the social climate developing on the island, and her continued wish to move back to England. She wrote of her numerous illnesses, and complained of the fatigue, sickness, and oppressive heat that made her life so uncomfortable.

Catherine began reading with more care as she reached the time of her mother's pregnancy with herself.

September 1811

A physician has confirmed what I have recently suspected—I am expecting a child. Just when I thought I could not possibly bear one more physical inconvenience I have been told that I will bear a child in this wild and savage place. I had secretly hoped that the climate was causing my infertility, but it appears that is not so.

I have been quite nauseated, overwhelmingly tired, and unable to concentrate on anything. All I can do is lie in my bed while Esther fans me. Fruit is about the only thing I can stand to eat, and the smell of fish absolutely makes me want to die! How much can a woman possibly be expected to endure?

At least Cecil is keeping away from my chambers. I should have told him I was pregnant months ago!

Poor Elizabeth does her best to entertain me with the pianoforte we recently had shipped to Eden, but I can only stand to hear one song before the infernal noise positively ails me.

I cannot believe that I am going to feel this way for seven more months. It is truly a distressing thought.

December 1811

Life has become even more difficult now that I am expanding by the day. I do not understand how those pregnant slave women can work in such heat, under such sun, in such a condition! It just reinforces what Cecil believes about the purpose of such servile beings on this planet.

I watch Esther try to conceal her swelling abdomen along with mine. It is absolutely indecent that a slave woman like Esther, with no known male companion, is carrying a child. She is appropriately mortified and humiliated and is lucky that I have not abused her further by calling attention to the situation.

It is a wonder that more of the women are not walking around in her condition with the way they run around the fields half-naked and in such proximity to the males. My poor mother, God rest her soul, would be horrified if she ever knew all I was subject to witness in this place!

April 1812

I am nearing the conclusion of my confinement. Strange and terrible sensations have been gripping my abdomen since last night, and Esther has begun preparing the nursery. How she will deliver my child after just having delivered one herself is quite beyond my comprehension, but

Mary will assist her. The island physician is ill, so there is no telling when he will be out to Eden.

I am filled with a longing to lay eyes on this child that has grown and moved within me for so long. However, I am filled with much terror over the idea of labor. I only hope it will all be over quickly.

Writing in the face of such pain is becoming difficult, so I will put down my pen until after the baby has arrived.

Catherine turned the page and saw that the entry she had just read was her mother's last. She flipped back, wanting more, but sickened at the true nature of her mother. Some pages had been ripped out between September and December of 1811, but that was all. There was nothing more.

The thought of Esther's pregnancy with Leah began to trouble Catherine. She had always assumed that Esther had a companion who fathered Leah, and had since died. Catherine conjured Esther's dark face, and then Leah's face which was the color of wet beach sand. Catherine pushed the bed curtain out of her way and moved over to the open window. She strained her eyes to see through the rain, but found it impossible. Catherine closed her eyes and allowed the sounds of the rain pouring down to push the disturbing thoughts that had begun to emerge from her mind back into the dark places from which they had come.

A loud boom of thunder and a flash of lightning roused Catherine from her thoughts. Wondering at the time, Catherine slid the diary back into its original resting place, smoothed the bedspread, and crept out of her mother's room.

The entire house was hushed and dark. She thought that she heard the sound of movement coming from behind Cecil's closed bedroom door, but as her foot creaked the floorboards it stopped. Catherine moved down the long staircase and into the music room. Leah was cleaning and polishing the furniture, and looked up with surprise when Catherine entered the room.

"What time is it?" asked Catherine.

"Eleven o'clock. Where have you been?"

"I was resting upstairs. The weather has depressed my spirits."

Leah stared at Catherine, and returned to her work. Catherine moved over to the pianoforte and began playing. The sounds drifted through the house, up the stairs, and dissolved on the wind and rain outdoors.

～ ⌒

That night, since the weather cleared, the Dalls went to a dinner party at the Hall Plantation. The carriage rocked slowly over the mud as the night began to fall. Catherine said nothing to her father, and he was content to sip his drink. She watched the setting sun grow fat as it stole the color from the landscape and sank heavily into the ocean. Slaves were still working in the Hall fields as they passed toward the main drive. Their features were lost in the shadows on their dark faces.

Before turning up the main drive, Catherine could see the Whitting home. Three small, dirty children chased a goat around the front yard trying to tie it up to the fence. Mrs. Whitting bundled tobacco leaves on the front step. She looked up and waved at Catherine as she passed. Catherine waved back but her hand froze as Caleb stepped onto the front porch with a gun in his hand. His half-buttoned shirt hung over his breeches, and his face was fierce. He jerked his wife up by the arm and pushed her into the house. His children, who had succeeded in tying up the goat, ran in through the door without a word. Catherine looked away and was relieved to be swallowed by the trees lining the Hall's drive. When she turned to Cecil to see if he had noticed the exchange, she saw that he was snoring with his chin resting on his chest. His empty glass rolled on the seat beside him.

Catherine was not looking forward to an evening of mind-numbing conversation with the Hall women, but could think of no good excuse not to go. Mrs. Hall was insufferable in her obsession with marriage. She considered any woman not married by twenty to be doomed to a life of spinsterhood and misery. She admonished Catherine for not taking courtship more seriously. Mrs. Hall was determined to have her daughters married off—before twenty, if possible—to bachelors of the islands.

Mrs. Hall and her daughters stood in the foyer to greet the guests.

"Miss Dall!" exclaimed Mrs. Hall. "We were just saying how delighted we are that you could join us this evening."

"Thank you for your invitation, Mrs. Hall."

"You are an absolute vision!"

"I could not agree more," said Edward Ewing as he entered the room. The Hall girls looked at one another with wide eyes and wilted in their posture. The entire company greeted one another and settled into obligatory conversations on weather and other small matters.

As the guests talked, Catherine slipped quietly onto the balcony off the parlor. She had dressed that evening in a pale blue dinner gown that rustled over the floor, giving her the appearance of an apparition. If one had seen her on the balcony in the moonlight she would have seemed to be a ghost.

Mrs. Hall and her daughters had not noticed Catherine on the balcony and stood just inside gossiping.

"I have heard that Mr. Ewing is seriously beginning to focus his search for a wife," said Mrs. Hall. "You girls are a bit young, but your beauty and charming personalities should recommend you for eligibility."

"Oh Mother, please," said Fanny, the eldest. "Catherine is surely the object of Mr. Ewing's affections."

"I urged your father not to invite the Dalls. Edward Ewing doesn't need any more exposure to Catherine. It's scandalous the way she carries on with her slaves and that Leah—as if Leah were a right and proper member of society."

"With all that time Catherine spends outdoors, her skin is as dark as a nigger," remarked Lucy.

Fanny and Mrs. Hall sucked in their breath.

"Lucy, you are a lady. Negro will certainly do."

Burning with anger, Catherine stepped out from behind the curtain on the balcony. The Hall women were horrified and Catherine's glare did nothing to reassure them that they hadn't been heard.

Mrs. Hall announced dinner in a weak voice, and led her daughters to the dining room as quickly as she could. Edward was as delighted as Catherine was disappointed to find their places next to one another.

"You're red in the face beyond the usual scorch of the sun," said Edward. "What's wrong?"

"Nothing."

Edward leaned close to Catherine's ear.

"The Halls are insufferable, are they not?"

Catherine closed her eyes and shook her head.

"You sulk the same way at our dinner parties. I hope you don't find my father and me as miserable as the Halls."

"That's a different kind of misery."

First Edward laughed, but then he grew quiet for the rest of the meal. Catherine could almost hear him trying to think of a way to turn the conversation in his favor. When dinner concluded, they all retired to the music room as the Hall sisters attempted to entertain their guests with their musical endeavors.

Edward sat next to Catherine and again whispered in her ear, "I had thought the music of the bellfrogs to be quite sufficient for the evening."

Catherine grinned in spite of herself. Edward appeared pleased at having elicited a smile, and basked in the glory of his achievement for several moments.

"And after so heavy a meal, I fear this will quite do me in," he said.

Catherine smiled more broadly and gave him a reproachful look. At the conclusion of the song she said, "The only thing that could make this performance more perfect than it already is would be if some male accompaniment were added. I think we would all be delighted to hear Mr. Edward Ewing in concert with the Misses Hall."

Mrs. Hall jumped out of her chair.

"A more splendid suggestion could not have been made. Oh please, Mr. Ewing, indulge us!" Fanny and Lucy fidgeted with nervous pleasure as Edward glared at Catherine.

After the color left his face he walked to the pianoforte and suggested a song to Fanny. She and Mrs. Hall exchanged glances as Lucy began to play *I Have a Silent Sorrow*. Catherine's smile slowly evaporated as the song began. Edward's singing voice was superb, and the audience could not help but lose itself in the performance. He stared into Catherine's eyes throughout the duration of the song, forcing her to look away. At the culmination of the song, the audience clapped with enthusiasm. Catherine nodded in concession at Mr. Ewing. He bowed back at her and joined the gentlemen.

As the evening drew to a close Catherine wandered to the front terrace. She rested her head on a column and looked out into the blackness, straining her eyes to see the water.

"Are you all right?" asked Edward as he stepped out of the shadows.

Catherine looked at him, startled. "I just need a bit of fresh air."

"The air is cleansing."

"I must agree with you."

"I know our ancestors came from England, but Nevis is in our blood."

Catherine looked at Edward and then back at the horizon.

"I know I offend you in some way," said Edward. "I can only hope to find myself in your good graces. We have much to offer one another."

Catherine was saved a response as Cecil stumbled out onto the terrace. Edward ran to catch Cecil before he plundered down the great staircase. He and Catherine helped her father down to the carriage, and Edward and Thomas lifted Cecil into it.

"I will be sure to tell the Halls that you needed to get your father home immediately," said Edward. "I am sure they will understand."

Catherine nodded and climbed into the carriage. She glanced back toward the house and saw Edward standing on the front stairs until she was out of view.

9

Gwen Flynn, a student at Florida State University working on her doctoral thesis on Benjamin West, could barely contain herself during her phone call with Meg. Gwen told Meg that she was flying down on Thursday with one of her professors, art historian Dr. David Parfitt, who also happened to work for Sotheby's. They would be able to verify the authenticity of the work, and guide Meg in the sale of the mural.

Meg called Brian and told him as much as she drove to the Historical Society building.

"You've gotten a lot accomplished this week," said Brian. "If this is what you're like on vacation, I'd like to see you at work."

"I'm very motivated."

"I'll say."

"Will you still love me when I'm broke?"

"I'll love you more. You won't have as many distractions."

When Meg had first brought Brian to meet her parents at their waterfront estate, he had been noticeably uncomfortable. But Richard and Anne were warm and welcoming people, so Brian's unease evaporated. Brian was from a working-class family in Wales. His father worked coal, his mother was a musician and a poet, and they had always lived modestly.

When Meg first visited Brian's family home she was in awe of the vast, green, hilly country. She remembered running up to the middle of a knoll and singing *The Hills are Alive with the Sound of Music.* Brian had said, "Wrong country, Meg;" as she turned to face a weathered, tall, smiling woman.

"Mum, this is Meg."

Meg was appropriately mortified, but Mrs. Hyer was delighted. The rest of the holiday was spent getting to know the Hyer clan, drinking at local pubs, exploring the coast, and listening to music. Meg had surprised Brian for his birthday while in Wales by taking him to see his favorite musician, David Gray, at the Cardiff Arena. They checked out the ruins of Cardiff and Caerphilly Castles. Brian said he originally intended to propose there, but thought the Fourth of July in Annapolis more fitting for his American lass.

Brian's parents were smitten with Meg. His father, though much quieter than his mother, was more pleased with Meg than he had intended to be. He had gotten over his son not taking a Welsh girl as soon as he heard what Meg had said about Brian's accent upon their first meeting.

Meg thought of her trip to Wales as she drove to the Historical Society Museum with the diary double-bagged on the seat beside her. She glanced at it every few minutes to verify its existence, and nearly ran off the road when it fell to the floor after she drove over a rut. Meg scarcely put the jeep in park before grabbing the diary and racing into the Museum. Drew looked up with surprise as Meg charged through the door.

"I was just about to call you, Meg. I found something of importance."

"Me too. You first."

"In our archived letters I came across something from a Miss Fanny Hall to a Miss Eugenia Darrow of Darrow Hall. Darrow Hall was a plantation on the windward side of the island. Catherine Dall is mentioned by name in the letter. Here."

Meg took the letter and began to read it aloud.

23 January 1831

My Dearest Cousin Eugenia:

Last night a fire engulfed our mills, destroying the entire sugar industry of our plantation. Father says we are ruined and Mother is beside herself. I scarcely know what to think. Three slaves died fighting the blaze, but mercifully we lost no others. I overheard Father discussing the slaves' unruly behavior since the incident. Since there is no way to process the cane, it is rotting on its stalks while the slaves carouse as if they were free men and women. We are all forced to sleep with muskets at our sides, in fear for our own safety. Father is irate because he thinks this is either the work of an angry neighboring small farmer, or abolitionists. The blaze started in three different buildings—not at all accidental.

I've overheard rumblings of Father selling out to the Ewings of Goldenrise, but he is angered over the price they've offered, so I've no idea if that will take place. In any case we will be forced to move to England.

Mother said she will be glad to remove herself from this island, but I was born here and know nothing else. I've no interest in becoming a pauper in a foreign place with a cold, rainy climate. We wouldn't even be allowed slaves in England as they have been banned there.

You'd be interested to know that Catherine Dall was here last night. She organized the slaves to help care for the wounded while Lucy and I served refreshments. No doubt she made herself useful to appeal to Edward Ewing. Catherine is not getting any younger and probably can't wait to find a husband. I wish I could say that Edward did not notice her, but that was not the case.

I will write to you as soon as I know our fate. Give our love to Sissy and Auntie.

Yours,
Fanny Hall

"Fanny sounds envious of Catherine," said Meg. "I wonder whatever became of Edward Ewing?"

"I wondered the same thing," said Drew. "I checked the parish records and found that a Bartholomew Ewing of Goldenrise—presumably Edward's father—died of bleeding fever in February of 1831—there was some sort of epidemic. Then in March, there was this entry. "

Meg looked down at the weathered, yellow page. "Edward Ewing married Fanny Hall, March of 1831. I suppose Edward found a good way to acquire the Hall's destroyed estate."

"Marry their daughter."

"The name Edward Ewing is nagging at me," said Meg. "It sounds so familiar. Was he famous for something?"

"Not that I'm aware of," said Drew. "He was involved politically on the island, but I don't think he had any other fame."

"It will come to me. In the meantime, I found this in an upstairs room of Eden. I think it belonged to Catherine's mother. It's a diary."

Drew carefully opened the bags and slid the diary onto his desk. He turned the pages, scanning the entries and shaking his head.

"Meg, this is an extremely significant artifact. There is information in here on daily plantation life, home construction, and the personal lives of the plantation's inhabitants."

"I want to donate it to the Historical Society."

Drew was speechless.

Meg went on. "I found this stuffed in some old sheet music on the first day that I went in the house."

Drew looked at the abolitionist pamphlet.

"There's a note inside from a James Silwell to Catherine Dall. We've got to find out more about James Silwell. I think we're on the verge of finding something big."

"It does seem as if this story wants to be known," said Drew.

"Maybe that will quiet the ghosts," said Meg.

"You don't believe in ghosts."

Meg went back to the villa and made a *Golden Friendship* rum drink. She thought of the evidence they'd found and tried to make connections.

Edward Ewing married Fanny Hall and grew his estate. Abolitionists may have started the blaze. Catherine, a slave owner's daughter, received an abolitionist pamphlet. Esther the slave became mysteriously pregnant and had a baby girl the same time Catherine's mother was pregnant and had Catherine. The girls would have been close if they grew up at the same time and Esther was a house slave. A slave girl allegedly killed herself by jumping off the cliff.

Meg's cell phone rang.

"It's Drew. I missed something."

"What?"

"I turned the page in the tax records. Edward Ewing and Fanny Hall must have purchased Eden. I don't know what happened to Catherine and Cecil, but Edward and Fanny's names are listed with the house in June 1831."

"Edward Ewing came into all that land. He must have made a fortune!"

"Not only that. I looked back in the parish records. Edward and Fanny baptized Bartholomew James in September of 1832."

The line grew quiet as the realization suddenly dawned on Meg.

"I'm a descendent of Edward and Fanny Ewing," she said.

"It would appear that way."

"That's why his name sounds familiar. The family bible. I must have seen the Ewing name in it."

Meg suddenly felt very sick. It was difficult knowing with certainty that her family fortune was founded in slavery and her father's theft. It felt like everything she owned didn't truly belong to her. Meg knew she had nothing to do with the decision of her forbearers, but it didn't change the fact that she was responsible for the future of her assets.

"Are you okay, Meg?"

"I am. This is just a lot to digest. I need to think for awhile."

"I'm sorry if I upset you," said Drew.

"No, no—knowing is best."

After she hung up, Meg put down the phone and watched the changing sky. Knowing that she was descended from slave owners bothered Meg more than she thought it would. She had been hoping that her father had acquired the land on his own, but now saw that it had been passed down to her through her family for generations.

Clouds were creeping over the sky from the west in a dark shelf. The wind was picking up. On her drive to the villa, Meg had heard that a tropical depression was forming in the southeast. She had heard the report when the sky was clear, so she hadn't thought much about it. Now it was getting dark and Meg was getting concerned. She flipped on the news, but the weatherman just reiterated the radio report. He thought the depression would change course and head up to Florida, but reminded residents and vacationers to stay tuned for evacuation information. He did mention that if the storm changed course it wasn't due to hit the island for another six days.

10

Strong winds had entirely blown away the stench of the rat bonfire. The dew made a moist blanket over the grasses, palms, and flowers, enhancing the brilliant greens, purples, pinks, reds and yellows of the vegetation. Mist hung low around the great mountain, blocking its summit from view, and the distant waves of the Caribbean beckoned to the island.

Esther walked a bit straighter that morning at breakfast. Cecil arrived after Catherine and rambled incoherently. Something he said, however, caught Catherine's attention.

"There will be a ball this Friday at the Bath Hotel. Many affluent and important people will be there. I have made an appointment with the dress-maker for you this afternoon, so I will join you later."

Catherine found herself excited by the prospect of a ball. She longed for a bit of socializing to escape her duties on the plantation. She also found herself not unhappy at the possibility of seeing the Silwells.

Friday arrived and preparations were begun early for the ball at the Bath Hotel. While her father attended the formal meeting of the Council, Catherine allowed herself the pleasure of being doted upon to prepare for the evening's entertainment. She had bathed the evening before, and her hair was set early. Much fuss was made by Esther over the difficulty of removing the ink and dirt from Catherine's fingertips and nails, but the black was eventually scrubbed clean.

The dress arrived at two o'clock. It was pale yellow and complemented her hair. Catherine grabbed a shawl as covering in case of high winds, and paced around the house until five with Esther scolding her every time she tried to start a chore that would dishevel her appearance.

Thomas was dressed in elegant livery as he chauffeured Cecil and Catherine to the Bath Hotel. As the carriage pulled away from Eden, a movement in a window on the second floor of the house caught Catherine's attention. Leah gazed down at Catherine. When their eyes met she turned away from the window. Catherine looked down at her lap.

Since Esther's beating, Leah had become distant from Catherine. She spoke little, could not be persuaded to steal away for reading, and would scarcely meet Catherine's gaze.

"What could possibly be troubling so beautiful a specimen on such a fine evening?" asked Cecil.

"It is nothing, Father."

"Do not trouble yourself about Eden. I am quite sure the plantation can do without you for one night."

Catherine smiled weakly at her father and then turned her face to the sea. The rocking of the carriage was soothing and soon quieted her nerves. They moved down the road, occasionally speaking to admire some pleasing sight, but mostly sitting in the easy silence of old companions. The road they traveled was high and divided the three largest island plantations. Though it was heavily landscaped, glimpses of the various estates could be seen through the palms and shrubbery. It was a cool place to travel, as the trees and vines had begun to form a natural canopy over the hard, brown dirt.

Catherine began to ruminate on how pleasing a journey it had been thus far and felt her spirits lightening at the thought of the ball. As she commenced humming a waltz, a low droning noise drifted up on the breeze from a field below the road. The noise took on a frantic quality, and soon grew to an animal-like howl.

Thomas slowed the carriage and the three of them looked through the palms to a field on the Hall's property where a slave woman wept and struggled to carry the lifeless body of a young girl toward an overseer riding a brown horse. The slave girl's head hung facing the road, and a thread of green bile could be seen running out of her sallow lips. Her skin was ashen and sweat glossed over her emaciated, half-naked body.

The carriage had reached a stop, and Catherine looked on in horror as the overseer used his riding crop to pry the dead girl from the woman's arms and beat the hysterical woman over the head until she returned to her place in the cane. Through the slits of her eyelids, the dead girl's eyes caught the sun and glistened at the onlookers. Her body lay in a tangle by the cane until the overseer instructed two slaves nearby to remove her body from the field.

Cecil shouted at Thomas to continue onward and mumbled under his breath. Catherine watched the miserable slave woman's agonized face as she worked the cane with sharp slices of her blade. Her shoulders heaved and the sweat mingled with her tears to produce a slick sheen on her face. Gradually, a blank curtain settled over her features. Her eyes stared vacantly at the crop, her mouth hung slightly open, her shoulders ceased to heave.

The carriage rode away, and Catherine could feel a knot forming in her stomach. Of all the gruesome sights just passed, it was the vacancy that took over the woman's face so suddenly that most terrified Catherine and refused to leave her mind.

The Bath Hotel was a grand structure that towered over the verdant topography of the island. It provided a startling contrast from the landscape with its geometric stone design, and fortress-like appearance. It loomed over Nevis, daring the tropical winds to disturb its place on the hilltop.

Catherine wished she could command the carriage home as it approached the Bath Hotel. Well-dressed men and women were strolling through the gardens, and a line of carriages formed to deposit their elegant passengers. Cecil nodded at arriving friends and neighbors while Catherine's eyes swept her surroundings. As Catherine and Cecil descended from their carriage, Edward Ewing came forward and grasped Catherine's hand to assist her down the stairs. She noticed how handsome he looked and felt herself flush as she left the carriage.

"Thank you, Mr. Ewing."

"A pleasure, Miss Dall. I am thrilled to see you were able to make it."

"Is your father here?" asked Cecil.

"He's just in the entrance hall," said Edward. "We only arrived a few short moments ago, sir."

Edward began giving instructions to Thomas and his slave as Catherine took her father's arm and climbed the great staircase into the foyer. Though many greeted her as she moved through the foyer, she found herself sullen and in no mood to socialize. Catherine longed to leave the boisterous crowd, but knew she would have to endure the party for hours.

The strains of a small orchestra quieted the assembly and beckoned them to an enormous dining room blazing with hundreds of candles in shimmering chandeliers. Meats, seafood, fruits, and vegetables adorned the gleaming silver serving platters, and a large group of finely dressed slaves seated the guests. Sparkling flames twisted and danced on the candles giving the room a dream-like quality, and the crowd noise dissolved into a far-away murmur.

Catherine felt lost and lightheaded. The heat pressed upon her and her vision blurred. Her father talked and drank at her side, and the fumes from his alcoholic breath were dizzying. Feeling as if she was about to faint, Catherine began to rise from her chair, but felt a cool hand rest on hers. She turned and saw that James Silwell was taking his seat next to her, and his father, Albert, had already found his chair across the table.

"Are you quite well?" asked James.

Catherine nodded as her head began to clear.

"You looked as if you were about to faint," he said.

"I believe I was. It's oppressively hot in here."

"I agree—though the paddle fans are doing a bit to ease the temperature."

Catherine turned and saw slave children standing about the room waving large fans at the guests. She stared at them, and then addressed James.

"How is your stay? Are you making much progress?"

"Yes, thank you for inquiring."

Catherine felt eyes boring into her, and looked across the table at Albert. He smiled and nodded at her. Catherine felt a sudden surge of energy—as if she had been afloat at sea for days and found a buoy just as her strength was failing her.

"I'm glad for that," she said, and began her dinner with renewed vigor.

After the feast was cleared and the guests were escorted to a large room for cocktails, James addressed Catherine: "Could I interest you in a stroll through the gardens? It will be some time before the ballroom is ready for dancing, and the gardens at twilight are a stunning sight to behold."

"I'd love to."

The golden warmth of sunset dissolved into the cool stillness of nightfall.   Birds whispered and darted through the flowers as James escorted Catherine through the winding, leafy paths.

"I haven't seen you in my comings and goings at Eden this week," said James.

"I have been very busy," said Catherine, pleased to hear that he had been looking for her. "Are you finding your time spent here useful?"

"Very useful, though much that I see here surprises me."

"Really. What has been your greatest shock?"

"I would have to say that stumbling upon a young mistress teaching a slave girl to read would be the biggest surprise yet," said James.

Catherine looked at James with alarm. She stopped walking and tried to think of something to say.

"Allow me to speak frankly," said James.

Catherine nodded.

"I'm sure your motives are pure, but what you are doing will ultimately cause Leah pain. To elevate a slave through education, but keep her confined to servitude is cruel."

Catherine studied the ground. She was trapped. She was fearful of the consequences of her actions if he reported what he saw, yet she did not sense that he was in disagreement with her; rather, he seemed as if he was prodding her to understand her point of view.

Catherine thought back to James' smile with the Quaker outside of church on the first day they met. She thought of the abolitionist rumblings of her father and the Ewings, and felt she had nothing to lose by probing James for the truth.

"Why are you really here?" asked Catherine.

James looked at Catherine. She could see him searching her face.

"I have seen you play with slave children," he began. "I have witnessed you teach a slave to read. You seem at odds with your situation. It is as if you are attempting to atone for owning slaves."

"Maybe I am," said Catherine.

"You asked me why I came here. What I am about to tell you could get me and my father into serious trouble. I would expect your silent cooperation about my situation if you find it offensive, given what I know of your situation."

"You have my confidence."

"My father and I are abolitionists observing slavery on the islands. What we see will be used to make a case for banning slavery throughout the British Empire. We have strong support in Parliament, and expect to be successful in phasing out this abominable system."

The laughter of a woman could be heard on a nearby path, and Catherine and James resumed their walk.

"I'm not surprised," said Catherine.

"No?"

"I saw you exchange knowing glances with the Quaker outside of Services. You've had me suspicious."

"Well, what do you think?"

"I don't know," said Catherine. "I need time to think. But in the meantime, you need not worry. I won't expose you."

"You have my gratitude for that. Of course, I won't expose you either."

Catherine walked in silence for awhile, and then addressed James. "What will happen to the slaves and plantation owners once slavery is banned?"

"It is proposed that all slaves over the age of six will become apprentices to be trained in order to manage on their own. After a pre-determined time, the slaves will be freed totally. Slave owners will be compensated handsomely for being forced to free their slaves."

Catherine looked out to the horizon. She tried to imagine Eden staffed with paid labor. The first person to go, she thought, would be Phinneas.

"Have you heard of the New York Manumission Society?" asked James. "It was founded by Alexander Hamilton, a white man born of this very island."

"I haven't."

"They have established schools and other services for freed blacks in America. You may find some writings on the topic interesting reading."

"Are you trying to make an abolitionist of me, Mr. Silwell?"

"Are you willing?"

Catherine was silent again.

"When do you leave Nevis?" she asked.

"We are set to depart for England next month."

The pair found themselves arrived at the bath house. Steam hissed from the boiling sulfuric waters that churned and bubbled at the bottom of the staircase.

"This garden and spring are known on the island as the Gardens of Jericho," said Catherine. "Jericho was known as the City of Palm Trees. Banana, henna, sycamore, and myrrh were among the plants that grew there, and a spring ran through the gardens. These springs are said to have curative powers. Jericho was also the place where Jesus was said to have cured the blind man."

"Did you know that Dall means 'blind' in Cornish?" asked James.

"I did not."

The orchestra could be heard rising in the background as it began the melody of a popular waltz. Catherine and James exchanged glances and turned back to the hotel.

The ballroom shimmered in the candlelight. Catherine stared at the dancers moving about the floor and had the eerie feeling of one looking over ghosts in a once populated place. James solicited Catherine's hand, and they joined the throngs of well-to-do party-goers.

Edward Ewing circled the dancers looking for his chance to replace James. He soon found his opportunity when James excused himself to procure drinks for Catherine and himself. Catherine was caught up in Edward's arms during a minuet and he manipulated their position on the floor far from where they had started.

"You are positively radiant this evening, Miss Dall."

"Thank you."

"May I solicit another dance from you later in the evening?"

Edward breeched the rules of decorum by pulling Catherine in closer to himself. The dance floor was thick with bodies so he was not seen by anyone. Catherine's heartbeat quickened and she struggled to move out of his grasp, but he had her too tight.

"I'm sorry," she said, "but I've already promised my dances to another."

Edward pulled her even closer and leaned close to her face.

"I can't hear you. The music is too loud."

Catherine turned toward Edward's face and was just inches away from him. She felt dizzy and was afraid that she would faint.

"I've promised my dances to another."

Edward's eyes grew dark. "That is a pity, especially since Mr. Silwell will be leaving in less than a month. It seems rather a waste of time to further his acquaintance, does it not?"

"I am sure I did not ask your advice," said Catherine. "Kindly refrain from imparting it on me in the future."

Catherine removed herself from Edward's grasp and moved off the dance floor. After searching the crowd for a half hour Catherine finally found James.

"I'm sorry I've taken so long," said James. "I've been looking all over for you."

"It is I who am sorry. I was danced away by Mr. Ewing, and had to pry myself away from him quite impolitely in order to find you."

James smiled and handed Catherine her drink.

"This heat is intolerable," said Catherine. "Could we return to the outdoors for a while?"

"I thought you'd never ask."

Catherine and James returned to the gardens under the light of the moon and strolled around in silence. One path led them to a point overlooking the sea and the city of Charlestown. Charlestown was aglow with life, and its music drifted on the island breeze to the spot where Catherine and James stood.

"Have you been to Charlestown?" asked Catherine.

"I go some evenings with some of the younger men staying at the hotel. There is a small pub at the edge of town where we go to hear the sounds of a small Welsh group of musicians. I have not ventured further into town. I hear some of its establishments are quite shocking."

"Aside from the ten steps I take from the carriage into church, I have never been able to set foot in that city. I have always longed to go to a pub and hear music." Catherine looked at James with a sly glance.

"If you are suggesting that I escort you there you are quite mad."

"Mr. Silwell," said Catherine, "It is only a short carriage ride away. We could be back before the conclusion of the ball. No one will ever know we left."

"Absolutely not. I would be drawn and quartered for allowing you to go to a place like that."

"Father would be amused, if anything. He spends quite a bit of time in Charlestown himself."

"Even if I wanted to take you, it is completely inappropriate for a lady to take a carriage ride alone with a practical stranger to a bawdy town like Charlestown."

"First of all, you are not a stranger," said Catherine. "You spent a great deal of time at Eden, and because my father is an abysmal judge of character, he trusts you completely. Second, we would have a chaperone in our carriage driver. Finally, standards of decorum on the islands are quite different from those in England. We are a liberal society as you have well noticed."

James considered her arguments and shook his head as she led him toward the carriages parked in front of the hotel.

"I cannot believe I am going to be a party to this," mumbled James.

~☙~

The pub was a rickety structure of wind-beaten wood situated overlooking Gallows Bay. Music spilled out of the shuttered doors into the street where the carriage came to a stop. James helped Catherine down from the carriage and into the dark paneled interior of the pub. Candles flickered and danced to the lively beat of the instruments as James led Catherine to a well-shadowed table near the musicians.

Several people glanced at Catherine with mild interest, but her appearance went widely unnoticed. James brushed off her seat before allowing her to sit, and then ordered drinks.

The pub provided a stark contrast to the stuffy and elegant setting from which they had just come, and James looked into Catherine's face to see if she regretted venturing to the pub. His eyes were greeted with Catherine's glowing face and total ease of posture. He smiled, shook his head, and turned back to the music.

"Do you know why the bay is called Gallows Bay?" asked Catherine.

"I can only assume it's to do with hangings."

"Pirate hangings. Centuries ago pirates could be regularly seen dangling over the bay—hanged for their misdeeds. Pirates are still a bit of a problem throughout the Caribbean, though less so now than years ago."

"You are a wealth of island lore."

Catherine smiled and then turned to watch the dancers. Several couples weaved in and out of one another. The women's clothing was dirty and scant, and the men looked and smelled as if they needed baths. One particularly grimy and diffident young man approached Catherine and solicited her hand to join in the dance. She joined him while James looked on with amusement, until he slipped onto the dance floor and joined the group.

After a few circles around the dance floor with the young man, Catherine found herself pushed into James. He smiled and moved back like a gentleman, but Catherine pulled him closer. Unlike her dance with Edward, Catherine had no wish to pull away.

"I think I like your liberal society," said James.

"Then stay."

"Don't tempt me."

The time passed quickly and Catherine knew they must take leave of the pub. She gave her small bouquet to the young man and bade the pub's patrons farewell as she boarded the carriage and set off with James back toward the Bath Hotel. They didn't speak on the ride back, but instead let their hands fall together on the seat between them.

<hr/>

The wind blew the stench of pub smoke, alcohol, and perspiration from Catherine and James, and the two were purified by the time they arrived back at the hotel. They snuck in and found their fathers who were engaged in amiable conversation near the rear of the ballroom.

"Catherine!" exclaimed Cecil. "We had lost you in the crowd for a spell."

"We lost ourselves in the crowd, Father," smiled Catherine. "And we had to step out for a bit of fresh air."

"It is rather stuffy in here."

"It was a lovely ball," remarked Albert. "The entertainment and food rivaled that of the London society."

As the crowd began to disperse, the Dalls and Silwells exchanged farewells. Catherine was glad that she was able to enjoy the evening, but the road back to Eden reminded her of her troubles, and her mood again blackened. She reached into her evening bag and ran her fingers over the small slip of paper that James had given her, mentally weighing the consequences of being found attending the meeting named on its surface.

~ ❧ ~

A series of thunderous knocks on the heavy oak front door of Eden awoke Catherine and her father. She and Cecil stumbled down the stairs, holding candles—Catherine in her dressing gown and Cecil in the rumpled clothes in which he had passed out earlier that evening. Thomas emerged from his room behind the stairs and met them in the foyer. Cecil commanded Catherine to stand back in the parlor as he cocked his musket and pointed it at the door. Thomas loosened the locks, and as the heavy bolts slid out of their restraints, Edward Ewing announced himself through the door. Cecil put down the gun and allowed him entrance.

Edward was winded and covered in perspiration. His normally meticulous appearance was disheveled from the hurried manner in which he must have dressed. His horse stood panting on the crushed shells of the drive next to Bartholomew and several of their slaves on horseback. The group looked strange and ghostly white in the moonlight.

"It's the Hall plantation," said Edward. "The mills, the boiling house, the storehouse—it's all on fire. We need you and every able-bodied male on the plantation."

Catherine gasped, and Edward, just noticing her in the shadows, nodded his head.

"I'll be right there," said Cecil. "I must fetch Phinneas and the rest. Thomas will stay with Catherine."

Edward again looked at Catherine and nodded. As quickly as he'd arrived, he was gone.

"Catherine, take the musket and keep it with you at all times," said Cecil. "I suspect foul play is at work here. The Council's ruling on thatched houses was made law on Friday, and many small planters are angry."

"Please let me go with you, Father."

"You must be out of your mind, Catherine. You must learn that there are situations that simply aren't suitable for your attendance."

"Father, I will be safer near you than at Eden by myself. Besides, the Hall women may need support."

Cecil considered his daughter's words.

"You raise a good point," he said. "If there was foul play, you would not be safe here with most of the able-bodied men gone. Dress quickly, there isn't time to spare."

Catherine ran up the stairs, dressed, and again ran down the great staircase. She collided with Phinneas in the foyer, and had to remove herself from his clammy hands. He was thick with the odors of stale tobacco, sweat, and old rum. His shirt clung to his body in sticky patches.

"Where do you think you're going?"

"Father said I could accompany him to the Hall plantation."

Phinneas eyed Catherine as if she were mad.

"I will be able to comfort the Hall women, and I'll be safer there."

Phinneas was about to protest when Cecil rounded the corner and confirmed what Catherine had reported. He ushered them all outside where three horses were waiting, along with twenty slaves on horseback, two-by-two.

"Is this all you summoned, Phinneas?" asked Cecil.

"I wanted the others to remain at Eden and guard the mills. If foul play is at work we cannot afford to leave the buildings unguarded."

"Excellent, Phinneas."

The riders made a swift exit, and clopped down the dirt road under the quarter moon at a rapid pace. Catherine was charged with adrenaline as she raced to the Hall plantation. The moist, tropical air filled her lungs and her heart pounded with fear and excitement.

The group quickly arrived at the Hall plantation. Cecil commanded Catherine to enter the plantation from the front as he and the others took the path down to the mills, and she veered toward the palm tree lined drive alone. As the horses were swallowed by the path, Catherine was left to venture to the house in solitude. The acrid smell of the burning buildings reached her as she dismounted her horse and tied him to a nearby post. She patted his mane and whispered in his ear as he found his breath, considering what she would do next.

Cecil would be occupied with the fire for hours; therefore, Catherine had some freedom. She knew that the wisest choice would be to enter the house immediately, but the lure of the action was too much for her to ignore. Creeping through the tangled forest along the left side of the house, Catherine began to make her way toward the sugar buildings.

An orange glow rose up over the tree tops amidst great bellowing gasps of black smoke, and the shouts and calls of the men punctuated the stillness of the night. Catherine stole along the grounds creeping closer and closer to a clearing that would give her visual access to the fire, while still concealing her form.

She stumbled rather suddenly upon the clearing, and had to jump back into the shadows of the jungle to avoid exposure. Her eyes felt the sting of the smoke and she had to suppress her coughing as she gazed upon the shocking inferno.

Rising to the sky in a monumental pyre were the flames that had engulfed the heart of the Hall plantation. In spite of the dark forms scurrying around to put out the fire, it was apparent that all was lost. Catherine could see that controlling the blaze and keeping it from touching the surrounding trees was the only possible course of action that remained. She began to tremble as she realized that the Halls would be ruined. The cost of purchasing and building new sugar manufacturing equipment would be exorbitant, and Catherine knew from her conversations with Cecil that the Halls were already in debt to the Crown for unpaid loans.

The flames were hypnotic, and Catherine lost track of time as she stared into the hellish conflagration. A figure hurrying toward the house, however, roused her from her trance and sent her scurrying back through the shadows. She reached the front of the house, let herself in the front door, and followed the glow of the candlelight to the parlor, where she found Mrs. Hall and her daughters hysterical over the tragedy. Mrs. Hall rose from the settee where she had been clutching her daughters as Catherine entered the room.

"Oh, Catherine, how did you manage to come here under such dangerous and horrible circumstances?"

"I insisted that I come to unburden you and your daughters, and keep safe myself."

"How could you possibly be safe here? We've been ruined!"

Mrs. Hall began weeping again and returned to her place of mourning.

"All the men from our plantations are here putting out the blaze," said Catherine. "It's better if we all stay together."

Heavy boots thudding down the gallery caused the women to turn toward the door. Edward Ewing strode in, covered in sweat and streaks of ashes.

"We are doing all we can, Mrs. Hall. I was sent to check up on you and make sure you were safe."

Edward looked startled to see Catherine sitting in the parlor, and smoothed his hair and shirt.

"Miss Dall, I must assume your father knows that you are here."

"He insisted I come for my safety and for the comfort of the Hall women."

"An excellent idea. I do not mean to scare you, but this fire was most likely the work of vandals displeased with the recent rulings of the Council. When we find out who did this, there will be severe retribution. In the mean time, it is best that you are not alone."

Mr. Hall soon entered the room looking dumbfounded and numb with exhaustion. Catherine solicited the two Miss Halls to help her procure water, bread, and towels for the men as they began to enter the house. All were worn, weary, and blackened from the fire.

Catherine busied herself distributing water and towels to the men, and soon found that her assistance was needed in tending to several injuries. By that time, a small group of slave women had replaced the Miss Halls and Catherine serving refreshments. Catherine had two slaves fetch the plants needed for the scrapes and burns suffered by the men. As she bandaged Edward's forearm, he looked searchingly into her face.

"You are too kind," he said.

"It is nothing."

"Everything has been destroyed," Edward whispered. "The Halls are ruined."

She stopped working and looked at Edward's face.

"What will they do?" she asked.

"The only thing they can do is return to England. Mr. Hall's debts will cause his land to be seized and sold. They will become paupers."

Catherine finished bandaging Edward's burn and looked at the Halls. The women wept as Mr. Hall stared at the parlor floor.

"There has been talk among the men that this may be the work of abolitionists."

Catherine snapped her face back to Edward's.

"What do you mean?"

"The Quakers and Methodists on the island have been rounding up small groups of black-loving fools. Some are militant in their opposition to slavery."

"Surely the religious would not perform so violent an act to further their cause."

"Throughout history it has always been the religious most violent in furthering their causes. Besides, they are not the only abolitionists. There are many involved in secret groups."

Catherine finished bandaging Edward's arm in silence and then traveled with two of the Hall slaves to tend to the injured slaves down by the smoldering mills. Three of the Hall slaves had died from smoke and many others were injured from their efforts. Catherine saw the irony in these people working so hard to save the family who enslaved them. It sickened her.

After a short time Cecil sent for Catherine and told her that it was time to return to Eden. She checked on the men back at the plantation, and then set out for home. Cecil and Catherine did not speak on the ride home, and proceeded upstairs once they arrived at Eden. Cecil kissed Catherine's forehead, and trudged to his chambers, leaving her standing in silence at the top of the great staircase, looking down into the darkness, and turning over all she had seen that night.

~~~

The flames danced along the walls and flickered over the faces of James, Albert, Jonas, and several Quakers. Each time the door opened on its salt-rusted hinges, James looked at it, hoping to see Catherine. He knew his hopes were ridiculous—it would be unspeakably dangerous for a lady to travel at night to meet with men who were practically strangers for a cause she was just beginning to embrace. Still, though, Catherine had an adventurous spirit, and seemed intrigued by the meeting when she had spoken with James at the ball.

James also turned over the possibility of betrayal. Catherine could tell her father about the meeting and have the Silwells run off the island, or worse. The men on the largest plantations were often inebriated and armed—a deadly combination. Albert's faith in Catherine, however, was what had led James to tell her of the meeting, and put his trust in her. Albert was seldom wrong about the character of others, so James allowed that knowledge to quiet his mind and put his confidence in Catherine. Her support could provide valuable testimony in London if she would cooperate.

But the meeting passed, and she did not come.

~~~

Unable to sleep from the evening's occurrences and her troubling thoughts, Catherine slipped from her bed, and moved through the darkness to her window. She opened the shutters, sat on the window sill, and stared out into the blackness, searching for the ocean. In her hand she folded and refolded the slip of paper inviting her to the abolitionist meeting earlier that evening.

1:00 AM   Bath Hotel   Room 10

James' fine penmanship was slightly blurred by the moisture of the island air, and the paper was growing brittle from Catherine's frequent handling.

It did not seem possible that James and his father would orchestrate so violent and sudden an attack against her neighbor, but the evidence was there—the charred remains of the nucleus of the Hall plantation were smoldering in an ashy heap on the same night that the meeting had taken place.

Catherine felt her fear turn to anger. Was this a warning to her? Was James putting on a gentlemanly façade to conceal the true reason behind his visit to the island? England could certainly receive payment for her debts a lot sooner if the plantations were snuffed out by fires, rather than shut down by the long and tedious process of the law.

But somehow, Catherine doubted her ponderings. It seemed much more likely that a small neighboring planter took matters into his own hands to sabotage those bullying him; and Catherine found that she could not entirely fault him.

Exhaustion stole over her, and Catherine moved back to her bed. Sleep came much easier than she had anticipated, and she passed out before she managed to pull up the quilt.

Mrs. Whitting turned over in her bed as she felt her husband's weight collapse the mattress next to her. The musky stink of exertion and the ragged, wet sound of his labored breathing filled the room. A pungent, ashy smell emerged from beneath the sweat, and Mrs. Whitting found herself shivering in spite of the close heat.

11

Desmond Foxwell arrived early. Nothing irritated Meghan more than someone arriving early for a meeting. She had just finished drying her hair and was still in a bathrobe when she heard a knock at the villa door.

Fifteen minutes early.

Meg threw on a sundress and ran to answer the door.

"You're early," she said.

"If that's a problem I can wait for you in the car."

"No, no, you're already here. Have a seat. I'll be out in a minute."

"This is a beautiful little place," said Desmond.

"I like it. Help yourself to some tea if you'd like. I just made a pot."

Meg ran back to her room, threw her hair in a ponytail, and reappeared minutes later in the living room.

"Before I take you on a tour of the property, I want you to know that the appraiser said I could ask about a million per acre," said Meg. "There are fifty-seven acres. Would Grand Star be able to afford that?"

"Does that include the old plantation house on the property?"

"I'm meeting with someone to discuss the value of some of the paintings in the home, so those may or may not be included in the price. That price does, however, include the house."

"With some negotiations, I feel that Grand Star could make you a very reasonable offer."

"All right then," said Meg. "Let's go."

Meg drove Desmond over to the property and gave him a tour. Much to Meg's relief, Desmond seemed content to simply peek in the windows of the old plantation house. She felt protective of the place, and he felt like an outsider. He was impeccably dressed, and Meg wondered to herself how he could stand hiking around the grounds in his long-sleeved starched shirt, long pants, and shiny, black shoes. Little drops of sweat were beginning to seep through his shirt, and he alternated between dabbing his shining face with a handkerchief, snapping photos with his digital camera, and scribbling in his notebook.

After the tour, Meg drove Desmond back to the villa.

"I'll get back to you as soon as I speak with my partners about this project. I'm optimistic that they will be willing to take it on."

Meg was forced to shake Desmond's sweaty hand. He nearly crushed her fingers with his grip. After he had gone, Meg went into the house and called Brian. He did not answer his home or cell phone numbers. She plugged in her laptop and checked her email, but there were only a few work messages. Her office was respecting her vacation time. There were only a few minor questions her administrative assistant had for her on email.

Work. What to do about work?

Nelson had been elected to another term as Governor, but Meg was feeling unsure of her position at the office. She couldn't bear the thought of going back to work for him, but was unable to quit her job due to the recent problems with her estate. She loved political work, but was becoming convinced that politics corrupted those it allowed to rise through its ranks. A knock at the door interrupted Meg's thoughts. It was Gwen Flynn and Dr. David Parfitt.

David was balding and kept his gray hair trimmed very short and neat. He had a carefully edged black beard and black framed glasses. Despite the severity of his appearance, he had a warm and engaging manner. Gwen was tall and thin with a shock of long red hair that she had attempted to confine in a low ponytail. She was dressed in black from head to toe, and looked rather like Klimt's Danae.

"You've no idea how eager I am to see the West," said Gwen.

"Alleged West," said David with a smile. "Miss Owen, are there any medical facilities nearby? Miss Flynn will surely have a stroke if the mural proves to be authentic."

"There's a number by the phone," teased Meg.

Gwen and David smiled.

"May I offer you a drink, or would you like to go right over to Eden?" asked Meg.

"Eden?"

"That's the name of the plantation. The mural is painted directly on the wall in the dining room of the house."

"There are no records of West having ever traveled to Nevis," said Gwen. "This will be an exciting find for art historians if it proves to be his work."

"I found something interesting," said David. "West and a student of his, James Heath, published a work in 1811 entitled The Death of Lord Viscount Nelson. I found this significant because Lord Nelson was famous for his marriage to Frances Woolward Nisbett, a widow from Nevis, at the Montpelier Plantation. Perhaps West was inspired to take on Nelson as a subject due to his time spent on the island."

The group traveled to the house. David carried a small black bag that looked like an oversized, old-fashioned doctor's bag. Meg led Gwen and David through the foyer, parlor, and the empty library. They admired the house and its furnishings and speculated about its owners. As they rounded the doorway to the dining room, Gwen stopped and let her mouth fall open

"It's him."

David walked up to the painting and stared at it.

"It would appear that way," he said. "I'm afraid, however, that I'll need to do more to verify its authenticity than simply state its similarities to West's body of work."

David opened his bag and removed a camera, tripod, and light meter from its insides.

"May I photograph the art?" asked David. "I will take as few pictures as possible. I wouldn't want the imaging to damage the mural."

Meg shrugged. She had snapped about fifty photographs of the mural without even considering the effect it might have on the painting.

David took six shots of the painting—four up close at various points of the mural, and two from far away. One of the shots was exclusively of the signature and date.

"The signature looks authentic and is positioned in a way typical of the artist," said Gwen.

David took out a magnifying glass from the bag and inspected the painting, while making notes. Gwen walked along the mural inch by inch.

"Have you seen this?" she asked.

Meg and David directed their eyes to where Gwen was pointing on the painting. Meg couldn't believe she hadn't noticed before. There was an angel hidden in the dark foliage on the perimeter of the painting. She was difficult to see because she was dark-skinned.

"A black angel?" asked Meg

"Not exactly Ralphaelite," remarked David.

"And look at her foot," said Meg. "It looks as if she is stamping out sugarcane. Was West an abolitionist?"

"I've never come across information stating that he was, but that means very little," said Gwen. "Abolitionists weren't especially popular."

"But that must have some other meaning," said Meg. "I mean, the man was presumably commissioned to paint a mural in a plantation home, funded by slave owners. Do you think that he would insult them on their very walls? Perhaps the paint has faded."

"The angel's features are African—faded paint or not," said Gwen. "And Meg, how many times have you looked at this painting? You've never noticed her before."

"You're right. I've looked at the painting and photographed it at least a dozen times. I've never noticed her."

"By the time the family could have noticed her, if ever, West could have been long gone. He surely didn't spend a substantial amount of time here. There is no historical record of it."

"That means nothing," said David. "History reveals itself in small ways. What we know of the past is a mere glimpse. We postulate, make connections that aren't necessarily appropriate, and run with it. The body of history is so much more than we can ever see."

That night Meg, Gwen and David dined together at Eddy's Bar & Grill. It was a local hotspot, and Karaoke night. They ordered wings, fries, and Carib Beer.

"It's so good to be away for a few days!" said Gwen as she slid her hand around David's neck.

He leaned over to kiss her and rested his hand on her leg.

"We have to be very discreet in Florida," said David. "The whole professor/student thing doesn't go over well."

"And you're old enough to be my father!" laughed Gwen.

"If I conceived you at twelve."

They laughed and watched a large woman and three slim men sing *Leaving on a Midnight Train to Georgia*.

Meg felt herself relax. Spending time having wings and drinks at a bar with friends reminded her of being home and happy. She and Brian were very close with a man from his department at St. Johns and his wife, and the couples enjoyed spending time in casual bars for happy hours, poetry readings, or even karaoke.

"Singing is one of my hidden talents," said Meg.

"Really? What are you going to sing tonight?" asked David.

"Ask me after a few more Caribs."

The waiter brought over a round of shots and told them they came from a friend. As Gwen passed them around, Meg scanned the room until her eyes settled on Desmond. He smiled widely once she noticed him, and proceeded over to the table.

Meg leaned in to the table and was able to whisper "This is the guy I told you about earlier—the one from Grand Star," just as Desmond slid into the chair beside Meg.

"We keep running into each other," said Desmond.

"I was just saying that to my friends," said Meg.

Desmond was actually quite charming that evening. He bought drinks for everyone, told stories of local island lore, and even sang a surprisingly good rendition of *It Had to Be You* with a reggae beat.

"Now I've heard everything," said David. "Reggae Frank Sinatra."

"Have you heard that Eden's haunted?" asked Desmond.

Meg gulped her drink and smiled sheepishly at the table.

"Meg neglected to mention that," said Gwen.

"That's because there's not much to mention," said Meg. "Islanders say that the ghost of a dead slave who threw herself over the cliff wanders the house, but I've never seen her."

"Maybe it's the slave angel in the mural," said David.

"What mural?" asked Desmond.

Seeing that Meg was uncomfortable, and clearly hadn't wanted Desi to find out about the mural, Gwen said, "It's your turn," and pushed Meg up to the DJ.

Meg didn't know if she was drunk enough to sing karaoke, but decided she would rather sing than discuss the property with Desmond. After a brief exchange, the music began, and Meg began *Son of a Preacher Man*. She started out with a few sour notes, but picked up steam as the song continued. When it was over the crowd went wild. Meg bowed and walked over to a standing ovation from her table.

After last call, David decided they should take a taxi home since none of them were in any condition to drive. The driver was named Allan, and he led them all in Caribbean drinking songs as he drove. Gwen and David were the first stop, and after they left, the van became suddenly very quiet.

"Thanks for allowing me to hang out with you all tonight," said Desmond. "My business partner is not much fun, I'm afraid."

"It was our pleasure," said Meg, surprised that she actually meant it.

"The island must be doing you good," said Desmond. "You seem much more relaxed since the last time we met."

"I feel more relaxed," said Meg. "Of course, the alcohol helps."

Desmond laughed and the taxi pulled up to his hotel. He had to crawl over Meg to get out. Underneath the bar smoke, he smelled good.

"Would you like to come up for a drink?"

Meg could see the taxi driver looking at her in the rear view mirror with a smile on his face. Desmond leaned against the edge of the van waiting for her reply. She twisted her engagement ring on her finger and thought of Brian.

"No thanks, Desi," said Meg, putting her arms around Allan from the back seat. "My date might get angry."

Allan started to laugh, and Desmond smiled. "Maybe next time." He closed the door and watched the van drive off.

When they got to Havilla, Meg thanked Allan for rescuing her, tipped him the cost of the fare, and stumbled into the villa alone.

12

Of all the insults to her body and soul, those miserable flies threatened to push her over the edge. With every flicking thump against the thatched walls of her hut each morning, their buzz amplified until she crawled right out of her skin and into the blistering sun. Only hell could hum and drone worse than those noisy fly-filled mornings with those little, winged demons—fresh from rotten cane, sweating livestock, unidentified carrion, or human shit—thudding into her face, and nauseating her.

Killing flies only seemed to beget more, so she simply tried to ignore them, unless she found some maggot filled, hollowed out piece of old fruit or dung pile. Those she destroyed. Creatures born of shit should not have a place in the world. Her thoughts would often turn to Sarponte—that miserable, fiendish overseer—as she stamped out maggot piles. Though, wasn't he more of a snake?

Waking each morning sore from sleeping on hay, weary from yesterday's work, nauseous from hunger, and sick of her own filthy stink to an army of flies did not start her days well. Waiting on Catherine should have made it worse. It did on some levels, but mainly she liked being with her. They had started their lives days apart, nursed from the same breast, sat at Esther's feet side by side as they grew, made mischief, explored, worked. Catherine taught her to read. She taught her to write her name: L-E-A-H.

After Esther had Leah, she was back at work two days later with Leah tied in a sling around her waist. But after Catherine's mother died from a hemorrhage, Esther had to care for Catherine as well. Master allowed Esther to live in the house and gave her a room where Catherine and Leah slept. Catherine had a cradle, but Leah slept with Esther in bed. Esther said that Catherine used to cry all night long, until she finally brought her into bed with her and Leah. That made Catherine happy. Esther would sleep with the girls tucked into her—their tiny faces inches from each other breathing each other's breath back and forth.

When the girls turned one and no longer needed to nurse, Catherine's aunt, Elizabeth, sent Esther and Leah back to the slave village. Miss Elizabeth was Master's sister-in-law. Her husband, Master's brother, died of yellow fever shortly after arriving on Nevis Island in 1810, and left Master to build a plantation on his own. She was jealous that she was never able to become mistress of the house, jealous that Catherine loved Esther most.

Leah felt the brunt of that jealousy when Elizabeth was alive. Elizabeth abused the child when others were not around. She beat her and belittled her. Elizabeth chastised Catherine for sharing so much of her life with the slave child. She appointed Leah her personal servant, but was forever displeased with Leah's service.

Leah walked along the path to the house. It rose before her as it did every morning. She rubbed her back with her rough hands and spat on the dirt.

Catherine sat with her slave lists, updating births and deaths and writing detailed notes about each man, woman, and child at Eden. The Triannual Lists needed to be sent to England to keep an accurate account of slave ownership. Catherine knew these lists would be used if slavery was ever banned. The scribbled writing on the list was troubling her. Phinneas' broken and practically illegible handwriting had replaced that of her father's. Now that Phinneas oversaw the trade of the Dall slaves, Catherine had lost a degree of control of the plantation. New faces would appear and disappear from the village each month, and the records did not reflect as much slave activity as she was sure transpired. Catherine did not trust Phinneas, but was having difficulty convincing Cecil of this.

She scanned the list once she had finished and counted 202 souls in all. 202 men, women, and children who were the property of Cecil Dall. 202 men, women, and children who labored without compensation under extreme conditions for the profit and comfort of one small family.

The sharp clash of shattering glass pulled Catherine from her thoughts and into the hallway, where Leah knelt over a pile of broken China. Leah's face fell when she saw Catherine emerge from the study, and Leah began to fumble an apology.

"Are you all right?" asked Catherine.

"I'm sorry. I don't know why I've been so clumsy."

In spite of Leah's protests, Catherine knelt to help Leah collect the broken plates.

The girls worked in silence as they picked through the broken shards of the plates. It had broken into large, easily handled pieces, but smaller fragments concealed within the mess began to bite at the girls' hands, causing small specks of blood to stain the debris.

Catherine reached for Leah's hand and saw that it was not only Leah's fingertips, but her own which were wounded.

She turned over Leah's callused hand and pulled a small shard from her palm. Leah looked down and pulled her hand away.

"I'll get the rest. Please leave me," said Leah.

Catherine stood and watched Leah for a moment. Then she turned and left her.

"The blaze consumed everything of value on the plantation, with the exception of the house," said Cecil. "It won't be long before the Halls will be forced to leave the island."

Albert and James looked at one another with troubled expressions as Cecil prodded the soil along the edge of the cane field with a large, cut stalk. The wind was blowing strong which made it difficult to hear.

"Have they any notion of who would do such a thing?" asked Albert.

"The most obvious suspect is the small planter, Caleb Whitting. He is openly hostile to Mr. Hall and quite vocal about his anger over the Thatched House Law. An investigation is already underway, but frankly, I don't know how it will turn up anything."

The men looked down over the acres of rustling cane. The slaves toiled hard amidst the crop, and their droning song could be heard behind the wind—low voices, sorrowful voices, monotonous sounds. An old black man raising his voice above the others—eyes closed, face turned to the sky— stood in the middle of the cane with his scythe high, then lowered it back to its task. A young woman shook her head, sweating, singing along. The slice of the blades moved in concert with the weary chorus.

"My God, that sound depresses the soul," whispered James.

Cecil looked at him. "They are singing. That means they are happy."

"A happy man doesn't sing a song like that."

"Our slaves are the best kept on the island," said Cecil. "Only days ago Catherine finished sewing new dresses for all the women working the fields. They are all permitted to grow small gardens on their plats to sell vegetables at the market. The rod is spared in many cases, when it should be used."

"I'm sure we hope to model our plantation after yours, Mr. Dall," said Albert. "My son and I, though in favor of using slave labor, are not in favor of unusual cruelty toward them. We shall try to maintain a peaceful settlement in St. Christopher."

"We find it helps keep everything running smoothly if the slaves are well-treated. Of course, it is sometimes necessary to set an example. But that is where Phinneas comes in. He is not afraid to use the whip every now and again to show the others what will not be tolerated."

The men looked at Phinneas on his horse. He weaved through the working slaves issuing commands and overseeing the field hands. When he saw that he was being watched, he tipped his hat to the gentlemen.

"There is a lawful limit on the number of lashes allowed, is there not?" asked James.

"Yes," replied Cecil. "About twenty years ago a planter on the island had his slaves flogged at the market in Charlestown. He was said to have whipped some of the slaves over 200 times. One of the women died as a result of the beating, but a jury found the planter innocent. Shortly thereafter an amendment to the Melioration Act of 1798 passed limiting the number of lashes on a slave to 39—but who's counting," laughed Cecil. "At any rate, you may feel free to explore. I must away to the house for a bit of business.   Meet me in the parlor at tea time for a bit of refreshment," said Cecil.

James and Albert watched Cecil stagger back toward the Great House, humming and swatting at the cane with his cut stalk.

———·✆◯

Catherine looked out at the cane fields and inhaled the scent of molasses from the nearby boiling house. She looked down at the fields and saw that the men and women working the cane were hunched over in the most unnatural way. She touched her back as she watched theirs, and then slipped back into the path by the lagoon to escape the weight of the sun.

Catherine was on her way to Mary's hut, but she did not wish to be seen by anyone. She felt sullen and heavy and was tiring of the battle being fought in her conscience. She was beginning to feel that island isolation—an intense claustrophobia—that she had only heard others speak of but never fully understood until now. She badly wanted to escape.

Catherine pushed through the hanging vines and monstrous leaves around the thatched dwelling, and was just about to step out of the growth when the low vibrations of a man's voice coming from within the hut stopped her. It was difficult to make out his words, but Catherine was able to ascertain that it was the voice of James Silwell conversing with the aged slave woman. She strained her ears to attempt to make out the particulars of the exchange.

"Two-and-a-half months?" asked James.

"Yes, nearly three months," said Mary, "but I cannot remember exactly how old I was—maybe nineteen."

"And you were captured?"

"Yes, many villagers feared the night. We knew of the kidnapper ghosts who haunted the villages in the night. But I was headstrong and foolish. I snuck to the watering hole to gather herbs in the moonlight. I was blindfolded and taken to a large camp where I was shackled, boarded on a ship, and sent here...so many lifetimes ago."

"And how did you endure the Middle Passage onboard the ship?" asked James.

"Death would have been better than what we lived through on that vessel. We were shackled together and forced to lie in pits beneath the ship's deck at night and during bad weather. We were allowed up to the deck to exercise two times a day. The exercises caused much pain to the wrists and ankles. We were fed twice daily if we were lucky, but were mostly required to lie in the filth and disease below the deck.

"I remember one morning I awoke to find that the slaves on either side of me had died, and I had to lie chained to them for three days because of a storm at sea. The stench of decay and human waste nearly killed me."

Catherine lowered herself to the ground and leaned her head against the hut as Mary continued.

"Slaves who died were tossed overboard. On my ship, three women tried to kill themselves. The third was unable to make it over the railings before being grabbed and flogged by a trader who did not want to lose any of his cargo."

"And did you ever wish to end your own life?"

"Many times on that ship I wished to die, but I could never take my own life. It is too large a thing. And being foolish, I always had a bit of hope."

There was silence for a few moments, followed by a soft exchange that Catherine could not decipher. As James exited the hut, Catherine sunk into the undergrowth and watched him walk away. She stood and crept along the foliage, tracking him as she went. He stopped at a few huts along the way and chatted with several slaves. They seemed at ease with James, making it clear that he had been spending a lot of time in the village.

The end of the lane opened to a sprawl of cane fields, and James stood surveying the acres of green stalks. Suddenly his posture stiffened. Catherine was unable to see what caused James' face to distort itself, but saw that he was greatly appalled. Whatever he stood watching called him to some sort of action as he was swallowed by the rows of cane.

Catherine emerged from the vegetation and started after him. She began to run, but stumbled over a roll of cane stalks and landed in the dust. Peter, an aged slave nearby, rushed to help Catherine.

"Please, I'm all right," said Catherine as she continued after James.

The cane leaves slapped at her face and clung to her hair as she made her way through the field. The sun was nearly unbearable, but she pushed onward. She had not taken the time to see what it was that had so troubled James, but she could only imagine that it was something horrible since she could hear shouts rising over the cane.

An opening in the rows came abruptly and Catherine stumbled upon Toby, a large field hand, lying naked in the dirt and covered in blood. James was struggling with Phinneas over a whip as several slaves watched. James was able to dislodge the whip from Phinneas' coiled grip, and both men glared at one another and panted from exertion.

Catherine's appearance caused James and Phinneas to straighten themselves.

"What is this?"

The men were silent. Phinneas spit on the ground, mounted his horse, and rode toward the lower fields.

Catherine ran to Toby and felt for his pulse.

"He's alive. Homer, Thaddeus, help Mr. Silwell carry Toby to his hut."

The men carried Toby to his hut and placed him on the ground in front of its flap, and Catherine ran to fetch Mary. When they returned, the women tended to Toby's wounds.

"Thaddeus, you must tell me why this happened," demanded Catherine.

"I know not, Miss Catherine. I came upon the scene just as you did."

"Homer?" she asked.

The man looked at the ground as if he did not want to speak.

"I demand that you tell me what you know," said Catherine, frantic with anger.

"Toby and Overseer were having words," said Homer. "Something about Leah."

"Leah?"

"Toby wants to marry Leah, but Overseer said no. They had words, and then Toby got beaten."

Catherine looked at James.

"I heard as much as I approached," said James. "I intervened when it became clear that Phinneas meant to do more than punish Toby."

"Leah has told me nothing of Toby's intentions," said Catherine. "But I do not understand Phinneas' objections. He's the one who says that male slaves need companions to keep their male energies suppressed."

The men looked with unease at one another.

"It's best you get back to work so that Phinneas finds no fault with you," said Catherine.

The men dispersed and James assisted Catherine and Mary with Toby. Once Catherine was sure he was not in grave condition, she and James walked back up to the house.

"He hit Toby more than the lawful amount," said James.

"That was apparent."

"Can he be reported to law enforcement?"

"You know as well as I that nothing would come of it. But I thank you for interfering."

"I only hope I did not cause trouble."

"The trouble has been there for some time," said Catherine. "I need to speak to Father as soon as possible. I also need to find Leah. I'm a bit stunned that I knew nothing of her relationship with Toby."

Leah heard James and Catherine enter the house as she wiped the spittle from her mouth with the back of her hand. She hid in the shadows of the staircase as they talked through the foyer. Her stomach turned over when the smell of her sickness hit her from the chamber pot. She got sick again and slid to the floor. Sweat ran down her face as she trembled in the darkness. She grasped her stomach as she felt the child move within her womb, and began to weep quietly. Leah knew that she could not conceal her condition from Catherine much longer.

13

Meg arrived at Drew's house at six o'clock to pick up the Edmeads for dinner. She was treating them to a meal at the Mount Nevis Hotel Restaurant. It was a clear, warm night and a light breeze moved through the open restaurant. The candlelight on the tables danced over the marine art on the walls creating an underwater illusion. The menu had a small but tempting selection of fare, and Meg had difficulty choosing a meal. She finally settled on the leek and potato soup, the grilled mahi-mahi with the ginger garlic glaze, and the chocolate torte with Chantilly Cream. Drew and his wife ordered the butternut squash soup, beef tenderloin, and coconut banana crunch cake.

"We always seem to want the same things," said Drew.

"No, you always want what I want," said Dorothy. "That's how we first met, you know. We were at the market looking at a table of island art. I needed a gift for my cousin's birthday, and was reaching for a painting of a machineel tree when this man stole it right from under my fingers."

"I did not steal it. The woman lies. She took it from my hand."

"Bah—you could you see me eyeing it, you old thief."

They laughed and Drew put his hand over Dorothy's.

"I only grabbed it so you'd be forced to talk to me," said Drew. "And didn't it work out?"

Dorothy smiled and she smoothed her gray-black hair with her hands.

"Who ended up with the painting?" asked Meg.

"Who do you think?" asked Drew as Dorothy smiled.

The first course arrived and the group savored the warm, delicious soup.

"Any more meals like this, and I won't want to go home," said Meg.

"But you have a companion at home, do you not?" Dorothy eyed Meg's engagement ring.

"You nosy woman," said Drew.

"I don't mind," said Meg. "I do have a fiancée."

"And when are you getting married?" asked Dorothy.

Meg was quiet for a moment, and then explained everything to the Edmeads. They expressed their concern as she told about her parents' death, the called off wedding, the inheritance, and ultimately, the lawsuit.

"Sixty-eight million dollars?" asked Drew.

"Yes. I'm going to have to sell the property here. I have a buyer—someone from Grand Star Resorts wants to put a hotel on the property and call it the Paradise Plantation Inn, or something like that."

Drew and Dorothy exchanged looks.

"I know all about the local perspective on that, but it may be my only option."

"You know, you may have another option," said Drew. "My nephew is a politician and has big ideas for the development of the island, where the islanders' best interests are paramount. I will have him call you, if that's okay. He may have another idea."

"I would be glad to speak with him."

"I've heard the house is in great condition for its age," said Dorothy. "I can't believe you got Drew to go on that property with you."

"What do you mean?"

Drew and Dorothy looked at one another and then back at Meg.

"Meg, it was our child who died on the cliff there," said Drew. "It's been fifteen years. I haven't been able to go to the property since the accident, until the other day, with you."

Meg felt terrible as she looked from the tired, heavy eyes of Drew to Dorothy. "I had no idea. I'm so sorry to have brought you there."

"No, you couldn't have known. I actually felt very peaceful while I was there. I tried to encourage Dorothy to go back with me."

"I'm not ready," said Dorothy. "I'll go some time."

The sun had set and a steel drum band began playing by the pool. The waiter brought out the entrees, and the conversation ceased while they ate. Meg stole glances at the Edmeads trying to imagine their pain—the pain of losing a child. She was nearly crushed under the weight of her grief over her parents, but thought it must not even compare to the pain Drew and Dorothy must have felt. Meg thought they all made an interesting group of parents and children— their losses filled in by each others' presence.

"So Meg, what next in your research?" asked Drew.

"Some art historians are here reviewing the mural of The Fall to see if they can positively identify the artist and appraise it. Then I need to find out more about James Silwell, and then the Ewings."

"Did you find out any more about the abolitionist pamphlet and Alexander Hamilton?" asked Drew.

"I did some research online and found some information about an African Free School in New York where runaway or freed slaves were able to receive an education. Alexander Hamilton was involved in its establishment through the New York Manumission Society. The New York Historical Society has archives from the school from the early nineteenth century. But I'm not sure if that would have anything to do with the history of Eden. I plan on spending tonight looking up information on James Silwell."

"And when do you plan on resting?" asked Drew.

As it turned out, the post-dining induced stupor ensured all that Meg would be able to do was rest. After dropping off the Edmeads and stepping through the door at Havilla, Meg decided to turn in early and leave her research on James Silwell for the next day.

But something was wrong.

Something had changed in the villa since Meg had left earlier that evening. She thought she may have left the door unlocked, and wondered if someone had been there. Nothing seemed out of place, but Meg felt like someone or something occupied her space. There was a presence that seemed to absorb the noise and render the villa silent—an energy that was everywhere.

Meg thought she would go back to the Edmeads, but realized that she had already traveled to her bedroom, and no one was there. She stepped back out of the bedroom and looked around the main room. The sheers over the sliders had been drawn, and she thought that she could see light flickering in the back of the house. Suddenly, the music of a steel drum band began on the back lawn. Meg drew back the sheers.

The night blew into her face, soft and warm. The band was just behind the plunge pool. Candles were drizzled over the back porch and around the back yard. And lying in the middle of it all, smiling up at her, was Brian.

14

James and Catherine separated in an attempt to find Cecil more efficiently. They intended to meet one another at half past the hour. Catherine again left the house, looked through the storehouse, checked the stables, and finally, went down the path to the beach. Catherine did not think her father would be at the beach, but wanted to leave no area unchecked. She looked in the cave, thinking back to the time he had gone missing for hours and had been located in it, passed out and nearly unconscious with an empty cask of rum on the ground beside him. It had been Leah's birthday, and Catherine had made her a honey cake as a surprise. She was just about to turn fourteen, herself, days later, and wanted to share some of the uneaten cake with her father. He had been found just before the tide came in. He would have drowned.

Cecil was not there this time, however, so Catherine climbed back up the path and to the lagoon. A pair of small green eyes peered at Catherine through the shadows of the rainforest. Phinneas curled himself around a palm. The creatures were silent around him as he wove himself through the vegetation. His desire for Catherine had been growing since his first meeting with her. He had seen her bathe in the lagoon waters on several occasions, and was hoping to see her do so now, but she only stood at the banks of the water staring into the waterfall.

Thomas suddenly exploded out of the path, breathless and sweating. Phinneas recoiled into the shadows as Thomas ran to his mistress. Something he said caused her to run with him back to the Great House.

"Where is he?" asked Catherine.

"Your father has taken him to the guest wing upstairs," said Esther.

Catherine ran up the stairs. She hurried into the closest guest room and found Cecil and Albert staring down at James as he shivered on the bed.

"When did this start?" asked Catherine.

"Only moments ago," said Albert. "He was overcome with a sudden outbreak of chills."

"Cover him."

Catherine ran to the kitchen to find Esther. Esther, who already knew of James' symptoms, produced a pot of boiling water and poured it into a pitcher for Catherine. Catherine went to the herbal pantry and located a container of quinine bark. Working with haste she finely chopped the bark and placed it in a cup. Catherine hurried back to the room where James lay and poured the hot water over the bark.

"Once this cools a bit, I will help James to drink it."

"What is happening to him?" asked Albert.

"It looks like malaria. The sudden onset of chills is characteristic of the disease. The good news is he is getting help immediately, and he is young and strong."

"What will you make him drink?"

"The bark of the cinchona is very effective at treating malaria," said Catherine. "It has some unpleasant side effects, but it is a powerful way to treat the illness."

"We have both had malaria and recovered," said Cecil. "But James will be bedridden for weeks. There is no way he will be able to travel to the hotel."

"Can he be transported once the fever breaks?"

"Absolutely not," said Catherine. "The fever returns over and over again over the course of several weeks. It would be too much of a strain to force him to travel such a distance in his condition."

"You and James will simply have to stay at Eden for the duration of your time on Nevis," said Cecil. "It actually makes good sense, since the plantations under your observation are all nearby. I will send Thomas for your things immediately."

"This is entirely too much of an imposition," insisted Albert.

"Your son's life is at stake," said Catherine. "I insist that you remain at Eden."

Albert looked with concern from Cecil to Catherine to James.

"I am sure I cannot express my gratitude enough. Your kindness will never be forgotten."

"Think nothing of it," said Cecil. "Now, I will take you immediately to Thomas to retrieve your belongings from the Bath Hotel. Catherine, please stay with James. I will send Esther up soon to see what assistance she can provide."

Catherine nodded and sat at a chair near the head of the bed. When her father and Albert departed, Catherine checked the patient. James looked at her through wild, bloodshot eyes. Sweat ran off of his face and drenched the bedding. He quaked so violently Catherine worried he would fall off the edge of the bed.

"It's all right," said Catherine. "I am going to take care of you."

Catherine replaced the drenched blanket with another, and brought the hot liquid concoction to James' lips. Carefully lifting his head, she supported him as he drained the cup. She eased him back down on the pillow and wiped his forehead with a damp cloth.

"You will drink this bitter liquid daily until you are healed."

James nodded and closed his eyes.

"You are not suited for this climate," she said. "But I will see to it that you are able to return to your home."

⁓

The golden rays of the setting sun illuminated James' room. Catherine watched him as he slept. His chest rose and fell as he shivered in his sleep. Occasionally he cried out through his fitful rest. Cecil had again disappeared, and Catherine reasoned that this was not the time to discuss what she saw between Phinneas and Toby. Albert returned after dinnertime that evening, and rushed up to see how James was faring.

"This will be extremely tiresome and difficult to work through for James, but I am very optimistic," said Catherine. "It seems that early treatment in such cases is the best way of fighting the illness."

"I am sure any treatment at your hands, Miss Dall, will restore my son."

Catherine nodded and turned to James.

"His fever appears to have broken for now, but the fever tends to reoccur every few days with malaria. He will need constant attention."

Albert nodded and dropped himself into a chair by the fireplace. He buried his head in his hands.

"I will never forgive myself if something happens to James. He didn't want to come here in the first place."

"We are all called to places by forces bigger than ourselves," said Catherine. "Your son would not have come if he was not destined to do so. He will fight through this."

"You are most reassuring," said Albert. "Thank you for your kindness."

"You must not forget to take care of yourself, Mr. Silwell. I will see to it that your belongings are brought up to the room next to your son's. Leave the adjoining door open through the night so you can monitor him. If you need me at all, no matter what time of night, I am just down the hall."

Catherine left the room and returned after a short time.

"Thomas has carried your belongings to your room, Leah is unpacking for you, and Esther will come up shortly with a tray of food for you both," she said. "We will try to rouse James to eat before you go to sleep for the night."

"Thank you."

James' eyes began to open. He gazed around the room with some confusion, until he realized where he was. He smiled feebly at Catherine and Albert.

"There are other ways of getting yourself invited to stay with us," teased Catherine. They all laughed as Esther entered with food for Albert and James.

"You will need to leave the room for awhile, Catherine," said Esther. "I am going to assist Mr. Silwell in changing James' clothing, bathing him, and changing his bed linens."

"Certainly, Mami," said Catherine. "It's actually quite late. Goodnight everyone. I'll be back first thing in the morning. Don't hesitate to call if you need assistance."

The winds were brutal. Catherine turned all night in her bed, certain that she heard James calling to her. When she would rush out into the hall with her lit candle, she was met only with silence. Catherine would then return to her bed for another bout of nightmares.

In Catherine's first dream, James called to her. When she went to his room he was gone. A sound urged her to the window, and upon opening the shutters she saw James stumbling across the back lawn and disappearing into the night. Her second dream was more distressing. She quarreled with Leah, but could not make out what they were saying over the howling winds. Leah fell back as if she were struck, and then ran away from Catherine into the dark, damp night. Rain began falling as Catherine found herself in a blinding storm. Vines and leaves lashed at her face preventing her from seeing. She could hear a mournful wail on the winds of the storm, but was lost and unable to find her way. She finally broke into a clearing where James looked at her and turned away. She felt a hand at her shoulder and turned around to face Phinneas with lightning crashing behind him.

Catherine bolted upright in her bed. A gust of wind blew open the shutters of her bedroom. Catherine jumped from her bed to close them, and sat down at her window sill to steady her nerves. She lit a candle in her room and paced around the floor. A muffled noise reached her ear and she opened her door and peered out into the blackness. Something caught her eye at the base of the stairway. She strained her eyes to see a form hurrying out of the house.

Stepping out into the hall Catherine thought she saw candlelight snuffed under her father's bedroom door, but realized it must have been her imagination. She crept down the hall and peered into James' room. She heard his deep, regular breathing. Catherine stole back to her room and crawled back into bed, anxious for the morning's arrival.

———∽◯

Catherine's days went from plantation management to patient management. She spent all day at James' bedside nursing him back to health. Every fourth day James relapsed into violent chills and fever. During the days in between he was bedridden with headaches and nausea. Catherine did her best to keep him comfortable. She fed him, forced him to ingest the quinine, read to him, played the pianoforte for him, and conversed with him. Esther and Albert changed and bathed the patient after his fevers, and after two weeks James was regaining his color and strength.

Each evening Catherine talked with James and Albert of politics, religion, literature, Nevis, and England as they played cards. They spoke of their families and pasts, and grew in their intimacy with one another. Catherine questioned the Silwells openly about their abolitionist pursuits when she was sure Cecil was out of the house.

"There is a school that Alexander Hamilton and the New York Manumission Society established for free and runaway blacks," said Albert. "We spent some time there last year, and were greatly moved by the students. We established a relationship with an instructor there who assists runaway slaves in transitioning safely into their boarding house."

"That sounds dangerous," said Catherine.

"It is, but it is easier than you would think to change the identity of a slave," said James. "The average slave owner hasn't the time, money, or connections to pursue runaways once they've moved beyond their own states. Most slaves are caught, but those who are able to cover enough ground are often able to make it."

"But many slaves have distinguishing marks or injuries," said Catherine. "The body of a slave often tells a story of his past."

"That is a problem they often confront," said James. "They do the best they can."

Leah entered the room to clear the dinner trays. She moved quickly through the room. All eyes were on her until she left.

"She's angry with me," said Catherine.

"She does seem especially melancholy. What is it that angers her?" asked James.

Catherine looked from James to Albert.

"I am ashamed to admit that something I did caused injury to Mami."

"To Esther?" asked Albert.

"Yes. I had asked Leah to summon me when Rebecca, one of our field slaves, went into labor so that I could witness a birth. I knew that Esther would not approve, but I also knew that once I was there, she would not refuse my assistance. Leah came to get me the night Rebecca was in labor. Esther was upset that I was there, but just as I anticipated, she let me stay. She did worry, however, that Phinneas would find out that I was present at the birthing, and would punish them. I was foolish enough to think that he wouldn't find out, but somehow he did."

"And Esther was punished," said Albert.

Catherine nodded and looked down at her hands. The only sounds came from the dying fire.

***

The next morning, Catherine traveled down the stairs to the kitchen, hoping to intercept Leah in bringing James' breakfast tray. She could smell ham baking as she passed through the cool stone hall, and grabbed a piece from the plate as Esther swatted at her hand. Catherine smiled, but it soon evaporated as Leah entered the doorway from the path outside. The morning sun outlined her dark frame and hid her face.

"I'll take Mr. Silwell his breakfast tray this morning," said Catherine.

"It's already been fixed," said Esther. "It's over on the side table."

As Catherine crossed the kitchen and picked up the tray, she could feel Leah's icy stare. Leah remained in the doorway until Catherine exited the room. As Catherine traveled down the hall she thought she could hear Esther scold Leah, but was unable to make out what she was saying.

James was sitting up in bed that morning, looking much healthier than he had the day before. He opened his eyes and smiled when he saw Catherine enter the room.

"I have become quite spoiled by you," he said. "I will be a horrible nuisance when we return home."

"You're a horrible nuisance now," teased Catherine.

She crossed the room and set down the tray on the bedside table.

"I've spoken to Esther about a carriage ride for you today, and she advises that we wait a few more days to ensure the fever does not return. I think that one more day of bed rest should be sufficient. You have not had a fever for four days. If you do not get one today, you will surely be ready to go outdoors again."

"I feel better than I have in weeks," said James.

"We don't want to rush your recovery. Your journey home is fast approaching, and you need to be strong for the return voyage.

"I must say, on behalf of my father and myself, that you will be heartily missed."

"As will you," said Catherine as she looked down at her hands.

James' hand moved from under his sheets and slid something into her skirt pocket. She reached for it, but he grabbed her wrist and gave her a look to dissuade her from investigating as Cecil entered the room to inquire after his health. Catherine left Cecil and James, eager to see what James had given her. She went to the parlor, sat at the piano where she would be shielded from anyone entering the room, and reached into her pocket.

It was an abolitionist pamphlet with radical quotes from Alexander Hamilton and Benjamin Franklin on slaves and emancipation. Catherine began reading through the booklet, but boisterous laughter emanating from the hallway caused her to shove it into her music book and slide it into the piano bench. She stood quickly behind the piano as Edward Ewing and Cecil entered the room.

"Good morning, Miss Dall," said Edward. "You are looking fresh and lovely as a tropical flower this morning."

"Mr. Ewing has come by to personally make sure that we will be attending the Darrows' gathering this evening" said Cecil. "I have assured him of this fact."

"Is that tonight?"

"Had you forgotten, Catherine? Honestly, your mind is slipping. You used to count down the minutes between social outings. You need to get more rest."

"I'll try, Father."

"Mr. Ewing has also brought over some lovely blossoms for you," said Cecil.

"How terribly unnecessary, since our home is positively surrounded by them," said Catherine.

Edward shifted awkwardly on his feet and addressed Cecil to take his leave.

"Well, I must be off. I look forward to seeing you all tonight. Good day."

Cecil led Edward to the front door and closed it after him.

"Mr. Ewing is a fine gentleman," said Cecil.

"I suppose so."

"He and his father have amassed quite a fortune, and the fact that they are neighbors is quite comforting."

Catherine did not speak, but looped her arm through his, and led him to the dining room for breakfast. As Catherine was finishing, Leah passed through the room carrying an empty laundry basket. Catherine excused herself, and hurried after Leah. She soon overtook Leah and pulled her into the parlor.

"Leah, we need to talk."

"There is nothing to talk about."

"Then why are treating me this way? I am sorry for what happened, but I am trying to make it up to you and to Mami. I will never compromise your safety again for my own personal adventures."

Leah looked as if she wanted to reply, but abruptly turned from Catherine and left her alone in the parlor.

15

Meg's shock left her speechless for several minutes. Somewhere, in her wildest fantasies she had envisioned a scenario like this, so it took some time for it to register with Meg that she was not dreaming. Once she regained her speech, she was able to reassure Brian that she was elated that he came to Nevis. She ran inside to put on her bathing suit, and joined him in the pool, marveling at the candles and the band.

"I can't tell you how much this means to me," said Meg, wrapping herself around Brian.

"I'm relieved you think so. I was worried that I would be unwelcome."

"It's my fault for making you feel that way. You are always welcome."

"Just in case, I got a room for myself at Sunshine's."

"Cancel it."

"Well, I wanted to talk to you about something."

The music ended and one of the players cleared his throat.

"Excuse me," said Brian as he jumped out of the pool and spoke with the musicians while they began to pack away their instruments. Brian said something that caused the band leader to laugh, and shook his hand. He was back in a few moments.

"They've got to go, but I hope we'll see them again soon," he said.

"They were a nice touch."

"Oh, I nearly forgot to tell you, I brought some information I found for you on James and Albert Silwell. You mentioned that their names had been nagging you."

"You've been doing research for me?"

"The college is on winter break, and with you gone, I didn't know what to do with myself. Anyway, you may have heard of the Silwells because they were instrumental in seeing slavery ended in the British Colonies. They worked closely with Thomas Clarkson on behalf of William Wilberforce, and saw The Slavery Abolition Act of 1833 through Parliament. There is a lot of information out there on the Silwells. I wrote down the websites for you. There is also a museum at one of their former residences in Cornwall with a catalogue of archives on the website. You would have to pay a fee to join the Silwell Society and get access to the archives. I didn't sign up. I thought I'd leave that up to you."

"What a great new lead," said Meg. "I was at an impasse with my research, but you've given me a new direction. Drew will be very excited."

"The man from the museum?"

"Yes. I'm afraid I've pulled him into this, too. For some reason, I just can't let this rest."

"You've got us all involved," said Brian. "I looked through your artifacts on the table before you arrived. I'm hooked."

Meg and Brian began to shiver, so they decided to get out of the pool. After dressing, Meg made two *Caribbean Romances* and joined Brian on the back porch.

"You started to tell me something that sounded serious before we were interrupted by the band leader," said Meg.

Brian's face was shadowed, so she was unable to read him.

"Meghan, I've made some phone calls about getting married on the island."

For the second time that evening, Meg was rendered speechless. A thousand thoughts raced through her head, and within moments she realized that it would be the ideal time and place to get married. Her parents were gone. She no longer wanted a big wedding. And she had fallen in love with the island.

But there was the matter of Brian's parents.

"I've already spoken to them about it. They support our getting married alone on this island. They just made me promise that they could throw a big party for us the next time we visit."

Brian looked at Meg, searching for a reaction.

"There are a few legal formalities, but it's very simple. Father Joe at St. Theresa's is free. We can be married on Friday."

"And why don't you want to cancel your villa?"

"I'd like to be a bit old fashioned about all this," said Brian. "I don't want to ride in your jeep with you to our wedding ceremony. Besides, I have all my wedding planning papers at my room. They'd get all jumbled up with your historical research if I were to stay here. "

"By the way, how did you get here? I didn't see a car."

"I took a taxi-van. Great guy. We made a lot of stops along the way to chat with the locals, and nearly killed a family of goats strolling down the road, but I made it in time."

Meg stood up from her rocker and climbed into the hammock with Brian.

"Is there anything you didn't take care of?" she asked.

"I've no idea what you'll wear. You'll have to work that out."

Meg and Brian would be married on Friday at Saint Theresa's with a reception following at Sunshine's on the beach. They booked the steel drum band, and invited David, Gwen, and the Edmeads. Meg and Brian sat with Drew at the museum and Meg asked Drew if he would give her away. He was touched and his voice trembled when he agreed.

"I don't know if Meg told you," said Drew, "but our son died fifteen years ago on the property at Eden."

"She did," said Brian. "I'm sorry for your loss."

"It's still painful after all these years. I don't imagine you ever get over losing a child. But I feel like I have a daughter now."

"And since my father is no longer here," said Meg, "I can't think of anyone I'd rather have walk me down the aisle. I feel like I was supposed to meet you, Drew."

"Me too."

While they discussed the plans, Roland Pinney, Drew's nephew, arrived to talk about Meg's land. Meg was pleased to learn that the land could be subdivided and parceled out to investors and locals for residential or commercial uses. He said that he had a group of local investors looking to start a Nevis-owned hotel, and were ready to make someone an offer once the right land was found. Roland thought they could begin the zoning and subdividing processes within days.

"I'm so relieved about this," said Meg. "I was feeling very uneasy about selling to Grand Star Resorts for it to build yet another 'Plantation Inn.'"

"It really is a double edged sword," said Roland. "Grand Star could put up a nice hotel and pay nice wages, but it is better to give the local people a chance to reap the benefits of tourism entirely. I don't hate the people who've made the Plantation Inns. It's just a higher lever of sensitivity and a good business move for us to start something all on our own."

"My only concern is that I need to move as quickly as possible on this," said Meg as she looked down and started wringing her hands. Brian reached over to her and slid his hand between hers. She smiled at him and turned back to Roland. "To be completely frank, my family's estate is facing a huge lawsuit because of my late father's business practices."

"And this will move quickly," said Roland. "This investor group has been searching the island for perfect land for over a year. They are ready to move. And this is a small island. Everyone knows someone who can help the process along."

"I'm supposed to be returning home in less than a week. Will I be able to do this from the States?"

"Certainly, though you may need to give someone power of attorney to sign documents if you are unable to return yourself."

"That shouldn't be a problem," said Meg.

The group spent the afternoon discussing the zoning and possible buyers. When Roland left, Meg felt much better about selling the land. She called Desmond Foxwell, but he didn't answer. She was relieved to be able to leave the bad news on his voicemail.

David and Gwen joined Brian and Meg that night for dinner at Sunshine's. They ate lobster and drank Killer Bees—the rum drink for which Sunshine's was famous.

"Are you ready for our appraisal of the mural?" asked David.

"I think so," said Meg, feeling the butterflies beginning in her stomach.

"I feel confident that the mural is a West. I've detailed my findings, used the best research manuals around, and consulted with several of my colleagues over the phone. I was also able to send photos of the mural on email. After researching and consulting with several auctioneers, I found that an oil of West's sold in 2000 for $800,000. A pair of West studies sold for $140,000 in 2003. Both sales were of works significantly smaller than the mural. The context of the mural itself would probably add major value to it, in addition to the fact that it has been previously unknown. We think you could get at least two million for it."

Meg closed her eyes and smiled. "Is there no end to the good news today?"

"But who would buy it?" asked Brian. "You can't remove the wall from the house."

"Oh, there would be plenty of private art collectors willing to buy such a treasure. Of course, they may need to buy the house and land with it. There is where you could run into some trouble."

"And there is an end to the good news," said Gwen. "Have you watched the weather report lately? There is a big hurricane coming up the Caribbean. It's supposed to hit the island on Saturday or Sunday."

"She's worried to death about the mural," said David.

"We are scheduled to leave on Sunday," said Meg.

"You'll probably have to postpone your departure," said Gwen. "I know we have. We're staying through until next Tuesday."

"If you all want to leave sooner, you don't have to stay because of the wedding."

"We know. In truth, it looks like the storm will head out to the Atlantic before it even hits Nevis," said David. "It's not only your wedding that keeps us here."

"Gwen, that house has withstood two-hundred years of hurricanes," said Meg. "I wouldn't worry."

———⌒~⌒———

Meg lay awake in her bed tossing and turning all night. She was not troubled—she was very much at ease—but so much was happening so suddenly. Around four o'clock she slipped on her robe and padded out to the kitchen to get a glass of water. She saw her laptop on the table in the great room and decided to email her office that she would have to stay longer due to the weather.

Political fundraising seemed so far away from where she was. Meg found it difficult to imagine returning to her life in Annapolis, but she knew she needed a salary—especially now.

Meg decided to email Howard and tell him the good news about the land. Though she would probably see a bit less than Grand Star could deliver, Roland thought Meg could probably get over fifty million dollars for the land from all the buyers. Meg recommended to Howard that they try to reach a settlement agreement with all parties. She was willing to sell everything down to the rugs in her house if they could keep the lawsuit out of court. Meg couldn't bear the thought of that.

After sending her emails, Meg opened the slider and stepped onto the back porch. The sky was deep pink along a rim of clouds on the horizon. The sun was beginning to rise. It was windy and the blowing palms made a rustling sound, but there were pauses in the gusts. In the pauses, Meg could hear Beethoven's *Sonata*.

16

Albert decided to stay back with James while Cecil and Catherine attended dinner at the Darrows' estate. Catherine was surprised to see the Halls in attendance at the gathering, but she supposed that since they were cousins it made sense. The Halls, however, cast a shadow over the gathering with their glum faces. The group did its best to avoid the difficult subject of their removal from the island, but as the evening progressed, it was spoken of more freely.

The Halls were planning on putting their land up for sale by the end of the month. Catherine watched Edward and his father cast knowing looks at one another as Mr. Hall discussed the sale of the property and their relocation to England. Bartholomew whispered something to Edward that made him sneer, and the tension between the Ewings and the Halls was obvious.

On the carriage ride to the Darrows' house earlier that night, Cecil had informed Catherine that Bartholomew Ewing had made an informal bid on the Hall land, but that Mr. Hall was insulted by the price he had offered. When Catherine asked why the Darrows had not made an offer, Cecil informed her that, like the Halls, the Darrows were in great debt. Cecil mentioned that he wished the property was closer to Eden so that he could make use of it, but that it would be a rather awkward acquisition for them.

"We don't need any more land for slave labor," said Catherine. "Even if we are fortunate enough to escape arsonists, we could face a similar fate."

Cecil quieted Catherine and reiterated his belief that the ban on slavery would never happen, and that he was becoming increasingly aggravated about her involvement in such matters. He was irritable the rest of the carriage ride, and Catherine's mood blackened knowing that her only ally for the social outing was cross with her.

That night, Catherine learned that Caleb Whitting had been detained and questioned at the jail for two days, but that they were unable to find sufficient evidence to convict him of the arson of the Hall's plantation. A barrister working for the Halls told them that they should not hold out hope. That there were too many with motives to destroy the mills—from the slaves, to the small farmers, to abolitionists—and that it was possible that the fires erupted from natural causes. The irony was that the thatched roofs on the outbuildings had caused the fire to spread and grow out of control—which was the very reason the Council had given the small farmers with thatched homes the order to re-shingle or rebuild.

When the men retired to the billiard room, Catherine was forced to stay with the women. Tired of listening to the insufferable conversation between Fanny and her cousin, Eugenia, Catherine excused herself to the back veranda and walked outside. Wind blew through the garden, and the moon gave a blue glow to the landscape. Catherine found a bench with an unobstructed view of the coast and sat on it.

It felt as if she hadn't sat in weeks. Caring for the plantation, caring for James, fighting with Leah, the increasing tension with her father, and her confusing feelings for James began to weigh upon her.

Earlier that day, as Catherine prepared a tea tray and light sandwiches for James and Albert, she had stumbled upon the surprising and turbulent realization that she was going to miss the Silwells. Catherine spent the afternoon indulging in wild fantasies about leaving the island with them and traveling to England. She was unable to spend too much time contemplating her thoughts, however, since she was interrupted constantly for counsel on household matters.

A movement caught Catherine's eye, and Edward Ewing slipped from the palms.

"You'd better not let Mrs. Hall find that you've been sitting out here with bare arms and no covering between yourself and the tropical night air."

Catherine felt the tension that had just relaxed its hold on her return with Edward's appearance. She did not want to be alone with Edward, but there was no way to avoid him.

Catherine had known Edward since they were children. They played together quite a bit growing up, as Catherine was always more interested in romping through the jungle than participating in the more feminine activities her aunt wished she would embrace. But since childhood, there was always something sinister lurking beneath Edward's charming exterior. He was bossy with her and unkind to Leah. By the time they were teenagers, Catherine made sure their meetings were as infrequent as possible, but she was forever being surprised by him sneaking up on her in the lagoon or at the beach. His appearance now reminded her of that, and made her uncomfortable.

Edward walked over and sat next to Catherine.

"Our island is one of great beauty." said Edward.

"It is."

"I'm usually too busy to sit and admire it, but I must make more of an effort to do so."

Catherine did not respond to Edward.

"Catherine, I need to speak with you."

Catherine rose from the bench. "I'm sorry, but I was just going back indoors."

"This is tiresome."

He had her attention.

"I'm not going to dance around this any more," said Edward. "I need to speak to you about something of great importance. Sit."

Catherine knew she could no longer avoid the conversation, and lowered herself back to the bench, as far away from Edward as possible.

"I spoke to your father this morning."

"Yes, about the dinner party this evening."

"You know as well as I that the dinner party was ancillary to our discussion," he said. "I've tried to be gentlemanly about this, but you clearly are not interested in being wooed by me, so I need change my approach. I'd like to make you a business proposition."

"You must be joking," said Catherine.

"On the contrary, I'm quite serious. My father and I are about to acquire the Hall's land for our good uses. Our estate is nearly as profitable as yours. If we combined the three estates there would be no limit to our financial possibilities. As charming as this island is, and as much as I enjoy plantation life, you know as well as I that it is not going to last forever. The slave system is in serious danger, in spite of what our fathers would like to believe. The land is not yielding as much as it did years ago, and the threat of hurricanes is constant. It is a miracle that our families have prospered as long as they have. I propose to you that we marry, combine our estates, manage the plantations for a year or two more, sell out, and relocate to England."

"My father and I do not need to combine with your plantation to do as you've suggested. I've no reason to marry—"

"Your father is not well, Catherine. He is not long for this world, and the sooner you understand that, the better off you'll be."

"My father is a young man. He has had virtually no health problems his entire life."

"Your father is drinking himself to death, and you know it. What will you do alone on your big plantation once your father dies? Who will protect you once he's gone?"

"And who will protect me from you if we marry?"

Edward brought up his hand to strike Catherine, but stopped himself. His angry countenance gave way to laughter.

"What, I beg you, could be funny at this moment?" she asked.

Edward grasped Catherine's hands. "You and I would get great enjoyment out of one another. Think about it."

Catherine pulled her hands away and moved farther down the bench until she nearly slipped off the end of it. Edward rose and stood over her.

"If we marry, I would not only take you in, but also your father. I would bring him with us to England. Don't be a fool."

Edward turned and walked away.

By the time Catherine regained control of her nerves and reentered the Darrows' house, Cecil was stumbling and needed to be taken home. Edward helped Cecil into the carriage and gave a knowing look to Catherine as he did so.

"Tomorrow night our families will dine together. My hope is that you've come to your senses by then. I know you are not a stupid woman, Catherine. Use your head."

Catherine climbed into the carriage and commanded Thomas to drive. Cecil passed out as soon as the carriage was in motion, and did not wake even as he was carried up to bed by several slaves. Catherine was relieved that Albert and James were asleep. She went to her room, opened the shutters, and looked out into the night.

What Edward said about her father was true. Edward was smart enough to see that the slave system was in danger. His plan was a good one. Any other woman would think Catherine mad to refuse him. But she was sickened at the thought of marrying Edward. He was loathsome, cruel, and violent. He looked on her as a piece of property. His marriage proposal would be nothing but a business arrangement. Catherine knew that she would be miserable for the rest of her life if she were forced to spend it with him.

But her father would be taken care of—she could be taken care of, in a sense. The inevitable death of her father would not only leave her broken-hearted, but abandoned and in a terrible position, if she were alone. And she knew that her father wanted her to marry Edward.

But what about James? She dared to think, again, of leaving the island with him. She had grown quite attached to him, and felt certain that he felt the same about her. But he had made no proposal, and she did not know what would happen to her father. She knew she could never leave Cecil on the island, and yet she did not know if he would be welcome to come with her. And the thought of leaving Leah, and Esther, and Mary, and countless other slaves that comprised her extended family, filled her with dread.

Through the open window, Catherine could hear James cough. As if his cough summoned her, Catherine lifted her candle and tread softly to his room. The door was cracked and the faint flicker of a dying candle danced across the walls. Catherine pushed the door so it opened enough to give her access to the room.

The pounding surf and night creatures were silenced by the closed shutters. James was sleeping in the bed. His lips were parted and his chest rose and fell with deep, regular breaths. The dark circles that had rimmed his eyes for weeks were disappearing, and his forehead lost its furrow to sleep, leaving behind a peaceful and youthful countenance.

Catherine's heartbeat quickened as she neared James, and nearly stopped when a floorboard creaked. She stopped and held her breath as James readjusted his position from his side to his back. Catherine waited a few moments, and then continued her trace-like progression toward the bed. When she reached the side of the bed, she sat down on it and stared down at James. Without thinking she moved forward until she was inches from his face. Holding her long braid close to her nightclothes, Catherine leaned in and kissed him. She remained there a moment and then pulled away, stood up, and crept back to her chambers. As she closed the door, the sleeper turned and smiled.

The observing slaves tried to disappear into the shadows as Phinneas whipped Abraham. The glow of the fire illuminated his fiendish face as the whip sliced through the flesh of the helpless man. He hung by his wrists and tried to stifle his cries.

As Toby watched, his memories took him back to Jamaica, years earlier, where he had begun his life as a slave on a failing tobacco plantation. His master was a pure demon—pitiless on the men and women who served him. Toby recalled the night he was forced to witness his father's punishment for running away. He shuddered at his memories and tried to silence the agonizing cries echoing through his head. He recalled that his father's blood had splattered on his own slight, adolescent body, and that he had thought his father would be always with him because of it.

Fresh cries pierced the night, as Phinneas panted fast and hard. When he had exhausted himself, Phinneas looked at the dejected men before him.

"Does anyone else wish to challenge me?" demanded Phinneas. Mr. Sarponte slunk around to face the whimpering mess before him. "I know it is the middle of the night, and I do not care. You will work when I tell you to work. The rest of you better get back to that cane unless you want to join him."

The men dispersed like startled mice to the cane fields illuminated by the eerie glow of the moon. Phinneas climbed onto his horse, cut the strings holding Abraham, and spat on him as he rode away to the fields.

After he was far away, strong hands lifted Abraham and carried him to a hut. He was eased to the ground on his stomach as he groaned in pain. Dark hands wrung out the hot towel and handed it to coarse hands that began to cleanse his wounds.

Rebecca entered the hut with her infant son and gasped.

"He will be okay. His back was scarred before," said Esther. "Tougher surfaces can't be as easily hurt."

Rebecca knelt over Abraham and kissed him. She reached for his hand and settled next to him. Tears leaked from his closed eyes and onto the dirt floor. The baby began to cry, and Rebecca nursed him for comfort. Esther rocked herself and continued humming as Mary tended to the wounded man.

Deep in the black jungle, Leah tried to control her shaking. She hugged her swelling abdomen and wept on the ground as she watched the grimy boots stride away from her. Phinneas mounted his horse and was swallowed by the shadows.

17

To make use of her insomnia, Meg spent the remainder of the night searching the archives of the Silwell Society. James and Albert Silwell left behind an impressive legacy in the campaign for human rights. Before Albert's death in 1843, he saw the end of slavery for the British Empire. He had numerous writings on the subject—all heartfelt and deeply personal. His letters to his fellow politicians, family members, and friends always ended with a request for prayers for the end of slavery throughout the world.

Fewer letters and writings by James survived, and his writings bore a much harsher tone than Albert's. While Albert concentrated on the gains in the campaign, encouraging events and people helpful to the cause, James' writings detailed all that was left to be done, the corruption of the planters, the stumbling blocks to success—his writings were angry and sparse. Meg did see a note that a recent batch of his letters were found and would be loaded onto the website soon, but for now, she had few to work with.

Meg noticed the light in the room and looked at the clock.

6:07.

She decided that she would work until 6:30, and then go for a run. She fixed herself a cup of tea, stretched, and sat back down at the computer.

Thirteen more pages of archived text.

Meg scanned James' letters to his brothers and sisters, hoping something would jump out at her. His negativity was prevalent, but his deep love for his family was apparent. He loved his nieces and nephews and inquired about them often. He wrote a touching letter to his sister when she lost her husband. His sense of humor was evident in his letters to his brothers. But his sadness and anger surfaced frequently.

It was 6:30 and Meg was about to turn off the computer, when something caught her eye. In a letter to his brother, a clergyman, dated several years after James had left the island—in one of the last letters the Society had archived—Meg saw the word *Nevis* just below the date. After reading the letter, Meg called Brian and Drew and asked them to meet her at Eden at 7:30.

18

Layers of clouds hung low over the island, creating the illusion that those on land were at the bottom of a tumultuous sea with waves breaking high overhead. The turbulent and perilous waters of the Caribbean mirrored the sky, and the usually transparent, aquamarine sea was murky with sand stirred up by violent waves.

James and Albert were at the breakfast table that morning. James was looking nearly restored to his former self, and showed no sign of knowing about Catherine's kiss. Catherine was quiet, and Albert asked her if she was feeling well. She assured him that she was just tired.

Catherine and James agreed that a carriage ride in such threatening weather was not a good idea, and instead settled on the rear veranda to watch the landscape respond to the steady gusts of wind. Catherine had a basket of peas she was shelling, and James had a book.

"England is known for its frequent rain showers, but I must say that its good weather is so divine that it erases all memories of the bad," said James.

"Rain does not daunt me," said Catherine. "I only keep myself away from the elements to recline by my sickly companion."

James laughed and returned to his reading.

"As a matter of fact," said Catherine, "The moment you fall asleep—and you shall soon be asleep, for I see you nodding—I am going to steal off to the slaves' quarters to call on Mary."

"I was trying to keep you from noticing my fatigue. It bothers me considerably that I am so slow in recovering."

"Your recovery has actually been quite swift. You forget that malaria kills more than half of those who contract it. You're lucky."

James was thoughtful for a moment. He watched the palms and flowers thrashing in the winds, and observed a small monkey creep out of the shrubbery before darting back into its shelter.

"I don't have much time left on the island," he said, "and I'm usually much more diffident when it comes to women, but I fear I'm running out of time."

Catherine stopped her work and looked at James.

"I don't know how to flatter and make long speeches, so I apologize for this awkwardness." James pulled himself up in his chair and moved to the bench where Catherine was seated. He tried to take her hand, but it was full of peas. Both of them laughed and Catherine threw them onto the ground and grasped James' hands.

"I know you'll think I'm mad, but would you consider marrying me and returning to England with me as my wife?"

Catherine began to cry.

"Please don't cry," said James. "I'm sorry to have upset you. Of course you wouldn't want to marry a practical stranger."

James moved to get up, but Catherine pulled him back on the bench.

"You misunderstand me," said Catherine. "You and I are of the same heart."

James smiled. "That took far less convincing than I thought it would."

They laughed and Catherine wiped her tears.

"Do you understand what I asked you?" asked James.

"Of course I do. And my answer is yes."

"What about your father?" asked James. "I would certainly extend the offer for him to accompany us home to England, but somehow I fear that he would not want to quit this island."

"I had not wanted to acknowledge that, but I fear you are correct. That, however, is not our biggest obstacle."

James looked at Catherine with a question in his eyes.

"Edward asked me to marry him last night," said Catherine. "He has my father's blessing."

"I take it that you have not answered him."

"No. My father and I are to dine there this evening. I'm expected to have an answer then."

James grew silent as he held Catherine's hands. She looked at him and then put her forehead to his. A noise startled them and caused them to stand up quickly. Cecil came out onto the veranda and made his way over to the pair.

"It looks as if it will storm," said Catherine.

"Perhaps," said Cecil. "Of course the clouds just blow over sometimes."

"An unlikely scenario in this case," remarked Edward as he appeared on the veranda. Catherine stood next to James and felt the color rise to her face. Edward's jaw clenched as he regarded the scene before him.

"I trust you are feeling better, Mr. Silwell," said Edward.

"Yes, thank you for asking," replied James.

"The Silwells appear quite at home at Eden, Mr. Dall," said Edward. "It is a pity they are leaving so soon."

"A pity indeed," remarked Cecil.

"We would like to extend a dinner invitation to you all this evening. Of course you and your father are welcome, Mr. Silwell, if you feel strong enough."

"I am quite certain we will be in attendance," said James.

"It is settled then. We will see you all this evening." Edward met Catherine's gaze and bowed his head. "Good day."

~⌒◯

After escorting James up to his room to rest, Catherine set off across the back lawn to the slaves' quarters. She carried a basket of plants with her that she intended upon leaving with Mary. The winds lashed at her face and blew her hair into her eyes, but she marched on, undaunted.

A sharp gust lifted Catherine's basket and scattered her plants about the ground as she approached the forest path. She stopped to pick them up, but stood quickly when she saw Phinneas' boots approaching.

"Allow me," he said as he gathered the fallen plants. Despite Catherine's protests, Phinneas collected them all and pressed them into Catherine's hands.

"May I carry your basket for you?" he asked.

"No. Thank you. I must be on my way."

Catherine hurried off along the path that passed the lagoon. It was dark and strange by the water. The air had an unusual chill. She thought she saw a figure out of the corner of her eye, but when she looked it disappeared in the mist of the waterfall. Catherine shivered, and was grateful when she emerged from the path onto the slaves' lane. Catherine made her way to Mary's hut and smiled as soon as the old woman came into view.

"Good afternoon," said Mary.

Catherine kissed Mary and sat at her feet.

"I have brought you some plants for your collection."

"Thank you. My supply was short."

Catherine began sorting the piles of leaves. Mary sat and listened to the rustle of the silk stalks as they slid apart. She heard the soft pat of the plants on one another as Catherine separated them. Children coming up the path were quarrelling.

"Why are you quiet?" asked Mary.

Catherine looked into Mary's clouded eyes.

"You are leaving us," said Mary.

"I am."

"It is how it should be."

A slave girl and her younger brother came walking up the lane burdened by a bucket of water. It splashed out of the basket over her legs and made a muddy path behind her. She heaved it down near a hut, and said something through the door flap. Two smaller children came out of the hut rubbing the sleep from their eyes. The older girl used a crude wooden ladle and the children drank from it.

Catherine stood and pulled a napkin of pastries and meats out of her pocket. She walked over to the children and set it down on a rock. Three more children appeared and the hungry pack devoured the food. Catherine picked up the bucket of water and moved it into the hut for the small girl, who looked at her with gratitude through large, tired eyes. She smiled at the child and returned to Mary.

"What will become of Father?" asked Catherine.

"His fate will not change whether you are here or not."

"But there will be no one to take care of him if I go."

"There will be no one to take care of you if you stay," said Mary. "Your father will be looked after by the people who have always looked after him."

"He does not know of my plans. I am going to tell him when I leave you, and then Mami as soon as I can."

Catherine stood and fetched the hemp string. She sat with Mary wrapping the plants in bundles. They worked in silence, and Catherine thought back to a day from her youth, just after Phinneas was hired, when she had helped Mary with her plants. Mary had stopped every so often to rub her eyes. Mary's vision was going, but Catherine knew she could see Phinneas approach on his horse.

"It is exceptionally kind of you to assist the beasts, Miss Dall, but do you not think that a lady belongs in the house. Your aunt would have been flustered to see you dirtying your hands."

"The beasts are down in the stable, Mr. Sarponte. I was not aware that father had hired you as a governess."

Such exchanges were characteristic of their relationship. Catherine had never feared Phinneas until she realized that her father would not always be around to protect her.

"You'd better go," said Mary. "The rain is coming."

Catherine looked up and saw it was about to storm. She bade Mary farewell and hurried back toward the lagoon. Along the path, Catherine found some large red flowers that she thought she would bring to Esther. The rain started to pat on the trees above her. Catherine picked the flowers and ran up the path. As she neared the house, a movement drew her eyes to the window of her father's room. She stopped as she saw Esther closing the shutters of Cecil's chambers while he stood behind her with his hands on her shoulders. Catherine released the flowers she had collected onto the wet ground beneath her.

Catherine prepared for dinner before her mirror. She felt numb. Leah appeared behind Catherine, startling her out of her thoughts. Leah's face was ashen and the bundle of linens she held before her looked heavy and burdensome.

"I am here to lace up your stays."

Catherine stared at Leah until she realized why she was dressing at all. Catherine moved to the bed and grasped the wooden poster as Leah positioned herself behind her mistress. Leah finished quickly and disappeared from the room as fast as she'd come.

Catherine finished preparing herself, and moved down to the drawing room where Cecil, Albert, and James waited. Cecil summoned the carriage as soon as she arrived, but as the party prepared to leave, James drew Catherine back to him.

"You do not look well, Catherine. Will you be alright?"

"I'm fine."

Catherine smiled and led James out to the carriage.

❦

The mood in the Ewing household was cold as the guests arrived. Like Cecil, Mr. Ewing was drunk, and appeared belligerent from the start. Edward was formal and frigid with the party. Dinner was heavy and uncomfortable, and Catherine's only solace was James at her side. After a lengthy silence, Edward addressed Albert and James.

"Have you learned a sufficient amount about plantation life to start one of your own on St. Christopher?"

"We have learned much," said Albert. "After we get our affairs in order, we plan on returning to St. Christopher in six months to set up our sugar plantation."

"Word has reached us that a ship departs for England in two days' time," said Edward. "Will you be on that ship or will you wait until the end of the week?"

"I am needed here until the conclusion of the week. We will leave on Saturday after all of our business is settled," replied Albert.

"I am sure you are eager to return to England."

"Though I look with great pleasure upon returning to our beloved home, I will certainly miss the wonderful hospitality of the inhabitants of Nevis, along with its breathtaking landscape and views."

The silver rang on the plates and the diners studied their meals.

"And will the marriage be performed here or in England?" asked Edward.

All parties ceased dining and stared at Edward. Catherine felt the hot color rising up her abdomen to her neck and face. James looked at Edward with anger. Albert narrowed his eyes, and Cecil began to laugh.

"And of what marriage would you be speaking, Mr. Ewing?" asked Cecil.

"Why the marriage of Miss Dall and Mr. Silwell of course. It is clear how they feel about one another."

Cecil's look of confusion contorted to anger. He slammed his drink to the table and turned to Catherine.

"What on earth is he talking about, Catherine?"

Catherine began trembling with fury.

"This is a family matter that clearly has not been addressed until now, Mr. Ewing," said Albert. "I am sure you did not mean to provoke a discussion on a subject that is no business of yours. This can certainly be discussed later."

"It can certainly be discussed now," said Cecil. "If any marriage was scheduled to occur, I should have thought it to be between Mr. Ewing and Catherine. I have given no consent to an arrangement between Mr. Silwell and my daughter."

"Mr. Dall," said James. "I had hoped to discuss this deeply difficult and pressing matter with you under your own roof behind closed doors, but since Mr. Ewing has forced the subject I suppose I must now ask your permission to marry Catherine."

"Marry Catherine? You have barely had an acquaintance of a month."

The room was quiet, until Catherine finally spoke.

"Father, I intend on moving to England with James at the conclusion of the week. I was hoping we could be married before our departure so that you could give me away."

Cecil looked with disbelief at the entire party. He slowly began grinning as he finished his glass and laughed aloud.

"I see, my dear. This is a joke on your silly, drunken father. Well done, everyone!"

The elder Mr. Ewing and Cecil began laughing until they saw that none of the other faces matched their amusement.

"It is not a joke, Father. I love James and wish to marry him and accompany him to England."

"England? What of the property on St. Christopher?"

"Mr. Dall, I've never intended on residing at that property," said James. "It is a business venture. My residence is in England."

"I will not allow it!" replied Cecil. "You cannot leave this place. You have grown up here all your life, Catherine. It is in your blood. How could you think of deserting your father and slave family for a man you have only just met?"

The guests shifted in their seats.

"We have no firsthand knowledge of this man's family or property," continued Cecil. "And how many times have you said you would never marry? You are going to throw away your entire life, and move to a gloomy, dismal country you have never seen to be someone's housewife?"

Catherine stood from the table. She walked over to Edward and slapped him across the face. She then strode from the room leaving the men in a stunned silence at her retreat.

As soon as Catherine left the house she began running down the drive, past the carriage where Thomas called after her, and toward Eden. She heard her father's voice shouting after her, but continued running away from the Ewing plantation.

A storm began as she ran down the road with the wind choking her gasps and the rain mingling with her tears. Her hair fell from its pins and flew at her face. After making her way with some confusion toward her home, at last the warm glow of candles from within Eden beckoned her to its safety. She ran with increased speed to the Great House and collapsed with exhaustion on the front veranda to allow her breathing to regulate itself. She remained on the porch for some time, but then gathered herself up and entered the quiet sanctuary of her home.

Closing the door behind her, Catherine gazed up the long stairway to the balcony above and leaned on the door, wondering how she could think of leaving Eden. She inhaled the sweet scent of flowers and looked over her familiar surroundings. As Catherine began climbing the staircase, she ran her hand over the smooth, wooden railing and felt the carpet sink beneath her muddy shoes.

Catherine felt frantic and conflicted. On one hand, the plantation had always been home to her, and the thought of leaving Cecil, Leah, and Esther was weighing heavily on her. But the thought of marrying Edward sickened her. And how could she continue to run a plantation on slave labor? It was evil. Traveling to England with James and his father would be a great adventure, and Catherine felt certain that she loved James. She thought of Mary's words, and James' face, and resolved to go against her father's wishes, and leave Nevis.

The pure white linens, rugs, drapes and netting in Catherine's room glowed in the darkness. She struck a match to light a candle, and began to remove her soaked clothing. She peeled away the sodden layers of material clinging to her body, and pulled on a soft, dry, warm, white nightgown. As the garment met her shoulders she stopped abruptly and strained to listen. Faint singing reached her ears, causing her to shiver. She finished putting on the nightgown and lifted her candle.

Stepping into the hall she gazed toward the guest wing. Blackness met her eyes, so she turned and looked toward her father's room. Catherine gasped when she saw that the door to her mother's room was ajar, and a candle was lit within. The humming drifted out of the door on a cold breeze and caused Catherine to shudder. Her heart began pounding as she approached the doorway. She reached out her hand and pushed the door.

The first sight to greet Catherine's eyes was the open window. The storm moaned outside as rain poured in, soaking the wall and rug. As Catherine entered the room to close the shutters, she cried out when her eyes met their second sight.

Leah stood before the mirror wearing one of Mrs. Dall's old nightgowns. The thin cotton clung to her massive abdomen, revealing the secret that Leah had been hiding for so long. Leah grabbed for her clothes and attempted to hide her stomach in vain. Lightning flashed outside the window and strong winds blew into the room. The two girls stared into one another's dark eyes as their hearts pounded in unison.

"My God, Leah. Is this what you've been hiding?"

"What are you doing home? I did not expect you for another hour at least."

"How did this happen? Who?" stammered Catherine as she grasped a nearby chair to steady herself.

Leah's fear transformed to disgust.

"Are you feeling faint? Can you not comprehend what swells before you?"

Leah threw her clothing on the floor and stood before Catherine.

"I am expecting a child in three months time—a child most likely thrust into my womb by that snake that preys upon us beasts when the mistress of the house is not looking."

Catherine began to weep as Leah moved toward her.

"While you have been frolicking about Eden with your young love, I have been writhing in the dirt like a pig at the hands of that repulsive man. I have been vomiting and sweating my way through endless household chores while you have been dreaming peacefully of your sweet James."

"Leah, I did not know."

"You would not know! You would not see what was before your very eyes."

Catherine shook her head.

"You think that playing a game of chase with some obliging slave children, bringing a few plants to an old woman, or teaching your pitiful mate to read redeems you from your family's sins? It does nothing to erase the evil you have inflicted upon us."

"Leah, please," sobbed Catherine as she reached her arms out to her.

Leah pushed Catherine's arms away and ran out the door. She pressed past James who was standing in the hallway. Catherine ran out of the room and collided with him. She looked for a moment into his eyes, and then pushed him aside and chased Leah down the stairs and out of the back of the house.

Panic seized Catherine as she followed Leah toward the cliff. The winds scattered her cries, the blinding rain pelted her face, and her nightgown clung to her body. She could see the white figure running for the cliffs ahead of her and screamed for Leah to stop. James was filled with dread as he neared the women and came to understand Leah's purpose.

The three figures raced over the sodden grass of the back lawn. Catherine could see Leah's progress toward the cliff's edge in each flash of lightning. James ran with all his strength, but was nearly struck by a falling tree branch and lost sight of the women.

With Leah just yards ahead of her, Catherine caught up to Leah and grasped at Leah's garment, pulling her to the ground just inches before the drop of the cliff. Catherine clutched at Leah as she tried to crawl out of her grasp. Leah pulled herself free and rose, and they stood at the cliff's edge, panting in the rain.

"Why can't you let me be?" screamed Leah.

"You are as dear to me as a sister. I've no choice."

Leah laughed in disgust. "I am your sister when it is convenient for you."

"I do nothing out of convenience."

"Do you think for one moment of the hell we are all forced to endure while you go to your balls and dinners and romps through the garden? While you are off being wooed by your suitors I am forced to endure the legacy my mother has endured in silence all these years. I am made to protect you from the ugly secrets of this place."

"I do everything I can to help you all Leah! I am a woman, I have no power!"

"You have all the power you need, Catherine!"

"I try to make your life better. Are there any mistresses on this island who do half of what I do for you?"

"Nothing you do or say can erase the raping, the beating, and the work that goes on to ensure that you and *our* drunken, slovenly father live in blissful comfort in your island paradise!"

Catherine slapped Leah across the face. There was a moment of confusion as Leah stumbled from the blow. The rocks beneath her feet gave way, and she slid over the side of the cliff. Catherine grasped at the air where Leah had been, but she was gone. Catherine couldn't tell her scream from Leah's, and crawled to the cliff's edge. She was unable to locate the body amidst the swells and rocks, unable to see through her tears and the night and the rain.

She felt as if she couldn't breathe. Her lungs felt as if they were collapsing. As she struggled to breathe she fell to the ground and began to crawl away from the cliff. The rocks tore at her hands and knees, and she could feel the sting of the cuts. Just before she collapsed, she met the horror-struck gaze of James as he stood before her.

19

Nevis. It has been three years, but that name still haunts me. The island I never wanted to visit. The trip I never wanted to take. This is my confessional, dear brother. I am ill and fear I am not long for this world. I wanted you to know why I have been so angry for so long.

I fell in love with a girl there, Catherine, a plantation owner's daughter. She was a good one—intelligent, industrious, compassionate, open-minded, beautiful. She quickly learned our true purpose for being on the island, but was not angered. When I contracted malaria, I was forced to stay at the plantation, Eden, where she cared for me and nursed me back to health.

Father stayed with me, and it was during that time that Catherine and I grew in our intimacy with one another. Catherine asked us about the Cause and was an eager student. I felt as if she would become an abolitionist.

I proposed to her, Brother, and she accepted. We knew it would be difficult with her father, but she said she would do whatever it took to join me in England as my wife.

But as you know, it did not work out that way.

You see, Catherine had just received a proposal from another man, to whom her father had given his blessing. There was a dinner party at his home, hours after she had secretly accepted my proposal, where her father learned of her intentions. A terrible scene ensued, and Catherine left the house and ran back to Eden. She did not know that I had followed her.

As soon as she returned, she learned that her slave sister, a girl named Leah with whom she had grown all her life, was carrying the child of the plantation's overseer. The girls began to quarrel, and Leah ended up running out of the house toward a cliff on the back lawn, intent upon killing herself. Catherine was able to stop her, but then the fight continued. After Leah told her that Catherine's father was also her father, Catherine pushed her over the cliff in her rage. Catherine was frantic about what she'd done, and when she saw that I had seen everything, she passed out on the lawn. I carried her back into her home, left on a ship for England two days later, and never heard from her again.

I would not have believed it possible for someone as dear and sweet as my Catherine to murder another, but it shows how evil and poisonous the slave system is. It corrupts all it touches. Even the most well-meaning masters and mistresses will wield their power inappropriately, and with deadly results.

Several months ago I sent an inquiry to a contact on the island to see what had become of Catherine and her family. According to church and local records, she, her father, their chief overseer, and twenty-six slaves on their plantation died in an outbreak of the bleeding fever just two months after I left the island. It is a strange thing to think that Catherine has been gone for so long. It is a strange thing that I have thought of her in the context of the present for so long, when she has been so far in the past.

My pain is acute. Now, not only must I mourn the life I could have had, but I must mourn Catherine's passing, and the knowledge that if I had taken her home with me, she would not have died in such a way.

I know what it is to love and to have it ripped senselessly away. I've devoted my life to abolishing slavery, and have met small successes along the way. I can't help but think of how my life would have been different if I could erase the events of that night, the night of the fall, but it is too painful to imagine.

May God have mercy upon her soul, and on all of our souls.

Yours,
James

20

Catherine stared into the fire with a quilt wrapped around her soaked, shivering form. The wood popped as the flames danced in the drafts. Tears leaked from Catherine's eyes down her face and neck. The storm calmed itself and the thunder rumbled far out at sea.

James sat with his head in his hands across the room. He glanced at Catherine at intervals, but looked away as quickly as his eyes met the back of her head. Albert stood behind James in the corner of the room, studying the dejected scene before him. Cecil sat haggard and drunk in a chair opposite Catherine. Finally Albert broke the silence.

"I must suggest that we all retire. This has been a difficult night that will be followed by many cheerless days."

James removed his hands from his face and looked at Catherine.

"I think that it would also be best if James and I return to the Bath Hotel tomorrow for the remainder of our stay," said Albert. "We have imposed ourselves too long at Eden."

"I agree. That would be best for us all," mumbled Cecil.

Catherine turned so James was able to see her profile outlined by the fire.

"That is an excellent suggestion, Father," said James. "It will be better to get closer to Charlestown, anyway, seeing as I will be departing Nevis on Tuesday at noon."

Catherine glanced at James and back to the fire.

"But our ship does not leave until Saturday," replied Albert. "We must stay to see our task completed."

"You may stay, Father, but I will be going. Several other businessmen are traveling on Tuesday at noon, so I will accompany them."

"Do not be rash, James. Saturday is the day we have set to go and Saturday is the day we will go."

"I am a grown man, and can make my own decisions. I cannot stay on this godforsaken island one moment longer than necessary."

"You cannot go—"

"I cannot stay!" shouted James.

Albert became quiet as James left the room and he shortly followed James, leaving Cecil and Catherine alone. When Catherine turned to look at her father, he was gone.

Catherine paced through the halls of Eden all night long. She tortured herself with the knowledge that she had nearly driven Leah to suicide, and that she ultimately caused Leah to fall to her death. The state of her mind grew worse throughout the night. Her hands trembled and she could not drive Leah's words from her head.

Cecil had fathered Leah while Catherine's mother was still alive. When had Leah learned that she and Catherine were sisters? How long had Esther forced Leah to hide it from Catherine? The image of Esther's sad face as she closed the shutters to Cecil's room with his hands gripping her shoulders flashed before Catherine. She shook her head and tried to suppress the image.

And Phinneas had been raping Leah. That was why he wouldn't allow Leah and Toby to marry. He wanted her for himself. Catherine's hatred of Phinneas surged through her. She shook with rage and despair at the thought of that disgusting creature forcing himself upon Leah, but her sense of helplessness increased upon the realization that she could not go to her father about such a matter. He engaged in the same atrocious behavior.

And James surely wanted nothing to do with Catherine after witnessing her dispute with Leah. He was determined to leave the island even sooner than his father to escape from Catherine. She would be left on Nevis with the pathetic shell of a man her father had become and his overseeing predator.

Catherine sobbed through the night. She mourned her sister, her father, and James. She finally collapsed into her bed as the dawn began to push its way over the horizon, and through the lingering clouds.

By the time Catherine had awakened the next day, James and Albert were gone. The house was silent and Catherine could not find a soul inside of Eden. She stepped out onto the back lawn and looked back at the house. Never before had she felt so intimidated by its soaring height, its empty, shrine-like rooms, and its dark shadows. It no longer looked grand and welcoming to her. It looked gloomy and mysterious, and ghosts whispered around every corner.

Catherine went back into the house and tried to find her father in the dining room, the parlor, and the billiard room. She finally found him in his office. The room was darkened by the closed shutters, and Cecil sat unshaven and confused amidst a sea of papers that he shuffled from pile to pile. He did not look up as Catherine entered, but instead poured himself a drink from the nearly-empty bottle before him. Catherine looked with disgust at her father as he swallowed great mouthfuls of liquor and mumbled to himself. Dark circles hung below his eyes and he appeared wild and unkempt.

"I need to speak with you, Father."

Cecil looked up at Catherine as if he was seeing her for the first time.

"Not now Catherine. I am attending to some important business."

"Nothing you are doing is more important than the present conversation."

He stopped moving his papers and stared at her.

"You now know that Leah was with child," said Catherine.

Cecil looked back down at his desk.

"Leah was pregnant because Phinneas had been forcing himself upon her."

He remained silent

"Leah told me some terrible things before she died. She accused you of fathering her. Is that true?"

Cecil looked up at Catherine with glassy, tear-filled eyes. Catherine's mouth began to quiver but she kept her tears from falling.

"Is it true?"

Cecil looked away from Catherine and brought his glass to his lips. Catherine moved forward and slapped the glass from his hand, shattering it against the wall. Cecil looked with shock at his daughter.

"My entire life I have worshipped a man who did nothing but lie to me, and abuse those lower than himself, and make money off of miserable, wretched, helpless creatures. How am I to go on living in such a world?" cried Catherine.

Cecil began to cry and buried his head in his hands, but he still did not respond to her accusations. Catherine stared with revulsion at her father. She backed out of the office and left him crying in the dark. When Catherine stepped into the hallway, she met Thomas and straightened herself.

"Could I trouble you to take me to Charlestown tomorrow morning?" she asked.

"Certainly, Miss Catherine. What time will you need the carriage."

"No later than ten o'clock. I need to get to Charlestown by noon."

"I will be ready at ten, Miss Catherine."

"Thank you, Thomas." Catherine leaned up and kissed Thomas on the cheek. He touched the place she had kissed, and watched her climb the stairs.

Catherine moved toward her room, but then turned and went to her mother's bedroom. She closed the door and dropped onto the bed. Her thoughts returned to her quarrel with Leah the night before, and she began to cry. How could she ever face Esther again? Or Mary? Or anyone? It was an accident. She knew they all thought Leah had committed suicide, but what did James think? His eyes had accused her last night, and he was leaving the next day. She thought that she had to go to him tomorrow, and explain what had happened. Then he would take her with him to England, and they would be married, and she could escape the hell that had become her home.

The winds howled and moaned outside of the Great House as Catherine tossed and turned in a fitful sleep. Another storm was picking up on the island, and moving closer to Eden. As midnight approached Catherine looked with wild, frightened eyes out of the curtains blowing open around her bed. She heard whispers and groans all around her. The floorboards creaked as if something treaded over them. A tremendous flash of lightning followed by a deafening boom of thunder illuminated the pale, wild, and soaking wet face of Leah staring right at her. Catherine screamed and covered her face. Shaking violently, Catherine removed the spread from her eyes inch by inch, and was relieved to see that the apparition was gone.

The images haunted her throughout the rest of the night, and when morning came Catherine was worn, sore, and exhausted.

James placed the last of his packed bags by the door and put on his jacket. Albert gazed out of the window over the glistening shrubbery of the garden below, and out to the cloud covered horizon. James cleared his throat and Albert turned to face his son.

"Are you sure I cannot persuade you to stay on until Saturday."

"Father, I have made my decision."

Albert sighed. "Are you going to turn your back on Catherine entirely? This decision could affect the rest of your life."

"It already has affected the rest of my life, beyond repair. The sooner I get away from this hell the sooner I will be able to heal."

"Is your love for her so fleeting?"

James stared at his father.

"I still love Catherine, but after what has happened I don't know what to do."

"I believe there is more to this than what you say," said Albert. "You cannot forgive her for what you saw, can you?"

James shifted his gaze out the window.

"James, it is very important that you listen to me. It is possible, and highly probable that Catherine did not push Leah."

"I saw it happen with my own eyes."

"Did you? How were you able to clearly see through the storm and the night? Perhaps Catherine slapped Leah. Perhaps Leah lost her footing. To accuse Catherine of murdering Leah—whom she loved almost as herself—sounds preposterous."

"You did not see what I saw."

"James, you have been saying since we first set foot on this island that slavery corrodes and corrupts all involved—from slaves, to overseers, to masters. What you believe is true, but you must be wrong in your assessment of what happened to Leah. I believe that Catherine struck Leah, and that she fell. When Catherine struck Leah, it was not the hand of a domineering mistress striking her disobedient slave—it was the hand of a woman striking a friend who had affronted her. I am not excusing Catherine's violent and childish behavior, but I am telling you that it was not abuse, and could not have been murder. The color of Leah's skin and her station in life had nothing to do with the liberty Catherine took in slapping her. I believe that Catherine's action was an unplanned and unpremeditated defense against what she took as an assault. The truth was too painful for her to hear, so she struck out against it. And Leah fell. And Catherine's memories will punish her for it the rest of her life.

Don't you think you owe it to her to at least hear what she has to say on the matter?"

James listened to his father's words and turned them over in his heart. A knock at the door broke his spell, however, as the bellman arrived to take down his bags. James looked from his father to the bellman.

"I must go."

"I will not let you go alone," said Albert. "If you are unwilling to stay, I must gather my things and travel home with you today."

Albert quickly packed his trunk as the bellman loaded James' belongings into the carriage down the stairs. Before the men set out for Charlestown, Albert penned several letters to the contacts he had made on the island, apologizing for his hasty departure, and assuring them of his continued correspondence. One of his letters went to the poor farmer, Jonas Dearing, making him an offer of employment at his Cornwall estate if his family needed to relocate. Albert also included a large bank note.

The men made it to Charlestown in a short time and watched as their belongings were loaded onto the ship. They waited to board, wishing to keep their feet on land as long as possible.

Thomas had the carriage ready for Catherine promptly at ten o'clock the next morning, but was full of warnings of rain as she met him in the foyer.

"Thomas, I know it may rain, but the carriage is covered. I am quite sure I will not melt."

Thomas loaded her bags onto the carriage with a furrowed brow as Catherine went to look for her father. When she found him, he was passed out on her mother's bed, snoring heavily.   Catherine approached Cecil and leaned down to kiss him on the forehead.

"Goodbye, Father," she whispered.

She took a deep breath, stifled a sob, and hurried down the stairs to the kitchen. Esther was not there, and Catherine did not have time to find her. She crossed the foyer, looked up the great staircase and into each of the rooms around her. She left the house, boarded the carriage, and did not look back at Eden as the carriage moved down the road.

Rain started falling just after Catherine's departure.

"Shall we turn back, Miss Catherine?" asked Thomas.

"No Thomas, keep moving please."

"These roads are mighty muddy, Miss Catherine. The horses are struggling to keep the wheels moving."

"I know Thomas, but we must keep moving. I have to get to Charlestown before noon."

The horses struggled and heaved their way through the deep muddy tracks on the road. They got stuck several times and Thomas looked back at Catherine with concern. Catherine tried to ignore his pleading eyes as she gazed around at her surroundings. She watched the familiar island foliage as it passed her and disappeared from her view. Memories pushed through her mind, threatening to weaken her resolve and send her back to Eden.

Catherine thought of how she and Leah would run through the rain showers at home as children until Aunt Elizabeth found them and punished them. She thought of the day that she and James were forced to seek refuge from the rain in the cave by the beach. She thought of the horrible night Leah had lost her life as the rain poured down on the island.

Was the rain a baptism? Was she cleansed of her sins? Was God weeping over them with each rainfall as her childhood myths would suggest?

In spite of the odds, the carriage made it to Charlestown. Catherine urged Thomas toward the city dock and looked at the vessels as they lifted and fell in the current. Two ships were parked at the dock. One was empty, and the other had only a few deckhands on board. Neither of the boats looked ready to depart and her heartbeat slowed with relief as she realized that she must be early. She directed Thomas to pull under an overhang out of the rain and strained her eyes in the direction of the Bath Hotel in expectation of seeing James arrive. Catherine did not have any idea what she would say to him, and had even less of an idea what she would do if he rejected her, but she sat on, waiting.

After some time had passed Catherine grew nervous. Perhaps she was mistaken on the time or date of departure. She was about to call to a deckhand nearby when her eyes met with those of the boy she had danced with at the pub that night with James. He was coming off the pier with a large rope on his arm.

"You, there," she called.

He saw Catherine and turned crimson when he recognized her face.

"What time is the ship sailing for England due to leave?"

"It's gone, miss," said the boy.

"But I thought it was to depart at noon today?"

"The ship and its cargo were ready early. They made for England just before eleven."

Catherine sat in stunned silence as she scanned the horizon. She could see a ship far off, and became numb.

James strained his eyes to catch a final glimpse of the great mountain peak of Nevis, and when it disappeared, buried his face in his hands. Some impossible hope had overtaken him as he had traveled to the ship from the hotel that morning, and dared to suggest that Catherine would meet him at the city dock. He surveyed the crowds for her that morning, but was disappointed. Even as he boarded the great vessel he scanned the faces for a glimpse of her face. He watched the island until it disappeared from view, and only then would he accept that he was going home without her.

21

After Meg read the letter to Brian and Drew, they all walked out to the cliff and stared at the ocean far below. None of them could think of much to say, but finally Meg spoke.

"You said every slave story is a ghost story, Drew, so who's the ghost? Catherine died shortly after Leah. Who's the more tortured soul? The murderer or the victim?"

"I would say Catherine."

"Why do you think that?"

"Beethoven's *Sonata*" he said.

"I thought that was you?" said Meg.

"I don't play in the middle of the night."

Meg shivered and turned back to stare at the Great House. She thought she never again wanted to set foot inside that place. She regretted finding out as much as she had.

"Let's get out of here," said Meg.

She and Brian turned to go, but Drew didn't move.

"I think I'll stay here for a bit. Pay my respects."

Meg looked at him for a moment. She walked over and kissed his cheek.

"See you tomorrow at the wedding?"

"Yes, tomorrow."

Brian wanted to see the beach on the property, so Meg walked him down one last time. She told him about Hamilton, and wished that he would appear as he had so frequently when her quest began. Meg told Brian about the manchineel tree, and showed him the cave. They walked up the overgrown path to the lagoon and admired the waterfall.

"It's a shame you have to get rid of all this," said Brian.

"I thought that before, but knowing what I know now, I feel as if it is all tainted."

They walked along the banks of the lagoon, until Brian pointed out a path that Meg had not yet discovered. It was covered in vines, but was clearly defined on the ground. Brian pushed away the vines and began moving down the path.

"Up for some adventure?" he called.

Meg followed him through the tangled foliage. The path twisted and turned and seemed endless.

"It looks as if there's a clearing ahead a bit," said Brian. "I can see the light. Do you want to keep going or turn back?"

"We might as well keep going now. I'm curious to see where it leads."

They moved forward and were panting by the time they reached the end of the path. They spilled out into an open lawn where the trees were sparse and the vegetation was neatly trimmed. Stone statues stood every few feet with plaques at their bases. Angels, tablets, trees, and crosses were arranged in rows through the clearing.

"It's a cemetery," said Meg.

She and Brian walked around the grave sites reading the names.

"It's relatively recent," he said. "I can't find a stone older than 1950. I was hoping to find the Dalls."

"They were probably buried at one of the churches in town. I can't believe I never thought to look."

A noise caused Meg and Brian to turn. Drew cleared his throat from behind them.

"Drew!"

He smiled and pointed to an angel nearby. It was a male angel—young, graying, pre-Raphaelite. Moss grew up around its base.

"My son."

Meg gave Drew a hug, and walked with him to the stone. The light shifted through the trees and over the gravesite. The fresh flowers in the vase before it trembled in the wind.

"My God," she said.

Hamilton Edmead.

<hr />

"May I fix you a drink?" asked Brian.

Meg shook her head.

"I'll take one," said Drew.

The wind was strong outside behind Havilla. Brian, amused by Meg's little drink matching game, made two *Hurricane Leah's.*

"I know it's early, but there's juice in it," said Brian.

"I'll drink to that," said Drew, as he lifted his glass.

Meg still had not regained the color she lost upon reading Drew's son's name.

"It could be a coincidence," said Brian.

"I know of no other Hamiltons on the island," said Drew, "But it is a possibility."

"There's only one way to solve this," said Brian.

Drew nodded and reached into his pocket. He pulled out a brown leather wallet that looked as if it was as old as Drew. He picked through a pile of small papers and felt into the pocket inside the wallet. Drew passed the worn photograph to Meg.

She knew it was him before the picture was before her, and began to cry once it was confirmed. Hamilton smiled at her through those shining white teeth. He had his hands on his hips. He wore a collared white shirt, and looked as if he was on his way to school. The picture looked well worn. The edges were frayed from a thousand handlings.

Meg began to cry and covered her face with her hands.

"I must be going crazy," she said.

Brian walked over to where she was sitting and placed his hands on her shoulders.

Drew put his hand over hers on the table.

"This is not a bad thing, Meghan," he said.

"I'm seeing ghosts, Drew."

"Remember where you are. That's not so strange to me. I only wish I could see him."

"Did you ever see a picture of him before, Meg?" asked Brian. "Perhaps Drew has a picture on his desk at the Museum. You could have seen it, and could be confusing the image with the boy you truly saw."

"I have no picture of Hamilton at work," said Drew. "You don't have to explain this away."

"I'm not trying to," said Brian. "I'm just trying to make everyone feel better."

"I feel just fine," said Drew. "Meg, when was the last time you saw him?"

Meg thought back to their time on the beach when he had warned her about the manchineel tree. She thought of them looking on the rocks for sea life. She remembered how he had disappeared before she could take his picture, and told Drew all of these things. Drew sat for a moment and stared at the picture on the table. He reached out and put it back in his wallet, which he folded and put back into his pocket.

"I'd better be going. I have a lot to tell Dorothy."

Meg stood and wiped her face. Drew turned to leave, but stopped and went back to Meg. He hugged her, and then walked toward the door. He turned before he left.

"Hamilton played the piano."

———⌒⌒◯

Meg was quiet that night at dinner. They ate early with David and Gwen, and they asked Meg if everything was alright. She and Brian had spoken earlier, and Meg asked that Brian not mention what had happened with Hamilton to David and Gwen. They were nice friends, but new friends, and Meg didn't want them to think she was crazy. As the night wore on, Meg allowed herself to relax and get excited about the night dive, and the next day's nuptials.

In Brian's research, he had found a company who did night dives on Nevis. He and Meg were good divers, and found out that David and Gwen were also advanced. They said that most people on the Florida coast were avid divers and had plenty of locations to pursue their passion. Meg was looking forward to the dive, but was a little nervous about going at night, which she had never before experienced. She thought the dive would be called off due to the coming storm, but the water looked strangely calm.

Scuba Safaris dive shack was located at Oualie Beach. They boarded the Island Hopper "Over Exposure" and were greeted by a charming man named Alex, his son, Saul, and an assistant named Matthew. Two other groups joined Meg's group, and they all introduced themselves as they boarded the boat. Alex discussed the dive and procedures with the groups as he pulled out into the harbor toward the setting sun.

They were on their way to Monkey Shoal, a two square mile reef that went to depths of 100 feet and offered the largest variety of marine life. Their instructor told them to look for hawksbill turtles, angel fish, octopus, lobster, parrot fish, eels, starfish, barracuda, and sharks. Meg was less excited about the prospect of swimming with barracuda and sharks than with angel fish, but thought the dive to be well worth the risk. The most exciting possibility was of seeing the humpback whales and bottlenose dolphins. The whales and dolphins were often seen during the early part of the year, and each of the divers secured a listening device to use to hear their sounds.

"The whales are most vocal at night when they are thought to be mating," said Alex, much to the amusement of the crew. "This could be an X-rated dive."

Meg and Brian launched together and swam down as far as they could. The visibility was excellent, the water was calm and illuminated by a full moon, and the sand was settled at the bottom. They didn't have to search far to see the marvelous variety of tropical marine life. Brian poked Meg and signaled below at a rocky ledge. A large turtle rested under it. Straight below a gang of lobsters scurried along the floor. The divers stayed relatively close together, so anytime someone from the group saw a sight worth noting, they were all able to see it.

A shadow passed above the divers, and they looked up and saw a nurse shark. It was close to six feet long, and Meg and Brian grabbed onto one another as it passed above them. She could see Brian's eyes smile under his mask. After the shark passed, Brian pointed up, and they moved to a shallower depth. Meg's listening device began to hum and she scanned the area around them searching for the source of the change in sound.

The noise came first—a moaning sound like something from a large creature heaving all its effort into making it, followed by some playful, high-pitched bellows. Another moaning sound came through, and then they could see them appear about fifty feet away in the shallower water.

Humpback whales, two of them, moved through the water. The divers found one another and came together to watch the great beasts. They had surprising grace for their size, but one could feel the effort of their bodies just watching them move. The whales did not seem to notice the divers, and disappeared into the black water as quickly as they'd come.

When the divers came up, they were all talking over one another. Alex said they had never seen whales swim so close to the divers, and lamented over not bringing the camera. As Meg unsuited and changed she felt renewed energy and peace. She was glad that they had gone on the dive. Brian sensed her ease and smiled at her through the crowd.

Meg dropped everyone off at their respective lodgings and went back to Havilla alone. She put on her pajamas, fixed herself a cup of decaffeinated green tea, and went out to the back porch. The trees were still for the first time since she'd arrived on the island.

The calm before the storm.

Meg thought of the time that she and Brian had dived with her family in the Cayman Islands last winter. Her mother and father were athletic and youthful, and loved being able to keep up with Meg and Brian. They had seen scores of turtles on their dives, and Meg thought she'd never seen anything so beautiful, until now.

Meg looked out at the night, and thought that everything would be alright, and heard the silence all around her, and knew that others were alright, too.

The winds picked up during the night, and by the time Meg awoke the next day, it was clear that the storm was approaching. Weather reports predicted a tropical storm for

Nevis. The hurricane had lost momentum and was heading out for the Atlantic, as David had predicted. It was recommended that residents of villas and small shacks go to local checkpoints the next morning, but those staying in hotels could stay put.

The wedding wasn't until three o'clock, but the storm wasn't due to hit until the middle of the night. She wasn't sure why she had a change of heart, but Meg felt the need to return to Eden one last time, alone. She pulled the jeep up to the ancient gate covered in vines and jumped onto the dust. Wrapping her fingers around the cool metal she swung it open and stepped onto the drive. She took in the plants and trees and looked for the house at the turn in the road. It appeared, looming with its empty eye windows, just as it had before, like the sad shell of an old woman who was once beautiful. The crunch of the gravel turned to the thump of the stairs. Meg gave the door just the right shove to open it, and stepped into the foyer.

The house felt completely vacant for the first time since Meg had set foot in it. No pigeons paced on the pianoforte, no rodents could be heard stirring amongst the walls and shuffling under the decaying furniture, and there was no electricity in the air. No cold winds, no feeling of another—just emptiness. Meg felt no fear, only sadness.

She looked up the great staircase and imagined the slave girl running down, chased by her mistress—her sister. She imagined them running through the dining room, and walked herself over to it for one last look at the mural as it was, before it was sold and restored, and before a line of people stood to view it—that mural of The Fall. How appropriate in this house called Eden, in this garden paradise, where so many had suffered.

Meg turned and walked through the passage to the kitchen. The cooking smells still lived in its stone walls—

damper, mustier, but hanging underneath all the years of quiet. She could see the slave women tending to the oven, moving around like ghosts in the inferno as the massive oven blazed in the tropical heat.

She stepped outside and followed the lawn to the cliff and stepped right up to the edge and looked down at the jagged ledges that led down to the boulders and the water and watched the waves roll over the boulders and crash into the cliff and turn into foam and disappear.

———~⸲◯

That afternoon, Meghan married Brian in the church with the steel drum band playing. Drew gave her to Brian, while Dorothy, Gwen, David, and a few parishioners who had been wondering by stopped in and watched. Meg wore a silk gown of pale ivory that she had found at a hotel shop. Brian wore a linen suit. After the photographer finished shooting, a taxivan covered in white streamers and tin cans carried the guests, including the priest and the band, to Sunshine's for the reception. They ate lobster and drank Killer Bees and danced on the beach in the wind under the light of twenty torches until the first raindrops reached the revelers. Everyone helped pack up the tables and chairs and said their goodbyes, and Meg and Brian went back to Brian's room and were up all night to hear the storm.

———~⸲◯

A warm shaft of light stole through the blinds and moved up Meg's body minute by minute until it reached her eyes and opened them. She rolled over and looked at the clock on the bedside table: *11:46*. Meg turned in the other direction and saw Brian still asleep, flat on his back, with one leg sticking out of the sheets. She kissed him and cuddled into his side, rousing him from his sleep. He grinned at her through his half-opened eyes. Meg sat up and wrapped the quilt around her body as she stood up from the bed.

"What, modest? After last night?" Brian teased.

Meg laughed and walked over to the window. She opened the blinds, slid open the door, and stepped onto the balcony. The water was rough—white capped and cloudy from the stirred up sand. It was still windy, but the clouds were few in number and moved quickly. They blocked the sun in short gasps and then moved on in a rush. Leaves, coconuts, and small branches littered the beach, and the drink stand out by the beach had collapsed.

"The wind must have been pretty fierce last night," Meg called from the balcony.

Brian appeared on the balcony beside her with the sheet wrapped around his waist. He scanned the horizon.

"Not as bad as it could have been, that's for sure."

While they stood watching the water, the phone began to ring. Meg looked at Brian with a question in her eyes, and moved into the room to locate her cell phone. It was under her discarded wedding dress, and Meg got to it just in time.

"Meg, this is Drew."

"Hi Drew. Is everything okay?"

Brian walked into the room and watched Meg.

"Um, not really. Can you come by my house?"

"Sure. I'll be there in a half-hour."

"Okay, see you then."

Meg hung up.

"It was Drew. Something's wrong."

Brian and Meg dressed quickly and drove to Drew's house. On the way, they were relieved to see that there was little damage to the island or the homes. The winds had been heavy, but just enough to stir up the landscape. They pulled up to Drew's house, and aside from some leaves strewn about the yard, it was untouched by the storm. He came to the door as they parked and motioned for them to stay in the jeep. Brian climbed into the back seat and left the front to Drew.

"What is it?" asked Meg as Drew sat in the passenger side of the jeep.

"Drive to Eden."

Meg looked back at Brian and put the jeep into reverse. They drove by Havilla and up to the familiar gates of Eden. The gate was open, so Meg drove the jeep carefully up the drive. Meg looked at Drew with concern, and then back at the road leading to the house.

As they rounded the corner facing the house, Meg slammed on the breaks, put the jeep in park, and jumped out of the driver's side. The sun blazed forth over the landscape, the birds darted between the trees lining the drive, and a monkey scurried up a nearby palm. The fountain stood as it had been, but the house was gone.

Drew and Brian got out of the jeep and joined Meg in the road. They began to walk toward the site where the house had been and now, only a pile of rubble remained. The trees and plants along the drive and around the perimeter of the house were intact. Only the house had been destroyed. Not one stair, chimney, or wall remained. All that was left of the house lay in a heap of torn wood and plaster.

"There have been far worse storms than this since the construction of the house. Why now?" asked Meg.

"There's no sense in asking those questions," said Drew. "It's over."

Meg walked closer and peered into the pile of rubble. Nothing recognizable remained.

"The mural," said Brian.

"Gwen," said Meg.

The group walked around what was left of the Great House for some time. They poked through the debris, but were unable to find anything in tact. Meg called Gwen and David, who came over to inspect the rubble themselves. Gwen wept. Not one piece of the mural remained. Morning turned into afternoon. There was nothing left to do but go, so they took one last look at the site, and left.

That night, Meg and Brian went to Drew's house for dinner. Hamilton was in pictures everywhere, but Meg didn't cry. Dorothy didn't cry either. She laughed quite a bit, as did Drew, and they talked late into the night.

Meg and Brian packed their bags the next day, and drove to the airport. They were both sad to go, and looked forward to their return, which they knew wouldn't be too far in the future. As the tiny plane lifted from the runway and circled around the island, Meg saw the land at Eden. She held Brian's hand and looked at the land until it disappeared in the shadow of Mount Nevis.

Epilogue

Meg sat in the stiff chair in the library of the New York Historical Society. She looked around her and saw a woman with gray hair leafing through old manuals, and a young man with wire rimmed glasses running his finger along the archives in search of some lost item. She turned her attention back to the papers in front of her.

African Free School.

The collection of materials from the African Free School was extensive and text heavy. Meg rubbed her neck and looked at her watch.

3:37.

She wasn't due to meet Brian until five o'clock for dinner. He was doing a guest lecture at NYU on *Paradise Lost & Regained*, and Meg had accompanied him since she had resigned from her political post three weeks ago, and had just finished signing Eden's settlement papers over to Drew's nephew and his investment group from Nevis. Meg had accepted a job with the Annapolis Historical Society, and was writing a book on slavery in the Caribbean in the late eighteenth and early nineteenth centuries. Her research tracing runaway slaves had led her to the African Free School in New York.

The New York Historical Society held the largest collection of archives from the school. Letters, newspaper clippings, and pamphlets comprised the bulk of the material.

Occasionally, and to the great interest of Meg, manuscripts and compositions from the students, themselves, surfaced.

She knew that she would have to come back tomorrow to finish reading everything, but wanted to stay until 4:00. She picked up the last, plastic enclosed text of the day, and as she read, had to contain her shaking. She brought her hand to her mouth to stifle a gasp, and began to cry. This is what she found.

16 March 1834

My Story

I was born from my mother in 1812, but I was born into freedom in 1831. To everyone's knowledge I died in Nevis over a cliff, pushed by my mistress, my sister, Catherine. It was an accident. Her anger caused her to strike me when she found out the truth of my parentage, and I fell over a ledge. Everyone thought I died. And I let them think that.

When I fell, I landed on a shelf sticking out from the cliff. I suppose that Catherine didn't see me there because of the vines and the storm and the darkness, but I was right there below her. She could have reached out her hand and pulled me up. I almost called to her when I saw her look over, but then I realized that I had been given a gift. God gave me my earthly death, so that I could have a new life.

I was with child, and began having pains, but I was able to pull myself back up to the top of the cliff by crawling up the rocks and thick vines. I crawled through the lagoon nearby, and to the hut of my mother. When I got there, I knew I could not go in. She would not have let me go, so God forgive me, I crawled further along until I reached Mary's hut.

Mary was wise. She knew that some things needed to be kept secret. I lost the baby that night. I was not far enough along for the child to survive, and that destroyed me, because it was a dark baby. I had no part of that overseer in me after all. It was hard to stifle my weeping, but I did, because I knew I had to.

Mary kept me there in secret, and at great danger to herself, for two weeks, until I was strong enough to run away. I don't know what she did with the child, only that she said he was back with God. When I had to go, I left at night, and traveled to the home of a Quaker who that man James told me of, if I ever wished to go.

He and his wife hid me for four days. They cut my hair and darkened my skin with ink. They passed me to a merchant named Richard Buxton and called me Martha, and I was to be known as his slave as we traveled to a place called Carolina in America. It was easier than I thought since I, Leah, was believed dead. No one was searching for me.

Mr. Buxton was a good man and I will never forget his kindness. He saw me safely to Carolina, and then up the Chesapeake Bay to Delaware. Once we reached Delaware, he passed me to Mr. Thomas Garrett. I feared him at first, but he delivered me safely along with all kindness and no harm.

I traveled along to New York with several other helpers. I finally arrived in the night, and was met by a small woman in her dressing gown and a low candle. Her face was that of an angel, and she was to be my teacher, and I have been here ever since in her care and tutorage.

I'm Martha now. It's hard to remember to answer to that name when others call me. I still mourn for my mother, and Mary, and Toby, and my boy, and my sister. I wonder if she's well, and if she married that man, James, and my prayers are with them all.

Acknowledgments

The fiction writer delights in manipulating the truth to suit her purposes. On two points did I knowingly and deliberately alter the past:

- St. Christopher (now St. Kitts) did not put a hold on land purchases for plantation development.
- The *Thatch House Law* was not enforced in the 19th century in Nevis.

To the best of my knowledge, all other historical references are accurate. I found these sources to be most helpful:

- *Sugar and Slaves* by Richard Dunn.
- *Swords, Ships, and Sugar* by Vincent Hubbard
- *Nevis: Queen of the Caribees* by Joyce Gordon
- www.encarta.msn.com
- www.pbs.org
- www.nevisnaturally.com
- www.nevisisland.com
- www.nevis1.com
- www.nevis-nhcs.org
- www.virtualtourist.com
- http://rain-tree.com
- www.golden-rock.com
- www.rumshop.net

Many thanks to AuthorSupport.com for the beautiful cover design.

Some of the places mentioned in present day Nevis are real. Many thanks to the following for allowing me the use of their good names:

- Miss June's
- Scuba Safari's
- Sunshine's
- Eddy's Bar and Grill
- Mount Nevis Hotel Restaurant
- St. Theresa's Catholic Church
- Museum of Nevis History

To Eric W. Baumgartner of Hirschl & Adler Galleries for his information on the sales of Benjamin West works.

To Diane Shaw of the Skillman Library at Lafayette College for granting me permission to quote the letter from the Marquis De Lafayette to George Washington, from the Marquis De Lafayette Manuscripts collection.

To Charlene & Robert Shephard, Patricia & Richard Robuck, Alexis McKay, Suzie McKay, Kiera Stewart, Jami Duffy, Kathy Brown, Kim Mattison, Rich Reilly, Mary Snead, Heather Pacheco, Linda Andrus, Patrick Kiley, Kelly Robuck, Aretha Elder-Noel, Michael Neff, Lisa Leitholf, Cara Tracey, and many others who read (and reread) my novel, babysat my children, housed me for conferences, questioned my choices, gave me real feedback, and helped shape the book into what it has become, I thank you.

To Scott for all of his patience, guidance, support and (often unappreciated) good advice; my gratitude always.

And finally, to God for giving me a story to tell.